D0933663

Redwood Court

Redwood Court

Fiction

DÉLANA R. A. DAMERON

THE DIAL PRESS

New York

Published in the United States by The Dial Press, an imprint of Random House, a division of Penguin Random House LLC, New York.

THE DIAL PRESS is a registered trademark and the colophon is a trademark of Penguin Random House LLC.

"Thirty-first Annual Chitlin Strut" was originally published under a different title in *Day One* (2017) and "Work" was originally published in *Kweli Journal* (2020).

LIBRARY OF CONGRESS CATALOGING-IN-PUBLICATION DATA
Names: Dameron, DéLana R. A., author.
Title: Redwood court : fiction / DéLana R.A. Dameron.
Description: New York : The Dial Press, [2024]
Identifiers: LCCN 2023012664 (print) | LCCN 2023012665 (ebook) |
ISBN 9780593447024 (hardback) | ISBN 9780593447031 (ebook)
Subjects: LCGFT: Novels.
Classification: LCC PS3604.A4398 R44 2024 (print) | LCC PS3604.A4398 (ebook) |
DDC 811/.6—dc23/eng/20230316
LC record available at https://lccn.loc.gov/2023012664
LC ebook record available at https://lccn.loc.gov/2023012665

Printed in the United States of America on acid-free paper

randomhousebooks.com

9 8 7 6 5 4 3 2 1

First Edition

"Listen: we were good,
though we never believed it."
—R<small>ITA</small> D<small>OVE</small>, from *Thomas & Beulah*

Contents

Characters

LOUISE "WEESIE" BOLTON MOSBY (B. 1937): matriarch. She is the daughter of Lady and Mann Bolton of Thomson, Georgia, but has spent the majority of her life in Columbia, South Carolina. Weesie has an older brother, Peter, of Columbia, and a younger aunt, Hazel, of Chicago, IL. She marries Teeta in 1957.

JAMES "TEETA" MOSBY (B. 1934): patriarch, Korean War veteran. He is the son of Queen and Oscar Mosby of Green Sea, South Carolina. He and Weesie purchase the house at 154 Redwood Court in the late 1960s.

RHINA MOSBY TABOR (B. 1962): first child of Weesie and Teeta. She is born and raised in Columbia, South Carolina. She marries Thomas "Major" Tabor when she is seventeen, in 1979. They have two daughters, Sasha and Mika.

THOMAS "MAJOR" TABOR (B. 1959): first son of Annie and Thomas Tabor. He is raised in Charleston, South Carolina. Major has two older sisters, Jesse and Olive, and a younger brother, Griffin.

UNCLE JUNIOR (B. 1974): Rhina's little brother by twelve years; Weesie's surprise child, born when she is thirty-six. He has a daughter, Destiny.

SASHA "SISSY" (B. 1980): Major and Rhina's first child, the first grandchild of the family. She is five years older than Mika and moves out right after high school to work and make a way for herself.

MIKA (B. 1985): second child of Major and Rhina. She is the baby of the family until Destiny is born in 1997, right before Mika turns twelve.

AUNT HAZEL: Weesie's aunt, though born several years after Weesie.

DAISY: blood relative of Weesie on the Bolton side, living in Tampa, Florida.

DONNELL: Daisy's grandson in Tampa. He is two years older than Mika.

REDWOOD COURT NEIGHBORS

REGGIE AND PEARL: Teeta and Weesie's immediate neighbors to the left.

MRS. JACKSON: neighbor to Reggie and Pearl, two doors to the left of 154.

RUBY: Teeta and Weesie's immediate neighbor to the right.

AUNT JESSE AND UNCLE QUINCY: Teeta and Weesie's neighbors across the street; Major's older half-sister and brother-in-law.

DOT: Aunt Jesse's immediate neighbor to the right.

CALVIN: Aunt Jesse's immediate neighbor to the left.

Stories Everyone
Knows and Tells

My grandpa Teeta says I am the second and last daughter
of Rhina, who is the only daughter of Weesie, who was
the first daughter of Lady, who is the secret daughter of Big Sis,
who was born to Sarah, who came from Esra, the adopted daughter of Ruth (who adopted her because Esra was a slave and was
sold without her mama, but the story was Esra's mama had thir-
teen children depending on who asked and depending on if you
counted those unborn or born dead). Ruth had five children,
three blood and two like Esra. Teeta says when we go back that
far it's hard to know who or what is what. That far back and it's
not a matter of blood relations so much as a matter of who
brought up who? Who protected who? Who survived with who?

I am writing all of this down.

I tell him I have to draw a diagram for my history project and
bring an artifact, one that traces my history all the way back to

whatever country we emigrated from to come live in the United States. I know we didn't emigrate *like that,* that is, of our own free will, but I ask him if he knows what countries at least we go back to.

"Baby, the way I see it, I don't know if us Negroes get to answer that question in this life," he said, pulling the cigarette from the corner of his mouth. I feel a way about his use of "Negroes," because I thought the right term was "African American." That's what I've been taught to use. Teeta says ain't nothing African about him but maybe his skin. The way *they* see him. To me, Negro sounds too close to the N-Word, but he says it's clearer to him to define himself this way. Folks saying "Black" these days and meaning . . . not always American. He takes a sip of Sanka coffee I fixed just right. Just like he taught me: hot water, two sugars to three scoops of the bitter powder.

"How far back do you know we go?" I ask.

Jenny, who knows she's Irish American, showed the class the family Bible where her blood relatives were documented back to the 1600s. Tucker, Dutch American, brought his grandmother's doll with tiny wooden shoes, holding flowers that looked like teacups on the stems—tulips. Next week, I'm supposed to present whatever I bring to represent the country of my origin. I had asked Daddy to help me first, but he won't no real help. Told me to just make a cowboy doll since he knows for sure he was born in Texas—what his birth certificate says. "That country, if they ask, is America," he goes. I roll my eyes at his answer, but I also understand that it's the only answer he has. I came to Teeta to see what he knows.

"We go back to Georgia for your grandma Weesie's side, I guess."

"And for you?"

"Sometimes I like to think we just emerged from the earth, like Adam. How we 'spose to go back."

"Don't you want to know more? Where we come from? Where we going?" I ask him. He squints at me how he does when he knows I'll be on a list of questions he can't answer. Teeta shrugs and says he don't know if he wants to know more.

"What I know about who on this side of the ocean suffered what they did so that I could live the life I got is good enough for me. Waving somebody else's flag ain't gone give me more purpose than the one I waved in the wars I fought." He pushes himself up a bit on the couch, but doesn't sit upright fully. "How I see it, I either wallow in the unknowns that I ain't never gone know, or I rest knowing my peoples over in Green Sea, South Carolina, is made of salt water and collards and oak-smoked ham."

What am I made of? That's not quite the question for the project, but it has arrived on my heart. How do I know what I am made of? I ask Teeta if we have anything written down anywhere—or if there was something I could bring in to satisfy the impossible-for-me assignment? What does it feel like to have a *thing* or *things,* like our own stories and books and whatever, to hold our histories that future generations can reference?

"Teeta, how do you think the future generations will know the lives we've lived?"

He sucks so hard on his cigarette you'd think he was pulling tobacco through it to the back of his throat.

"Baby, that's your assignment, I guess. You the future generation," he says. He leans his head back over the arm of the sofa, like how I watched a baby bird out my window calling for his mama, and puffs out Os into the still air of the den. "Whoever come after you, if that's your plan, that's the future, and whoever after that—that, too, the future."

"But Teeta, who will tell them who *we* are?"

I'm thinking about how Missy has a book she could bring to class that is as big as the Britannicas in Uncle Junior's room. Ms. Hunter showed us a book that was published and is sitting in the main branch library where her great-great-grandfather and all of the things—and people—he owned is listed.

What about us?

I didn't realize my voice raised so high at the end of my question. Daddy's cowboy-doll compromise meant I was coming to class saying I was just an American, nothing more. Nothing like my classmates who were American but also descendants of folks who chose to leave their known countries to be here. Teeta didn't seem to understand me when I told him bringing in a handmade doll wasn't the same as having something that people who lived years ago had touched and saved and put away and moved from country to country, house to house to house, until Timmy could bring it to class, and by that point—after all those generations and years and hands—it would be an *artifact*. That folks already had *historical* artifacts to bring in from home, that no one was *making* a thing to pack into their backpack.

He shrugged again.

"Someone made whatever it is them kids is branging in at some point to be passed down."

I am worried if I don't pass this assignment I'll ruin my perfect grade in history and—like how everyone warns—my chance at college, 'cause it'll be on my *permanent record,* and if I'm to be the first off to college, I have to pass every. Single. Class.

But this hurdle—the ocean between what's asked of me and what I can answer.

·   ·   ·

"BABY, SURE, YOU GOT THIS PROJECT. DO IT. MAKE A FAMILY TREE branch or whatever. The lines I just told you about. I trust whatever you submit will be fine like it always is. But I guess I'm saying, maybe there's a bigger something to go after that won't never be finished—that you'll make and make again and make some more, since you asking all these questions. You know, you sit at our feet all these hours and days, hearing us tell our tales. You have all these stories inside you—that's what we have to pass on—all the stories everyone in our family knows and all the stories everyone in our family tells. You have the stories you've heard and the ones you've yet to hear. The ones you'll live to tell someone else. That's a gift that gives and gives and gives. *You* get to make it into something for tomorrow. You write 'em in your books and show everyone who we are."

Part One

Redwood Court

It took thirty-two breaths to walk from Weesie's front porch on the farm in Thomson, Georgia, to the county line, where the postman delivered their mail. Mostly bills, but sometimes a postcard or letter from her aunt Hazel who lived in "Chee-cago," saying, *Things are good,* or *Send money if you can,* or *Snow reached our windows for the third day in a row.*

When Weesie stood on the porch, there weren't any other houses for as far as the eye could see. There were other things she liked: being at the end of the singular road, so that if she heard the *sherr* and crunch of rocks under tires, that signaled someone was coming all this way intentionally to see about them; you don't just pass by the end of a country road. And Weesie liked company. She felt her family didn't get enough of it and wanted more. Even from the little glimpses of whatever life Aunt Hazel lived in Chicago, Weesie was jealous of her escape from farm life and its cyclical monotonies. That's what happened with the younger generations. Yes, yes, Hazel was an "aunt," because she was Lady's little sister, but she was born a few years after Weesie. Because of the times and the place, Weesie, as young as she was, had to care about a harvest season, reaping and shelling the butter beans, cutting and drying the tobacco leaves. The long, drawn-out days of it all.

She never saw it with her own eyes, thank God, but the white folks were closing in on her family's little piece of farmland, increasing their public acts of violence in an attempt to recover their dignity, first post-Depression and now post–World War II. Nothing was ever enough. Weesie couldn't go into town unaccompanied, and Mann (what everyone called her father) had to teach her how to hold a steak knife in her waistband—instructed use: *for emergencies only*. Mann himself had to make sure all of his steps were ordered just to go and pay a bill or get some nails from the hardware store, lest he, too, be disappeared, and the family read about some hunter finding his body in the woods an indeterminate amount of time later. Lady (what everyone called Weesie's mama) scoffed: Won't it the tail end of the first half of the twentieth century? Still, they felt the need to tiptoe around. Was there anywhere Black folks could go to be free like they said they were supposed to be?

It was the body found hanging from the light pole that had sealed their fate in Georgia. He was so gone—the maggots having done their maggoty thing—no one who saw the body knew who he was. Signature white-folk moves. Story was told that whoever he was had been caught stealing a stamp from the post office. Later, folks learned Jacob was trying to write a letter to his cousin in Detroit, to see if any money could be sent down because the harvest won't as strong this June 'cause of the drought and the air was as dry as a sack of flour and even the drought-resistant crops gave up the ghosts and burnt. Could you believe it? That's what prompted Lady to start packing. Mann won't dare picture himself in the city or noplace where you could see into your neighbor's house just looking out the window, so he said he didn't know where *she* was going—whatever this place was called Columbia—but he won't be going with them. He had his shot-gun, he said. Let them white folks come.

A month later Lady, Weesie, and her brother Pete were in Co-lumbia, South Carolina, in temporary housing. They chose Co-lumbia because it was due east and the first "big city" they got to, and also because some other family had made their way there in 1946 after the war dust settled. It had taken Lady two years to make the leap herself. Compared to Thomson, there were so many houses and buildings with multiple stories, you had to look up where you were walking to know where you were going. Ev-erything in Columbia was hard roads and manicured trees. Folks were closer together; it was hard to see where you could go and where you couldn't. Everywhere signs were shouting COLORED ONLY / WHITES ONLY and so forth. In Thomson, you knew on one side of the railroad tracks was for the whites and on the other side of the railroad tracks, down the road and around the corner, was for Blacks.

Here, you'd have a department store for whites, and across the street a department store for Blacks. When Lady got a job at Woolworth's and needed something for the house, she had to clock out, walk across the street, and pay full price for the tea towels or frying pan. Then the white folks decided they wanted downtown to themselves, so she had to drive across town to buy the things she sold ten hours a day—only those items were WHITES-ONLY items; she had to go use up her gas in search of the Black ones.

For Weesie, though, it all felt shiny, different. The front-lawn grasses were watered so much that it was too green to look real. Even the brick rows of two-room residences felt like a luxury: the bathroom was *inside* the building, even if you had to share with a neighbor. You knew you had arrived if you had one of those plug-in stoves to get cooking, and maybe best of all, some of the houses were hooked up so you turned a knob over the washtub and the water was hot. Even though it came out brown first and they had to run it 'til it ran clear, it was hot, automatic water.

So this was heaven.

WEESIE LOVED TO TELL THE STORY OF HOW SHE'D FIRST MET Teeta at the collard-green stand. She'd say, "At the collard green in nineteen and fifty-two." Teeta was unloading the truck early one Saturday morning and Weesie was coming for her bundles for Sunday supper. Teeta was pulling out a patch of mustard greens just as Weesie was walking up, and before he could put the bundle on the wood table, Weesie scooped them up.

"These my favorite. They sweeter than collards. Don't need the sugar to take out the bite," Weesie said. She smiled at him. Teeta tipped his hat and kept unloading.

If Teeta were there when Weesie was reliving those days, he'd say something about how he didn't even know *what* Weesie was talking about. Greens is greens. He was just trying to make his five dollars for the day, so he could go to the pool hall later that evening before heading back to Green Sea on the coast until the next weekend. It won't until she kept coming back and kept trying to grab his hands *and* the mustards that he started to think something. Finally, one day she asked his name. "Teeta," he said, smiling. By then, Weesie had decided she would always be the one to make the collard run every Saturday, and every Saturday like clockwork, Teeta was there.

Until one day he wasn't.

When word got around that they were requesting more men to support in Korea, Pete suited up for the navy. Lady did some scheme with the other Negro women managing the enlistment paperwork and her baby Pete came back beaming: he could stay stateside and clean the ships and manage the goings on in the shipyard. He only had to go an hour and a half away. This was relief enough for Lady and Weesie, though it felt eerily familiar to the tension in the air in Thomson just before they fled: every day, another Black man raptured into the sky. The third Saturday came and went without any sighting of Teeta. And then a new gentleman arrived managing the collard-green stand. He was older, probably not draft age—Weesie could tell because of all the grays and the ways his jowls hung low like Mann's did the older he got. She asked the collard-stand owner where the young gentleman Teeta was these days and he said only, "They shipped him off."

The sweet potatoes in her hand just about fell straight to the ground.

OF COURSE, WHOLE LIVES WERE LIVED IN THE YEARS BEFORE Weesie and Teeta got married. But when Weesie tells it, it's as if her life started when Teeta came back to Columbia five years after they first met and looked for her at the collard stand. Truth was the army shipped Teeta back to Green Sea, where he floundered for some time trying to land but couldn't find a drop a work and didn't want to necessarily go back to the fields. He yearned to get back to the big city.

Teeta couldn't remember exactly what Weesie had looked like, only that there was a buttered-cornbread-colored young woman who always bought two collard bunches and one mustard, and took her time picking through the largest and roundest sweet potatoes. When he finally wandered his way back to Columbia, every Saturday he'd roll off his army brother's mother's couch and say he was going to work. It was something like work. He would go and help the elderly carry a week's worth of fresh vegetables to their trunks and get a few coins in thanks. He would walk up the road to the Winn-Dixie and offer to help bale the empty vegetable boxes, sweep—anything. Sure, he was getting whatever thanks the service offered for years of his life and pieces of his brain—and he gave up most of that for his share of the rent, for a few cans of Schlitz or Olde English, his ration of Marlboro cigarettes from the Shamrock Corner Store, and a few rounds of pool at night. It was when that routine got old and folks kept asking when he would settle down that he remembered the woman he had wanted to get to know before he was sent off to the war. Just when he had gotten the nerve to ask her to go steady, he turned eighteen and immediately was served papers. He figured it won't no use starting something only to go off and die in Korea and leave her broken.

But he'd survived and found himself in Columbia again, and once he got his sea legs under him, he thought, once he stopped hearing the rattle of machine guns at night even above the whirr of the floor fan, once he could go outside and see a high-yellow person walk in front of him and know they won't the enemy, then he could consider creating the life he'd wanted to build in the before. He had tried with a few women and failed. So he went to the collard-green stand and he returned and returned again and again—until, eventually, there she was.

As Teeta tells the story, Weesie was fussing, as usual, about the quality of the greens to the old man, insisting he look for a better mustard bunch, just one, and she already had with her the round sweet potatoes and two collards. They had exchanged names all those years ago, but he couldn't remember hers. He had, however, remembered to wear his best shirt, like he did every Saturday, hoping their timing would align.

Weesie takes over telling the story at this point, and always has to say that Teeta had come up a little too close behind her and she had reached for her steak knife that she still carried because white folks was crazy, especially as the rumblings of civil rights had started to make their way into town.

Teeta always shakes his head, remembering her reaching behind her back. He held his hands up and just said, "It's me, Teeta. I used to give you the best mustards right here."

And then once Weesie realized it was the man with the sweet greens, they laughed, and that exact day they went for a ride in her car. It was when Teeta tried to get too fresh that she stopped the car in the middle of nowhere and kicked him out.

Weesie would shrug and wink at Teeta. He'd let out a short huff, still in disbelief.

"I had to hitchhike back to our side of town," Teeta would say, smirking, shaking his head.

Three months after they met again, they were married and moved in with Weesie's brother, Pete, and his new bride, Viola, over near downtown Columbia, not far from the main Greyhound bus station. Two young couples with still-war-weary men at the beginning of their lives.

It was all a blur if you asked Weesie to make sense of it, to map out how four adults and five kids all did it. It was as if the house unfolded each time a new baby came, and there was room for everyone. Even if it felt like how she imagined her aunt Hazel's life in Chicago might be—busting at the seams with bodies crammed in each corner—she rested in the belief that it would be temporary, because she had set her sights on a new subdivision called Newcastle that was coming along on the other side of town in what folks called "the suburbs." Newcastle was an all-Negro residential neighborhood with three- and four-bedroom ranch-style brick houses with good-sized lots. Enough for a garden and more. If they just saved up and made the right moves at the right time—God's timing—they could have a new house, too. And word was, soon there would be a groundbreaking ceremony for a shopping complex around the corner, and a whole retail corridor just down the road.

When the street names started to be mapped out and signposts pounded into the ground, open houses popped up every Saturday and Sunday, competing with weekend shopping. If you were one of the early ones, you could choose your plot and wait for the construction and simply move in. Just like that. Weesie sacrificed a Saturday at the flea to go to the construction sites and get a feel for what she really wanted. She tried several of the names on for size: Weldwood Court, Newcastle Drive, Coolstream, Redwood Court, Devoe, and so on. Then she tried them in order of how you came into the subdivision, just off Shakespeare Road: Carlton Drive, Jonquil Street, Carnaby Court, Redwood Court, Newcastle Drive.

Weesie loved Redwood Court because she liked the way it sounded in her mouth, and depending on who she said it to, it could sound like a Columbian (and not country Georgian) accent, though she was still known to dip down her vowels even lower just for "Court" if she said it too quickly, and couldn't help that she added a half syllable. "Coat-eh." She had to think to say "cut" to get it to sound right. It didn't matter; when she found her house, she loved to say it out loud: "One fifty-four Redwood Court." Her soon-to-be new address. On a cul-de-sac with nineteen other houses—the most houses she'd ever lived close to.

Even though they nearly all went up the same year, 1968, this was back when there were craftsmen, and while everyone started with a bath and a half, a carport ("car pote"), three bedrooms, and a back patio, there was a uniqueness that showed care. You weren't just choosing any-number ranch house in Newcastle. You were choosing your lifestyle, your retirement, a part of your family.

One fifty-four Redwood Court was in the middle of the cul-de-sac on the right side, the east side. The top of the court faced due north, so if Weesie stood in her carport and looked right, she could see all the houses that rounded it out. Looking left, she could see the stop sign. The only other house that had nearly the same view was across the street; but they didn't have a magnolia, and they definitely didn't have a eucalyptus tree or a raised concrete patio that Teeta started sketching plans for an addition to even before they sat with the bank. Most owners on the Court, they learned, had kids or were planning to, or grands, and that made Weesie and Teeta feel not so bad about their six-year-old daughter, Rhina—alone, once they left Pete and Viola's house and moved into paradise.

ONE OF THE THINGS WEESIE BROUGHT TO REDWOOD COURT that had been instilled in her in Georgia was an overwhelming sense that where systems fail, people prevail. Maybe Lady said that phrase first, having gotten it from someone else when they had all chipped in a dollar to help pay for the burials of loved ones. At Redwood Court, Weesie saw it happen day in and day out: people cultivating their own bounties to share with one another. Reggie, their neighbor to the left, grew squash and cucumbers; Teeta set up with tomatoes, strawberries, and bell peppers; and Ruby, to their immediate right, had the tallest pecan tree Weesie had ever seen in her life—and in Georgia, she had seen some pretty tall ones. All of them born just after the Depression, which is to say all of them raised by parents grown enough to think they wouldn't make it through, yet found ways to survive: being strategic about where you might invest what little you did have, and always, always understanding the basic truth of living with less, which is that the sum of parts could make a whole.

If Weesie didn't know any better, it was like Redwood Court was waiting for her—the final swipe of paint on the Sistine Chapel. What men ruled at the church—deacons and trustees and so on—Weesie and now her neighbors Ruby and Dot had in Redwood Court: a kingdom. And so they organized cookouts hosted by different houses, and yard sales to make a few dollars. It was always funny to watch a trinket move from house to house to house until, finally, Weesie would catch it at the flea market in Lexington and watch a white lady pay five dollars for a mammy ceramic or some such.

Out of everyone who had found their way to the Court, no one had grown up in a real subdivision, so there was a level of improvisation when it came to establishing codes and conducts. Having the backbone of church upbringings certainly helped in that regard. For those folks on hard times, Weesie had gathered all the ladies of the houses and offered to be block captain for the benevolence fund, a kitty for folks in the cul-de-sac who had a specific need that they felt an influx of cash could support. Armed with her manila folder with ledger lines, she went door to door to collect any change, really, to purchase a bouquet for someone who had died, or to be able to hand over an envelope of the Court's "love offering."

Weesie knew the need mostly because she made it a point to make people her business. After a few years in the classroom as a primary school teacher's aide, she understood that she liked being of service to folks, but also relished the exchange that happens in the small moments. As an aide to Miss Hinton, a strict disciplinarian, Weesie found her special time with the students to be between lessons—during quiet-work moments, at lunch, before and after school. It was Weesie's turn to ask questions then. She loved getting to know the children and learning their stories, mostly because they gave her so much information.

One afternoon during a shared lunch with Vera, a student she helped often during class, Weesie learned that the girl once went into the candy store looking for a few pieces of penny candy and couldn't figure out why the clerk lied and said he didn't have any.

"Was it a white man?" Weesie had asked, knowing where this story might be going. Vera nodded.

In the store Vera had pointed to the candy she wanted—the ones she could afford and also the ones that happened to be her favorite—and asked, please, for two strawberry-flavored pieces. The clerk with the candy who said he ain't had none then grabbed his ruler and brought it down at a hard angle on the finger Vera pointed in the direction of her desire. The clerk had moved so quickly, Vera said that it won't until the brightness in her eyes had faded from the shock and pain did she realize she was bleeding.

"Don't you have no manners, girl?" Vera said the clerk had

asked. Weesie reached for Vera's hand and rubbed the child's fingertip, where she could still see the faint marks of a scar.

"And then, when I got home, Mama took a switch to me. I was bleeding and crying and trying to tell her how this man lied 'bout not having no candy and *she whippin' me,* talking 'bout I shoulda known better than to go to that store. But it was a candy store."

Weesie had thought about Miss Hinton and her style of teaching. If she had been a half shade lighter, she coulda passed, and maybe that's where her resentment came from? Every lesson, to accentuate her point, Miss Hinton tapped the sharp corner of a yardstick on the blackboard. Or whenever the students were too rowdy, she'd whack the edge of her desk and the noise would strike its way to the back of the class, where Vera was with Weesie, freezing up. Weesie understood why Vera had required that each lesson be repeated slowly, whispered in her ear like a lullaby. Moments like these made clearer to her a new path: cosmetology.

When parents and neighbors in Redwood Court understood that Weesie was gentle, even with the broken ones, and could whisper a child still even with a hot-iron comb a millimeter from their ears, they came two-by-two to the back door of the house each Sunday after supper. Weesie didn't mind—she was making a bit extra above her teacher's aide wages, and getting to know the neighborhood children who liked to play with Rhina. Plus, in between the sizzling pulls of the hot comb turning kinky hair straight, she could enjoy one of her favorite pastimes: gossip.

One time, Dot had brought over her girl even though Weesie had just pressed her hair the week before. Dot had all but shoved the child into Weesie's seat in the middle of the kitchen and started getting to *her* story. How Buddy had been taking to drink too much these days and it was starting to impact their marriage.

"You know, I make a bit extra cleaning those houses by the lake. I put it in my cigarette case 'cause I figure Buddy has his own, and I mine, so won't no use in being up in my case. I come in from sweeping the carport and I see it open on the counter. I don't leave it open; that's how they get stale. All but three dollars is gone. I had saved almost ten dollars, Weesie."

Weesie had just been brushing the child's hair, helping smooth out the few strands that were starting to loosen back into a curl. She couldn't put more heat on it so soon or she'd risk damage.

"Did you ask him 'bout it?" Weesie took a few pats of blue hair grease off the back of her hand and smoothed the girl's edges.

"Last I asked him any question, if it was a bad day, he'd take it to be a whole accusation of his character. It's like he'd blink and his eyes would look into the distance, *through* me, like he was back in Korea and I was the enemy."

"Yeah. Teeta goes there, too, sometimes. Once he was so deep in it, I had to throw a glass a water on him," Weesie said. She had finished the girl's hair.

"You dumped water on him like he was a cat?" the girl asked.

"I guess I did, baby," Weesie said, chuckling while raising her eyebrows at Dot. The next time Dot came off schedule, she was alone.

Folks kept coming, even before she was official with her license, spending their own hard-saved dollars for her hair work. The added bonus of getting to know folks, of being counsel or sister-friend, made the hours on her feet more joyful than a whole week in the classroom. It was how Weesie knew Mrs. Jackson's husband had gone in for a biopsy, how she knew that the first house on the right when you get to the bubble of the cul-de-sac had a kid who liked to start trouble (one day for the heck of it he set the bathroom curtains aflame). And how she could keep tabs a bit on Teeta without confronting him directly—folks would come into her kitchen and tell her stories, or more often lay they troubles down, as the song goes.

So, when Weesie heard (though not from them) that Johnny and June, also at the top but on the left of Redwood Court, fell behind on their mortgage and could face their house being taken away, and then Rhina would lose her best friend, Weesie got to thinking of what she could do—what Redwood Court could do—to keep them in their home. And she thought that a cookout and fish fry could be the perfect answer.

Armed with her manila folder, Weesie went up and down Redwood Court, skipping Johnny and June's, for a two-dollar investment from each house to buy supplies for the fundraiser. Some folks required a bit more convincing because this seemed like a bigger task—saving a house—than, say, sending a bouquet or a one-time cash infusion.

"Don't God tell us to lean on his understanding?" Weesie would start her story at the door. She'd refuse entry by waving the manila folder—showing her visit was a business one, not a social one. "Just think: two dollars today can help us make plates for all of Newcastle. They'd come, get a fish plate or a burger sandwich. We can save some for the Court kitty for future big events like this. If you give today, you can get your plate free on Saturday. And we can keep Johnny and June as neighbors. Can you imagine anyone else living there with those azalea bushes? Being in community with us?"

Most times it worked. Except with Clara, down near the stop sign, who always kept a rotation of rottweilers in her gated front yard, and so Weesie had to position herself in front of her screen door just so and holler *"Clay-rah"* just above the barking to get

Clara out the house to meet Weesie at the fence. Clara lived alone and never said why, but sometimes Weesie could get her to open up. Today, though, Clara was one of the holdouts, and Weesie had to get her arsenal of tools to convince her to participate. It was important that Weesie be able to report to the neighbor in need that 100 percent of Redwood Court had made the gesture. Clara claimed she didn't eat fish plates, even though Weesie knew it was a lie. She came back every Saturday morning from the river with a bucket and her poles and smelled of burnt oil in the afternoon. Weesie said there'd be something for her there, though; she'd make sure of it.

"Besides, remember when you had to get your gate fixed because your Prince kept jumping it?"

Clara nodded.

"I would never tell folks' business like this, you know, but June and Johnny was the first to chip in, and the most. 'Bout dumped the whole of their wallets into the kitty. Johnny went with Teeta to get the materials, and it was Johnny's post digger that got it done."

Weesie tapped the top of the fence post.

At the cookout that Saturday, Weesie told anyone who bought a plate that Redwood Court, all of them, took care of they own.

TEETA CAME IN FROM A FULL DAY OF YARD WORK AND CATCH-ing up with Reggie over the back fence. He'd enclosed the raised patio for an informal den space not long after they'd moved into 154 Redwood Court and got to working on a screened enclosure just off the side of the den. It would have room for off-season clothes storage, another full ice box where he kept what he called his "refreshers," and the extra tables and chairs that they pulled out whenever Weesie had it in her to host a cookout on the warm holidays, like Easter, or Memorial Day, or the Fourth, or Labor Day, in that order. Teeta especially loved that time of holidays strung along like tinsel because he could mask the increasing numbers of Olde Englishes he was drinking every weekend. Weesie saw it, of course, but chose not to make a deal out of it. She knew it was working in the morgue at Bull Street state hospital—bottling up bad brains and things, on top of the wounds from Korea—that made Teeta think he had to cling to drink like a totem. Like it would steady his shaking hands. Won't no use fighting the truth with folks not ready to see it.

Like Mrs. Jackson, who thought she could muscle her way through her husband's cancer diagnosis when sugar diabetes was making its way to her limbs. Weesie had called out to her one day when she was driving down the street, headed home. Mrs. Jackson lifted her hand and let it fall. Weesie took it to be something like shoo-flying her away and so started on her way inside the house. From the kitchen door, if she leaned just right, Weesie could see Mrs. Jackson's brown-and-blue station wagon in the driveway. They had a garage with a working door, and Weesie saw inside one day—it was packed so tight with boxes, she understood why the Jacksons never used it.

When Mr. Jackson went to the hospital the last time, Weesie watched the ambulance carry him out, and watched again when they brought him back. It took four men to lift him and his oxygen tank and stretcher up the three steps of the front porch. Because his black sports car was also parked in the driveway close to the house, it meant that Mrs. Jackson had to park behind it and walk almost from all the way at the yard curb to her door, some twenty-five or thirty steps, depending on how much her sugar was weighing on her gait.

"Teeta, she shuffling now. Mrs. Jackson. Look!" Weesie said, leaning further out the kitchen door. Teeta had come into the dining room rustling for a snack.

Weesie started dialing Ruby, but Ruby won't able to see past her yard, Weesie's yard, and Reggie's house, so she hung up to dial Dot directly. She was 'cross the street.

"Hey, Dot. Weesie. Yeh, fine. You know. Same-o. Say, can you see Mrs. Jackson out your window? Yeh. I figured she'd still be trying to get inside." Weesie covered the receiver and turned to Teeta, perched on the island, chewing on whatever he found—saltines, maybe. "Dot saying she bent over like the midmonth moon."

Teeta shrugged, nodded.

"Yeh. When I saw her, she was leaning on the car for support, but I guess without it . . ." She trailed off. "Hold on, Dot." Weesie handed the phone to Teeta to hold while she rustled around in the back porch. Teeta almost held the phone to his ear, as if to say his greetings. But he cleared his throat of the crumbling crackers and wiped his mouth with the back of his hand. Weesie emerged a few moments later with a set of crutches she kept from her day job in the salon at Crafts-Farrow State Hospital—one of the patients had started so fast from the sudden rush of warm water Weesie had put against her scalp that she punched her in the stomach. The force knocked the wind out of Weesie and she slipped and fell while still squeezing the sprayer. When she got up to chase after the patient-client, Weesie slipped back onto the floor with her foot directly under her butt.

"OK, Dot, I'm back. Wanted to see if I kept the crutches from when Dr. Johnson said I sprained my ankle. Yeh. They super short, so you can save your armpit. The first set I sent back 'cause I was so sore. He said to set it lower, and you know I had tried that! Anyways, maybe Mrs. Jackson can use them."

Teeta sucked his teeth. "I don't know why you keep trying with her, Weesie," he said. She rolled her eyes and leaned the crutches against the fridge, then reached for the counter cloth to wipe the stove—her busywork while on the phone.

"Maybe I'll take 'em tomorrow. Yeh. Yeh."

She stopped wiping.

"Teeta. Dot says Mrs. Jackson cain't even lift her legs enough to get up the stairs! We should go over." Weesie hung up the phone and contemplated taking the crutches over. It was already going to be a task to get Mrs. Jackson to accept any help, much less hand-me-down items that screamed with every *click-click-clack* and foot shuffle just how much help was needed. Maybe if introduced all at once, she wouldn't be able to choose what to deny. Weesie left the crutches this time, and before she could get halfway across Reggie's yard, she heard Mrs. Jackson's voice, as raspy as Sunday newspaper coupons crinkling open.

"I'm alright, Louise."

Mrs. Jackson was truly the only person to call her by her government name other than the pastor at her wedding ceremony in 1957. Even he had to catch himself when it came time for the couple to recite their vows. But when Mrs. Jackson moved to Redwood Court, Weesie brought her a basket of oranges and a few sprigs of her homegrown eucalyptus as a welcome gift. Mrs. Jackson half-smiled and didn't let her in. Weesie welcomed her anyways with her usual "Everyone calls me Weesie, so please—"

"I prefer we use real names," Mrs. Jackson interrupted. Caught off guard, Weesie said her name like she was spelling it out for a bill collector. "Louise Mosby. Married to James Mosby." Won't no need in saying Teeta either. "We over at 154, two doors down." Mrs. Jackson nodded.

"Nice to meet you, Louise. We should get on to unpacking. Thanks again."

Weesie knew when to push her luck and that day wasn't one of them. When she heard the same tenor from the steps of the front porch, where Mrs. Jackson had paused in her journey from car to house, Weesie slowed down, sure, but kept coming. Mrs. Jackson must have wagered that won't no use sending her away, and you couldn't, anyways, once Weesie had it in her to do something.

"I'm just coming to see 'bout Mr. Jackson. Must been weeks since sunshine touched his forehead, huh?" She tried to deflect while glancing across the street. Dot was standing in the screen door. Oh, Dot. Just showing all the cards.

"I said I'm fine, Louise. You can call off the hunt," Mrs. Jackson said while still doubled over, pointing her chin in Dot's direction. Dot waved.

Weesie reached down with her hands under Mrs. Jackson's armpits to straighten her up, like she did for Mrs. Cook, the white lady whose house she went to after work and some weekends and sat with sometimes while Mrs. Cook's grown children did grown-children things. Mrs. Cook, who was old but could still do much, like use the pot, only needed Weesie's help to get up and down out of bed or her sitting chair. Weesie grunted as she lifted Mrs. Jackson from her knees.

"My mama tried to hide it for so long, too," Weesie said. Mrs. Jackson was only protesting in theory. Weesie knew a body in protest and a body surrendered. "When sugar diabetes got to her feet, it was harder to hide. Your body gives it away in other ways: how the back curves to offset the balance we lose, the way our ankles expand with water and look like tree stumps."

Mrs. Jackson sighed.

"Lift the left foot now, like that," Weesie coached. "I got you. Yep. Now the right. We can take as long as it needs to take. Were you out getting groceries? Do you need me to brang them in?"

"The Coke prolly hot and ice melted now," Mrs. Jackson said, purring. "That's all he wanted: a ice Coke and hamburger from McDonald's."

"We'll take care of it," Weesie said and carried her inside.

Working My Way
Back to You, Babe

Weesie

It was when the first occupants of the house across the street from us came and left and I had not the mouse-crumb clue about who they were or where they came from or where they was going that I decided whoever was next to take the FOR SALE sign down and set they roots on Redwood Court would be *so known*. I wanted them to come on in and feel like family.

"Don't go over there smothering them like you won't to do," Teeta warned me like *he* won't to do.

I was trying to lean as far as I could out the kitchen door without tipping into the carport. "Shush, Teeta," I tell him, "I'm just looking. They got a big fat bulldog. He was waddling behind two boys. I'm just trying to see if the woman white, though. She so bright. Shush now so I can see!"

I do what I have to do to get the information I need. I call Dot.
"She white? She look it."

Dot laughs. "Who white gone move here?"

"Someone who marry a man the color of my Lady's seasoned
skillet and trusts to have his children. You got any word?"

According to Dot, who, with Buddy, introduced herself on
the first day, Jesse has lived a life of social work and church service. Yes, she's Black. That's how she call herself, anyhow. When
Quincy joined up into the service, she became a housewife while
he was sent over to war in the final days of Vietnam to help sort
out who was going home, in what condition, and where and
when. Soon's it looked like Saigon would fall, he hopped on a
plane back to the States as the country was burning, then went
straight to his staff sergeant's office to demand release. He used
every penny saved for his own little piece of Redwood Court.

Dot say Jesse from the low country. Them folks sound like
they got a mouth full of sweet grass. Ain't that funny? I'm from
Georgia, yet when I finally marched my tail over to speak to her,
I had to squint to be able to understand. You know how my
mouth go and I worry I'll get caught up saying something I ain't
mean to say so I stopped trying and chatted up mostly with
Quincy and relegated Jesse to a wave—but not a chat—from the
carport.

Teeta reminded me of how them first residents was so discon-
nected from us all that they left the yard looking like a landfill.
Won't I trying not to re-create history? I say, "I tried being
neighbor-like!" But I just couldn't fake it.

The stories started flowing around the neighborhood. Folks
whispering they theories on a phone tree: *Why is Weesie so distant
to the wife? She have a thing for the husband?*

Dot told me what was going round.

I said, "What I need another service man in my bed for?" I told her I already got one with episodes that come and go like the coastal tides—'specially after Junior come, and so late into our thirties. It was like Teeta just come back from Korea again. My hands was too full with a toddler ripping and roaring through the nights and waiting to know if Teeta gone come back from the pool hall or juke joint or be picked up by the police—or worse—for me to be trying to have a secret relationship!

Upon hearing the absolutely untrue gossip, I brought some biscuits over to confront it directly. What did pastor say? Seek the higher ground. Ain't that something? You sit in church all your Sundays thinking a sermon won't about you at all, but ends up, it is?

So, in broad daylight, I deliver the biscuits—just in case anyone want to look out they window. I know how they do. Do my knock. You know it: the triple-double knock. *Tap-tap-tap. Tap-tap.*

I was nervous. When Jesse opened the door, I showed her the biscuits and told her what they were. (Don't ask. I know folk eat biscuits in the low country.) She says, "I know," but it sounded like "a new"—low, guttural. Atlantic salt spray making her tongue sticky. I chuckled only when I'm telling Teeta later. At the door, I was a perfect neighbor.

"This how you in this predic'ment," Teeta says. He always say I'm picking at people who ain't got nothing to do with me.

I shrug.

But anyways, she mumbled thanks under her breath and reached for the biscuits and excused herself.

I report to Ruby that she ain't even let me see more than the corner of her kitchen countertop, and that was only 'cause I was leaning. Hard. I ask Ruby if she think *Jesse* got something to hide and started my recap down my phone tree, calling Dot next.

Dot ain't have any new information, so I tell her I'll try her back after church this Sunday coming. While the phone ringing, I set up the last pots for Sunday's supper and let the cabbage simmer to melt while starting my post-church rounds.

"Glad I had my handkerchief ready for Willie Mae when the spirit caught her and she fell like one of them thousand-year oaks," I said, ashing my cigarette and ignoring Teeta's eye rolls, flapping my hand like a hummingbird to send him outside if he ain't wanna hear my stories.

"Ain't you just left 'em? Ain't y'all saw and heard the same things?"

I tell him to let me have my Sunday like I like it. Full of gospel and gossip. He went outside.

Teeta sneaks back inside just as Dot is telling me about a new boy come across the street at Jesse and Quincy's. Not Junior's age. Not their boys' age neither. Round Rhina's age, maybe late teens, like just finished school. Dot say his look more serious than Jesse's—dark, arched eyebrows. Lips that stayed straight even when she smiled at him. He prolly a man, what with how he rolled up into the driveway with two duffel bags and a trunk.

"You think it was a standard issue or travel trunk?" I ask.

She say one of them old trunks, like what Buddy brought back from Vietnam. I agree, it's too old for the boy if it look like that, and here Teeta come from the den holding a sandwich, wiping mayo from his mouth, talking about it's gotta be his daddy's.

"Yeh, Dot. Sound like his daddy's own."

I shoo Teeta away, of course, 'cause he frowned at me when I said that. I smile anyway.

"Quincy cain't be his daddy. Who he look like? Jesse? You say sharp eyebrows? Frown face?"

There Teeta go sucking his teeth. I tell Dot when she hear him he must been choking on his tomato sandwich or something.

"He ain't dying, so I guess he alright. Anyway, yeh. I can't get a sense of how old Jesse is neither. That hair tar black and no roots showing. If it won't for those hips, I swear she white."

I tell Dot I know she ain't white, I know, but we need to meet this boy, 'cause ain't no doubt girls round here done smelt him already. I got to get Rhina to that graduation stage if it's the last thing we do: just one more year. But we gotta make sure we get to this boy—Tommy, she say—before Rhina do.

"I don't know how a man got a boy name, Dot, but we gotta check him."

The cabbage done softened to the fatback. Steam creeping out the top of the pot.

"Alright. Let me go. If you see that boy Tommy over there outside again, ring me so I can play in my front garden, like I do."

Rhina

Ma says 'cause the white folks redrew the lines there's gonna be a new school built closer to us. It's the unraveling of the Movement, she says. Some white man in some office drew a circle around a building and an X marked the spot for a new one and they trying to go back to their separate peace again.

That means I have to coordinate a carpool to transfer to the closer school, though laws still make the buses—empty now 'cause we choosing to change schools—roll up and down the street. I can drive. But Ma won't let me. Still got her eyes glued to me, or else sends her surrogates to be her eyes and ears. She thinks I don't know. I understand. She blames herself for what happened to me. She always says if she had seen the signs sooner, maybe . . . I don't know. I don't like to talk about what happened. Sometimes I pretend I was like Mary—called by surprise to bring life into the world. I told my friend Willa that and she shook her head; I said, "I know, it's hard for *me* to comprehend sometimes."

But when my belly was getting too large, I had to quit cheer-leading and got some of his clothes to hide it. I sent Willa to get a few shirts, and she came back saying he offered them only after she threatened to tell Ma what went down. He grabbed a jersey and a button-down and a T-shirt from his locker and tossed them at her, and so that's my new uniform—which ain't even right, because people think we're still together. We saw each other in the hallway and he walked away shaking his head, said don't talk to him ever again. When Ma confronted me about it, why I was wearing baggy clothes and not going to cheer practice anymore, I grabbed her and cried. I couldn't say. She said she understood then.

"Don't matter how it got there," she said. "No thirteen-year-old should have to hold this weight in her womb."

I tell her I don't want it. I didn't want any of it. She purred and held me longer.

It wasn't until the doctor's office I believed her when she said we was gone love whoever or whatever come out of me, even if we don't love the circumstances. I believed Ma, 'cause when the nurses and doctors shook their heads at me while going through the motions, I could feel the temperature of the room rising. They shook their heads at Ma. Asked her how old I was like I won't even there.

"Hostile," the doctor said. Weesie sucked in the air so fast I thought she was going to jump him.

The doctor held his hand up. "The womb. She's too young. Scarring. So on."

He reached for the paperwork.

"The baby is probably going to be premature. We could do a quick procedure to fix her once it's born so as to be sure this can't happen again," he said, looking at Ma over his glasses.

Ma snatched me off the table so quickly she almost forgot my clothes.

"My baby ain't a dog. Ain't something you can just *fix*." She flung the door open. "And another thing: y'all can stop her from future babies but won't stop her from having this one?" She slammed the door behind her. She walked me to the bathroom and held my face with both hands, making me look her in the eyes.

"Don't you never let anyone make you feel like any of this is your fault; you hear me?"

I sniffed. Trying to breathe.

"Never."

Tommy

Mama sent me up to Columbia to Jesse's to breathe different air. She's my sister but we didn't grow up together. Felt more like an aunt, really. But it didn't matter, it was someplace new. I was suffocating in Charleston's salt air. Mama had depended on me to fill in whenever Daddy disappeared for his long stretches, said I was the man of the house, was up to me to protect us all. How do you say that to a ten-year-old? I had tried all those years. Somehow I made it through school. But I think, later, it was how she looked at me and said this wasn't a place for "just a boy" to hold all of what I held: My baby brother Griff in and out of the hospital with a failed kidney. Big sister Olive out in Texas with a weak heart. I've somehow made it so far without these death sentences, but one day, when Daddy saw me square up to him 'cause he lifted his hand as if to strike Mama, he cursed me. Said I would be inflicted, too.

"It's the way of things, boy. You can't escape genes. Get your living while you can. I tell Annie that's how I intend to keep on," Daddy said.

His living was hurting us though. His coming and tornado-ing through the house, then leaving, hurt us more. Mama finally asked me if I wanted to get out of Charleston to pursue my dreams. I could start off at tech school, then finish up at Carolina. Be an engineer. Make her proud.

So here I am. Didn't feel like a choice but something like duty. Nearer to service to family, like what the army asks of you. That's what I know. I know Mama's trying to get me to know different, even though she don't say it.

Jesse gave me the lay of the land, which ain't saying much. She keep to herself. That's what service families inherit, I guess. A fear of putting in roots too deep before you shipped off again. I tell her Quincy retired, let your hair down. She shook her head.

"I ain't never lived anywhere with so many nosey neighbors. It's like I walk outside and all the blinds creak open," she chuckles.

The eyes turned on me one day when I was out tossing a football on the front lawn with the boys.

"That one across the street'll be by soon enough." Jesse laughed.

There was the girl across the street. I asked about her. Jesse said she belonged to Ms. Nosey and shrugged. Those the eyes I feel the most. One day I swore the two of them—Ms. Nosey and her daughter—was just standing in the carport discussing who I was, how I come to be here. I lifted my arm acknowledging them and they hurried about their day.

Looking back, I can't call it on who or what broke the ice, but the next thing I knew I'm in the passenger seat of Mr. Mosby's car because he asked to borrow my "young man's arms" to go to the lumber yard. The radio is so low it sounds like static. Mr. Mosby has two hands on the steering wheel and both eyes forward. Both of my hands are in a neutral position: on my knees. I'm reciting "The Value of a Friend," a poem I wrote the week before at the laundromat, and tapping my fingers.

> How many times has someone told you
> "I will help, on me you can depend"
> And though you fought the war alone
> You'll share the victory with "your friend"
> You stood with me in near defeat
> Yet we were apart in victory
> In your counsel I found wisdom
> To bring joy from tragedy.

Mr. Mosby asks me, what's that I say? "Nothing, sir. Just some poetry I wrote." He nods. We watch I-20 peel open in front of us.

"Son," he starts. I look over, continue tapping my fingers. "Son, do you have any intentions?"

I stop tapping.

"With my Rhina. I seen how she look at you," he says. He turned his head when he said that.

"Sir?" I ask, clearing my throat. I hadn't thought much about her, not like that. She was pretty, sure. Quiet. We caught eyes in the yards, but that's all. Mama told me to come up here and focus on my studies, so that's what I had *intended* to do, I guess.

"I hadn't thought—" I started.

"Well, if you *think,* son, I'll take y'all out together. Chaperoned. I need to know my baby girl's safe. She's been through some things I don't intend for her to suffer again."

Thankfully, we pulled into the parking lot and a yard guy started walking toward us, grinning.

"Mose!" he shouted.

"Johnny boy!" Mr. Mosby shouted back. He pointed to me.

"He don't know it yet, but this my new boy—" He hesitated and leaned in. Asked me my name again. I whispered it. "This Tommy! He come to lift all the two-by-fours you can stack into the back of my truck, yeap!" Mr. Mosby lit a cigarette and leaned against the truck while I loaded.

Weesie

Rhina tell the story of her and Tommy like something wrong sometimes. Call it an "arranged marriage." We was tiptoeing around for three years after the baby, and I wanted to make sure she knew what she wanted. Just 'cause I helped don't make it no arranged marriage, like this ain't a free country. I guess she feel a way because it happened so quick.

"It was! All the tests. The hoops. Daddy messing with him," Rhina would laugh, leaning on Tommy's shoulder with such love and care it almost made me forget what God sought her to suffer just a few years before. But at seventeen now, she has her whole life ahead of her—senior year of high school. Family building, God willing. Intentional family building. I tell her it will be different, whenever she ready, to consider to choose to bring to life a whole person. To choose where she wants to live (on Redwood Court, though, I hope). To choose what kind of mother she wants to be.

"Choice just makes love feel different," I said. "Makes your back stack straighter when you stand."

I meant it. I mean to let her know motherhood changes you, mostly in a good way. I mean to let her know what it means to be a helpmeet to a husband. Evenly yoked, those things. She used to joke about how quick we pushed it all. I ask, can she blame us? She wonders out loud what it all would have looked like with "more time," say it was like Tommy was playing football with those boys 'cross the street, then all of a sudden Teeta asking 'bout intentions, then I was ordering a cake and dress and mother-in-law corsages for me and Ms. Annie.

She didn't care it only took Teeta and me three months to get married. She herself only had, what, five? Tommy would slink over and sit on our porch and she'd be practicing her varsity cheers, or he'd be outside exactly when her little friend carpool drop her off, and finally one day, handing him a glass of lemonade, I just say, "Y'all might as well go steady," and his eyes lit up.

"Chaperoned, of course."

Rhina sucked her teeth.

Then it seemed just as quick I was boohoo-ing watching Teeta walk her down the aisle. Sooner than that, like I swear no time at all after he tossed the garter into the crowd and Junior grabbed it and Tommy's best man, Bebe, snatched it out of Junior's hand, Tommy signed paperwork over at Fort Jackson to enlist.

I was there when he showed them to us, like a certificate of achievement. Rhina asked him, "What about your dreams?" And Tommy replied, "I have to think about us."

He slipped out for the army during the small slice of quiet

between Christmas and New Year's 1979. I had hoped he'd stay at the fort, just ten minutes away, but because of how Tommy tested, they sent him to the Zone in Korea to be a lineman, just like his father, God rest his soul.

Teeta

I try to find the goodness of the cycles repeating, and Weesie tried to offer that least I would be able to give the boy some pointers about my experience. *Hmph.*

"That boy's Korea and mine are generations apart," I said, shaking my head.

Before he shipped off, I tapped the name tag stitched on the fatigues just over his heart.

"Major," I said. His spine unfurled like a beanstalk reaching to the sky. "I guess I'll call you Major now, huh? Major, don't let them trap you in this monkey suit, you hear? Yeh, yeh, *rah, rah,* country this, praise Old Glory that. Say the script. Do what you need. But I know at the heart of all this—salary, benefits, so-called comfort— we, *you and I,* give up something soon's this costume come on."

I tap my heart.

"Black men. Them white boys think—believe—they joined a family. Prolly said that to the lot of y'all. But just know ain't no family that bottle up they healthy boys an' ship them overseas at the start of they lives like this, just when you starting out with Rhina."

He try to justify it, say they gave him a bonus. Say Rhina will be taken care of. I stop him right there.

"Not if you dead, son. Or worse. They break you only so much that you off they payroll but on disability and can't work for yourself."

He turned his face away from me. I ask him to look me in the eyes.

"Your daddy. Me. All of us of a certain generation. Broken. Now it's coming for you. Keep your wits about you, your head down, and come back as whole as you can to my baby girl."

I couldn't help it but I tapped his temple with my right pointer finger.

"Whole."

Rhina

When it happened, doctors had warned me it was going to be a premature birth and before that I would carry small. The time came to tell Daddy what had come to me, that a boy I liked had gone too far and haunched and kissed and haunched and pushed his way until he was sweaty like a cold shower rag. Daddy stood as tall and straight as a cornstalk in July. Nothing could have prepared me for what he'd say next. I was expecting some big explosive reaction. Instead, his voice melted to a coo, how he talked to baby Junior.

"That won't love, baby. A love that hurt you like that ain't love at all. I can't wait for you to find a love that wants what you want."

Now I'm marrying Major. Daddy reminded me in the small moment before the church doors opened and we were to meet Major at the altar.

"My baby done found it," he said, smiling. I asked him, What? He said, "A love that wants what you want."

So when I tell Major that God had called me to have another child, our child, after doctors said it would be impossible, I had to tell him about David. Ma reminded me so often won't no use harking on the how or what. I started the story near the end of it.

Told him how nurses held up his newborn feet and shook him like trying to jump-start his little pulp of a life. He opened his eyes and turned to Ma. She had said in that moment she saw her daddy, Mann, come back to life. She was smiling. Everyone was happy he let out any noise at all, then he turned and looked at me. I tell Major, I don't know how, but he focused his eyes and my heart dropped. Before I could hold him, they stole him away to start CPR. Stopped. That's when Ma sent them out and told me he was gone. I could, should, still name him. He was somebody for those brief moments, he was somebody. She climbed into the bed, on top of my blood and all, and held me.

"Maybe what I think David came to teach me is that I can be a mother, even if I don't feel ready," I told Major. "And because I'll be home caring for this new child, I could care for other children, make it a thing, when we go to Arizona for your post. It can keep my mind busy, and the baby company, until you come back from Korea."

I only tell Ma first about the caretaker part, when I tell her I plan on shipping out with Major within the month. I tell her it's the lesson of David. Said it with such assurance she couldn't fight it. I know it. Know her. She knows you can't reason with grief so unknown—losing a child—what could she say? She had two questions.

"Won't you be lonely? Who will be your family?"

Weesie

Folks take family for granted when it's right there, always, and don't go looking for it until it's gone and it's too late and you on the other side of a country from anyone who knows what you look like when you just got out of bed. Won't no use arguing the inevitable: Rhina was always a touch-the-stove-to-know-it's-hot kind of girl. But I had to ask if she considered who was gone stand in for family, because I knew what was going on—knew she was pregnant before she told me. Mamas always know. She'll know soon, too. Right now she needs to believe I don't know. I let her. Instead I ask her who gone be her blood.

"Me and Major a family," she said. They held hands. Bless they hearts. I look at Teeta. He know, too. We had to let her have this. Touch the stove. We knew the way she pulled back, needing space to figure this family thing out. In love. However they can get it.

When the telegram come months later, screaming, *EXPECTING! CALL US WHEN YOU CAN. LOVE, US,* I squealed. Then sighed. Ain't always satisfying being right. I dialed the long-distance number and launched my fuss when she answered the phone.

"Why y'all aint tell me 'bout my grandbaby before you and Major hopped in that little yellow Pinto and drove out West like y'all some pilgrims?"

She laughed. "Pioneers, Mama."

Whatever. "Y'all could be new-age aliens for all I care, but you coulda let me celebrate my grandbaby while y'all was here on this side of the earth. I just knew it! I told Teeta I knew—"

"Don't be mad. It's just . . ."

I hummed. She finished after a pause.

"I needed different doctors, different plans. They say I'm carrying a healthy baby even if she comes a little early, a little small."

I squealed again and repeated: *She?*

"Yeh. I don't know what I'm going to do with a girl if she come out like me, but the doctors claim their biggest worry about the pregnancy is the Arizona heat and if we can handle it. I told them I'm from the Columbia frying pan and they said, 'Yeap!

The swampy land oven,' and we laugh, and he says we gone be alright."

I raised my right hand. "Praise God. Praise God."

Rhina

My belly round as a fishbowl, rounder than with David. I know now what Mama was asking me, asking about family. Who was to be my family in the room at the birth of my baby girl?

Major called last week from Korea. He has to wait until almost 2:00 A.M. on Monday morning where he is to reach me at Sunday breakfast. Every time we talk, we travel through time. I tell him each day I feel it, Sasha's arrival, coming closer and closer.

"I'll start the request now," Major said, I think. At least, that's what I wanted to hear through the static on the line traveling all those time zones to get to me. He tells me the staff sergeant there knew his daddy.

"He said all he had to do was look at my test scores and my last name and he goes: 'Yeh, y'all Tabors all the same—smart as a whip. Hell, smarter than a whip!' He says he's going to sign my release early 'cause I asked to be in the room, in case—"

Maybe the phone connection shorted for a second.

"We'll be alright, Major," I say anyhow, in the silence. "Just start making your way here. Any day now. Sasha's ready."

Even through the crackles I heard Major loud and clear. Our song.

"... you, babe / with a burning love inside."

You could hear his smile from across the world.

"Yeh, I'm working my way back to you, babe."

My turn. "There's a happiness inside."

We hummed the rest until Major drifted to sleep.

How Do You Know
Where You're Going?

On his way to pick up his grands in his brown Toyota pickup truck with its covered camper, Teeta hit a pothole in the road, and then he was in an army-issue truck in the back-roads of Korea riding between the mine-pocked fields. There were two young girls walking row by row with a hoe or shovel, testing the hidden mines. Later, the crew back at the base mocked what they heard happen: a bandana over their eyes, soldiers used a broom handle to reach 'round the mess hall, falling in laughter at someone's surprise *KABOOOM*, shouted from somewhere in the room.

But Teeta saw it happen with his own two eyes. There were two girls with hair as black as Mika's and a mule between them. Then there was only one girl. When he made it back to the base to shower and the blood-colored water pooled at his feet, several folks asked if he was OK. Had he been shot? He looked at the stained concrete and didn't answer. The foot had sailed through the air like a boomerang. Now Teeta can't see a flock of geese going north without thinking about those girls that day in the Zone.

The worst part was he won't supposed to even be there. Working janitorial and mess hall in the service as a Negro meant his days was mostly filled with waiting until prep for the next meal; the period between lunch and supper saw him with much silence to fill, and so he had made an excuse to go for a ride— potatoes or rice was needed to round out the plate, and the platoon just across the way should have some extra. They had lost more men in the first forty days, but they still shipped rations for the full troop.

"Mosby!" someone hollered from a back office as he put on his hat and fatigue jacket.

"Just going for some supplies, sir," Teeta called back. "Be back just so." He kept walking lest he get pulled into some other menial task.

"TEN-HUT!" the voice commanded. Teeta stopped and straightened his back. He snapped his arm into a right angle, his hand to forehead. He knew he didn't have to do the salute but added it anyway, for good measure.

"Sir! Yes, sir!"

Teeta loved the service, the way aspects of it ordered his steps, were regimented like the work he had to do as a young boy on the tobacco farm back home. Measured. Somewhat predictable. Like agriculture, the army gave Teeta a set of practices that he could do over and over until his body moved like a machine, but when weather, or the enemy, entered the scene, he could rely on muscle memory and his bullet-quick reactions. But he also understood that if he chose wrong, he could lose a whole harvest. Or his life. Riding the thin edge between order and chaos was often fine for him; a command could click you right back into place like a cog into its wheel. His army brothers, they used the call to make sure everyone was right of mind. His superiors, though—if they croaked the command when there was no drill or imminent danger, it was more about power.

"I said, Where you going, boy?" Asking it now, in the way he had, Teeta knew by the syrupy lingering of *boy*—how it was reserved for just the handful of Black-skinned soldiers—that whatever was coming next could be trouble, nothing, a game, a show, or more trouble.

"We need some more supplies, sir," Teeta shouted, refusing to turn around and face his audience. "Rice, potatoes, for dinner. Kitchen towels."

"You didn't notice before now, boy?"

There was no need to repeat it. Teeta knew. He tried a different escape route. "The convalescents need more sup' so they bodies can repair, sir."

"Well, I see."

Teeta relaxed his shoulders. It was just show. He heard the smile lift the phrase a few decibels, even if he didn't see the sergeant's face.

"Yes, sir." Teeta understood from the whites back home in Green Sea, South Carolina, that if you remain small when they show they teeth, you can most times get out unscathed. For Teeta, that meant never puffing his chest, and always adding "sir" to his answers.

"Well, Mosby. At ease. How do you know where you're going, son?"

The slight timbre of care. So quick. It was the flip-floppiness, like a fresh catch tossed onto a boat deck, hook still in its lips, that made Teeta dizzy. He was often prone to whiplash. Hot/cold. Boy/son. Soldier/nigger. He joked that if he had stayed in school instead of gone out into the farm fields and then into service, he might as well have become a head doctor the way he had learned so early to measure the degrees of hatred one might have in they heart by the choice of words. When the temperature of the exchange shifted, Teeta knew he just had to defer and could soon enough be on his way.

"Sir. Medic going over for supplies, too. I figured I would catch a ride. Sir."

Teeta tipped his hat and kept his neck bent in supplication but didn't turn around until the sergeant walked off. He hopped in the back of the covered truck, and it rumbled over the service road gravel. He beat his fist against the window after the truck hit its third pothole.

"Say, you sure you know the way?" Teeta asked right before he looked over his shoulder at the rice paddy and saw the two girls and the donkey and then the one and before the medic could answer Teeta had been lifted up in the camper and dropped down by the blast.

SASHA AND MIKA CLIMBED IN THE TOYOTA CABIN ALMOST AS soon as Teeta pulled into the yard. He didn't even have to honk; they were on the porch, ready to go. Mika bounded off the steps toward the truck, and Sasha moved slower—her older tween angst weighing her excitement to a slog. Mika, still small enough to sit in the middle, lifted her left leg over the gear shift and cradled it out of his way for the drive to Redwood Court. His truck won't built for three travelers, no matter how small, so Teeta instructed Sasha to put her seatbelt on and to hold her arm across

Mika. Most times, when it was just Teeta and Mika, Teeta would let Mika ride in the back camper. He set up a few cushions and a carpet. Every few lights, Teeta'd look back to see if Mika was upright. He often had to fight the urge to see the camper transform into the back of the medic truck on the day of the blast. But every time he opened the truck's rear gate whenever they got wherever they were going and Mika squealed, "Teeta! That was fun!" he understood more and more what the priest was trying to tell him in the recovery days after. That the future and the joy and risk and pain are worth it if our generations experience a greater freedom than we're allotted.

Sasha had swung her arm over Mika too quickly, and Teeta heard a thud before Mika cried out. Teeta had never grown up around girls, much less ones who squealed like nursing piglets.

"Aye, aye, aye!" he said in the tenor of the freeze-on-command callout he was so familiar with. The girls zipped straight. How was he to fill a whole day with the two of them?

Mika leaned out of Sasha's death grip.

"Teeta, did you vote yet? Mama says she's going to do it after work, and Daddy, too. We had a vote at my school yesterday. Bill Clinton won my grade but Bush won all the other grades. Teeta, who did you vote for?"

Too many questions for the start of the day. Teeta couldn't vote because of that night in the pool hall. The owner called the cops on him for pulling his pistol out when, two tables over, someone broke the game open so loudly several balls fell to the floor and it sounded like a machine gun. He had had enough to drink, alright, and so his finger slipped on the feather-light trigger. Luckily, he won't facing anyone in the room, so only a lightbulb caught the bullet; but because he didn't have his dog tags (that only worked in certain parts of town anyhow) he went straight to booking on trumped-up charges, and on his record it said something about "attempt to damage private property." And so went his vote. But Mika didn't need all that.

"Yeap! I voted. Lost my sticker, though. Now, let's go on an adventure!" Teeta said to match Mika's excitement.

From the truck cabin, oldies crooned and Teeta ashed his Marlboro out the cracked window. Mika sat forward and, as instructed, though probably taking advantage of said instructions, Sasha pushed her back against the canvassed cushion.

Teeta put the truck in park at the stop sign and turned down the music. The girls were so quiet and breathing with such intent that, even with Teeta's cracked window, fog started to climb up the windshield from the dashboard.

"Right or left?" Teeta asked. The girls looked over at him with bewilderment.

"Which way y'all wanna go?" Teeta asked again, clarifying. Mika and Sasha looked left, looked right, looked at Teeta.

"Sasha, you go," he insisted. She surveyed her options, nothing looking like any place she had been.

"Left!"

Teeta moved his hand to the gear shift. Sasha pushed it away.

"Right! Teeta, right!" She had gotten the adventure bug, too, now seeing the possibilities in the way the road opened with just one decision.

Mika was entertained but didn't push her way into the game, let Sasha play to see where it was all going. "Teeta has to know the way to where we're going," she said to Sasha. "There's only one way to Redwood Court from home."

On command, Teeta turned right and the girls looked on to see how far before they had to make the next decision. It would be a minute as they traveled down a winding back road with not too many houses. Teeta pulled up to another stop sign, waited.

"One day, you'll see," Teeta started. "We always meet a fork in the road." He heard echoes of the medic through the glass pane. The crinkle of a Korean map unfolding. The gear shift, the wheels grinding through gravel and sand.

Teeta stopped the Toyota at the next stop sign. Sasha yelled, "Right!" Mika countered, "Left, Teeta!" But he didn't move to the gear shift at first. He closed his eyes and filled his belly with air. Then pushed the air out, imagining cigarette smoke rings chuting out of his pursed lips one by one. The girls recognized this breathing exercise and simmered down. Teeta reached for the gear and the wheel, and pushed forward in silence.

Finally, they made it to Redwood Court—on time for lunch. Teeta had a taste for iron and checked to see if Weesie had bought any livermush to fry up. After a morning bouncing between Korea and the present, smelling the burning flesh of the girl in the field and simultaneously entertaining his grands, what he really wanted was an ice-cold refresher from the back porch. He'd settle for the blood-rich liver over onions, though, and fix up some baloney sandwiches for the girls. Then insist they all rest.

TEETA DREAMED THAT HE WAS FALLING OUT OF A PLANE, AND that woke him up. It felt like how he landed in Korea, but without a parachute this time. He gasped, opened his eyes, and Mika stared straight at him. If he had startled more, they would have headbutted, but this dream—of falling through the clouds, watching the ground target get bigger and bigger—came so frequently that it was when he didn't dream a man pushed him out the back of a cargo plane that he knew darker visions would come in its stead. The startle was the feeling of gravity pulling him to earth with increasing velocity, was all.

"Teeta, you were mumbling something just now. What did you see?"

He always slept on his back with his glasses in his front pocket. At first, he was somewhere between plane and earth, sleep and awake, when Mika's voice had appeared in the atmosphere as a bodiless character—that's what shook him out of it, a child's voice asking him, "What did you see? What did you see?"

Teeta grabbed his glasses on instinct and saw Mika through the fog. His heart rate rocked back to normal.

"Just an old friend," Teeta said, finally answering. "An old friend."

Face still crinkled with concern, Mika turned to her real reason for waking him: Sasha and Weesie left while they were asleep and could she go outside? All the grands of Redwood Court were out in their yards; you could hear the *tick-tick, tick-tick* of phone-cable double Dutch games. Teeta didn't know them all like Weesie, and now that Mika was solely in his care, he hesitated letting her go out on her own, even if she had done it hundreds of times.

"Let's go out back," Teeta offered in consolation. "Been meaning to take them training wheels off your bike anyhow."

Teeta felt it had been too long for Mika, at seven years old, to be on a bike with training wheels. He had gone from being carted around in a wooden wagon through the tobacco fields to riding a two-wheeler at four, so in many ways he couldn't understand why she needed the extra support, but if he thought about it long, it made sense—the house where she lived on Forestwood Drive was on a hill and just three houses in off the road, which was Highway 1. It was what Mika's father, Major, could afford after he was discharged from service and could only pick up work as a manager at Church's Chicken for a while. Redwood Court was zoned for better schools because most of the surrounding white neighborhoods were zoned to those schools, and they bused the students in "for diversity" by then, so the girls used the Court address, which meant Mika and Sasha didn't go to school with all of the other kids on Forestwood Drive. Those factors, added with school friends and the street-protected and flat cul-de-sac of Redwood Court, meant that the very day the girls got bikes for Christmas—Sasha a red ten-speed with brakes on the handlebars and Mika a Barbie bike with handle tassels and train-ing wheels—they were taken straight to the Court.

It also meant that Mika couldn't ride often, so her time with training wheels stretched and stretched. Once, she called herself trying to ride Sasha's bike despite their height difference. She knew how to hop on, but that was as far as she got. On her bike, she could backpedal and get a sturdy foundation. She was quick enough to hop on the saddle but didn't know where to go from there. When she backpedaled on Sasha's bike and the pedal kept going around the spin, Mika had no choice but to hop off before she and the bike ended up in the dust. Oh, if she had thought it through, it might have saved her and Teeta some embarrassment later. She hopped off the seat and the bar caught her *right there*. Reggie had been in his backyard washing his Cadillac and heard Mika cry out and asked her if she was alright just as she ran into the house—past Teeta, who asked what was wrong, and into the blue bathroom to see if she had broken anything down there. When she inspected the toilet paper, there were red and pink dapples of blood. Mika tossed them into the wastebasket next to the commode and stormed back outside, past Teeta again.

Looking for any clues as to why Mika was a tornado through

the house, Teeta searched the bathroom. When he looked into the wastebasket, he thought, oh Lord, was he to have this talk today with her? How she already getting her first blood? Or was this something like what Rhina went through early? Who hurt her?

Just as he was starting to think of what to say, what to ask, Reggie called saying Mika had been playing with Sasha's bike and wanted to check in about the fall. From the window, Teeta could see Sasha's back wheel disappearing into the shed. Next time they were together, Teeta decided, it would be time to move Mika up.

"Teeta, I don't know how to ride two wheels, though," Mika countered when he suggested going out back to take her training wheels off. "Nobody will show me."

He swatted the air. "Ain't a worry. We'll get you," he said and curled off the couch.

Between clinks of the wrench against the white-painted metal of the bike, Teeta started. "You been mostly riding two wheels on this one, since the trainers don't always stay on the ground nohow." He tapped the training wheel for emphasis.

"But I don't fall," Mika said.

Teeta nodded. Jerked the wrench a few times and the first training wheel knocked off and rolled a few inches across the yard.

"To steady, you have to use your feet. It's the feet, mostly. You keep moving. You think you gone fall—keep moving. Pushing the pedals. Falls happen when you try to fix a fall by stopping. Don't stop. Keep moving."

Teeta stood the bike up and held it for Mika to step through. He was glad no one had given her this: riding a real bike. A thing you keep with you forever, take with you everywhere you go. If he did it right and died tomorrow, she'd always get on a bike and remember he taught her how to move forward.

"Get on, don't be shy," Teeta urged. He pointed the front wheel toward the house. "Ride to the house, then come back to me. I'll give you a jump start. Getty-up."

He always wondered what he could give the grands. Weesie was the perfect gift giver, especially at Christmas. Major had smarts, was their daddy. Teeta had more time than anyone, sure, but most often he fretted about whether it was enough— worrying they might tire of spending time with him just as he was starting to figure out how to make room in his crowded head and heart for the girls.

Laid up in the convalescence hall after the blast, all he could picture was a house, that cornbread-colored woman he needed to marry, and later on, kids and grands and great-grands and so on. That's what kept him moving forward, toward home. When they came, and when he realized how crowded his head was every day with cobwebs from the war, he thought about what he had to give. Who would love him? How would he connect with the next generations? But he found it. He didn't often remember too much from his childhood outside of walking up and down the forever rows of tobacco leaves, but he remembered the moment his father set him up on a bike and pushed him into a new experience. Confidence. Balance. Wind in his face. No matter how short or long their lives, Mika had this moment with him and no one else.

"Teeta, I just push the pedals?"

"Yes. Keep going. To the house. You don't wanna fall, you got to keep pushing your feets and then steer, just like how you rode when you had trainers."

Mika stepped through, and Teeta braced his body to hold the bike, her weight, upright. Mika looked up from the bike saddle like she was about to be sent on a long journey into the unknown.

"But, Teeta. How will I know I won't fall? How will I know which way I'm going?"

Still holding the handlebar with one hand and the back of the saddle with the other, Teeta started to rock the bike back and forth so Mika could feel the pedals move, learning the beginning of the balancing act. Just like his father taught him. What did he say back then?

"When I push, you push on the pedals just like you know." He smiled.

Before Mika could turn back to ask another question or stall, he gave her a push.

"Keep pedaling and turn the bike back towards me before you hit the house," he called out. "Don't stop until you're right back where you started with me. It'll feel like flying, not falling. The wind in your face. Once you got this, you'll never lose it. I promise you that."

Cinderelly, Cinderelly

The first week of summer after fifth grade, Mama and Daddy took me and Sissy to Disney World. We all saved for it—Daddy had scavenged empty water jugs from his company and set them up around the house, putting one in the living room by the front door, and another jug by his nightstand. Every night he emptied his pocket change into the jar in his room, except for $1.50—enough, he'd explain, for a gallon of gas in an emergency. Sometimes, if he was feeling good, he'd slip a dollar bill into his jug. For the jug in the living room, we followed suit: emptying our pockets, purses, wrist wallets, fanny packs, etc., when we came in, but we were forbidden from taking anything out. No excuses. I guess we sorta obeyed the laws. (Except when the ice cream truck jingled its way down the hill and we could just tip the jug by the door for a Bomb Pop or a Chocolate Eclair bar.)

It took us three whole nights—two of those Daddy worked

overtime—to hand roll each and every coin. My hands smelled like wet pennies for days. Why Daddy didn't take them to the credit union or the Coinstar machine behind the checkout at Bi-Lo is beyond me, but I guess I understand. He ain't wanna give up one precious penny we saved in all those days. All told, when we stacked all the quarter rolls, dime rolls, penny rolls, and nickel rolls, we had exactly $1,934.62 for the trip. If you add to it my earnings from selling friendship bracelets, we had $1,945.85.

Mama and Daddy kept saying this trip would be the most special because it'd probably be our last. All four of us. Any future trips and Sasha gone be too old. Unlike our last trip to Disney World when I was little, this time I'd finally be old enough to remember and even enjoy the Spaceship Mountain ride, and maybe, everyone always jokes, I won't holler in fear while meeting Mickey and Minnie. I know all the words to *Aladdin* and started tinkering around with the melody on my flute—my music teacher says it's easier to learn vibrato when you play songs you know.

Anyways, I planned to pack and wear my Jasmine shirt. Crystal and I practiced and practiced on my front porch on Forestwood Drive. We flew our magic carpet and rubbed the terracotta planters like they were our magic lamps. Now, I don't do it every time I cross it, but sometimes before I left the house I paused on the WELCOME mat and hummed, "No one to tell us no, or where to go / or say we're only dreaming."

A whole new Disney World this time, 'cause I'd be older. I used to only be able to watch *Aladdin* after school at daycare. Mama and Ms. Kaye would dump all the staff kids in a room with the movie and animal crackers and cherry Squeezits until it was time for us to go home. I only knew any of the Disney songs because in the last year we got the Disney Channel at Forestwood

Drive. Daddy had rigged the cable line somehow. One day it would be TV snow where it was supposed to be *The Mickey Mouse Club,* and the next he'd grab his BB gun and go out to the yard and shoot a signal or flag or something and say, "Give it a day," and the next, Disney would be on. He said there was a flag on the cable post that tells companies who pays and who don't. He learned how to restore our premium cable channels without paying the bill from his daddy, so I guess he was passing it on. I only heard stories about him, but Daddy's daddy—my granddaddy, I guess—started in the army as a lineman and graduated to staff sergeant recruiter before he let alcohol take him away when my daddy was just a boy. But maybe he was around long enough to teach him some things from his time in all the wars and overseas and learning secret enemy communications.

Daddy says being a lineman back then meant putting cable posts in new, uncharted territories. Blacks couldn't do but so much in the army, Daddy said, waving his explaining finger at me. (It always pops up and I think of exclamation points or imagine a thought bubble above his head and a light bulb to accentuate the point.) Blacks couldn't do much, but they could dig holes for the communications posts, and they could carry a cable line for the radio, and they could understand how to move the cable line to their cabin so that Grandma Annie could get free call updates from wherever in the world his daddy was whenever *he* wanted. I guess this was some of the same work going on so I could have the Disney Channel.

It don't matter how we got it, because we had it and no one else on our street did. Sasha loved the older films: *Seven Brides for Seven Brothers, The Sound of Music, Old Yeller, Pollyanna.* I watched them 'cause we had to share the TV. Somehow I learned all the words to all the songs, and I was so mad they had to shoot that dog. We loved the musicals. Sasha sang in chorus when she was in middle school and so always took the solos, whatever. She always acted uninterested in whatever I was watching, but whenever *Newsies* came on we'd run around the house looking for Daddy's baseball or fatigue caps and throw them on backwards and kick around our playroom scream-singing, "Golly, wow! I'm the king of New York!" with one of the paper circulars that Mama swore she needed for coupons that she never, ever used. Whenever it was time for chores, we'd put bandanas over our heads and pretend to be Cinderella before the prince, and sweep the corners of the rooms, and wash the baseboards we didn't have. But we'd turn to each other and, with a wink, chime in unison, "A dream is a wish your heart makes."

We didn't have to look hard for clothes like what Cinderella wore either—two growing girls and a budget meant our nightgowns were Daddy's hand-me-downs. No matter the washes, you could still smell on them the carburetor fluid or engine oil or general "man musk," Weesie called it. As short as I was, it was a frock, as dusky looking as Cinderella's. I loved that word Weesie gave me. Dusky. She said it when I had packed one of Daddy's Church's Chicken shirts to spend the night once. "Child, take that dusky-looking shirt off right now and get in this clean shirt." She gave me Teeta's shirt but it was too small, so we settled on one of Uncle Junior's white tees.

But as I was saying, Sissy and I would be Cinderella, both of us, humming songs during those last days prepping for the trip. We was dreaming. I was dreaming.

There's this saying that Weesie always say when something go down: "On your way to glory there's trials and tribulation." Well, we had that when we finally got on our way to Disney World. Daddy kept saying he didn't like the way the map had us swinging through the backcountry of both Georgia and Florida. Not with four Black bodies in the car that technically ain't belong to the registered driver, because we borrowed Weesie's car for the eight-hour road trip. So, even though that was probably the quickest route, we went the long way, rounding us out closer to ten hours, Daddy predicted, looking at his map.

We had prepared for the journey with an icebox full of sandwich meat and bread and sodas so there'd be no need for stopping. And no trouble if we did stop. We would only pull up to gas stations that doubled as truck stops, because by Daddy's measure, truck drivers were mostly Black, so if there were businesses that allowed truckers to park and shower and sit in they lot, they might let us get gas without any problem. We thought we'd get to where we were headed without anything happening, and we almost did, until Daddy lost track of the gas gauge and I didn't think to look like I usually did on long drives, and so we stopped at a random Amoco station and Daddy told us to lean low in the car as we were pulling up to the gas pump. Just as we were rolling in, another car with a family of four—two girls in the back, probably parents in the front—was pulling in, and because it was a small station and because both cars had their fuel door on the same side, both cars were going to the same part of the station. Daddy got there first. He told us to get further down, below the window, he was just gonna get us enough gas to get outta that part of Florida to Orlando so he was gonna be quick. It could only have been so quick, 'cause Daddy's credit was still recovering from the bankruptcy claim after a car accident he was in cleared our accounts what with lawyers, insurance claims, etc. But the bank let us turn some of the rolled coins into traveler's checks. More secure, Daddy said—except now, because it meant he'd have to go inside. Daddy moved things around in the middle console, looking for change, and went in with a dollar bill and two nickel rolls, and from where I was sitting, he basically tipped his toe in the door, threw the money at the register, and rushed back out.

The guy driving the other car was just standing there looking at us. Mama didn't get down low. I swear she got taller. She sat up straight-backed, ashing her cigarette out the sliver of the open window. It got so hot I thought we were gonna suffocate if the air didn't start moving, so I reached to roll down the window and Mama sucked her teeth. I saw her face in the right-side rearview mirror, and she said with her cigarette hanging out her mouth that if I touched the window crank again she'd throw me out there to that mangy-looking man, and so I didn't move. I breathed shallower to reserve my energy, save the air. The guy was still standing outside his car and Daddy was pumping and I swear it ain't never take this long to pump five dollars' worth of gas as much as we go to a gas station with only five dollars to pump at all but this lasted a century. And I just wanted to get to Cinderella. I just wanted to get to Mickey and Minnie. To wear a tiara like Cinderella at the ball. I saw the white man's mouth move. Daddy never looked up at the white folks at all. Watching him go through it, I kept hearing his instructions in my own head, and I mouthed them, just in case he needed them. *Don't look them in the eyes, they get worse. Don't make any quick movements. Keep your hands out your pockets. Keep your head down. Do whatever you was doing when they came up, agree quick with whatever wild thing they saying, and keep it moving.*

The white guy's lips pursed in Daddy's direction in the familiar way that I've seen before, and I knew he had said the N-Word, and I leaned closer to Mama's cracked window, and then I heard, "Y'all niggers should go back where ya came from," and that's when Mama rolled down her window so fast you heard the crank squeal with each turn; she had to push the pane to get it to track faster.

Daddy hopped in the car, and as it started, she yelled, "Wouldn't you like to send us back? Wouldn't you like that? We're *American*. Just like you!" When Mama had finished saying that, the white man was behind us and I kneeled facing backwards to see and he was shaking his fist at us, and his face was red and he was still yelling something, but I couldn't make it out. Mama's hands were shaking, but she had enough adrenaline left to lean her head out and yell back at him, "Prolly *more* American!"

When we made our way back onto the interstate, it was a few mile markers before I saw Daddy's hands move from the top of the steering wheel back into a more relaxed position.

"He could have had a gun, Rhina," Daddy said.

"He woulda led with that, Major," Mama said.

Just like Weesie said. Ain't nothing worth having without a struggle. When we finally got out that gas station, I did wonder why Daddy didn't put up an ounce of fight.

"Why didn't you say something to that man, Daddy? Calling us the N-Word?" I asked. He raised his eyebrows and looked at me in his rearview mirror. "Why didn't you say something but Mama did? Now you fussin' at Mama when it was that man starting with us?"

He looked at me the way Teeta did whenever I would keep pressing and pressing for an answer to a question he didn't want to give. When he'd use the excuse that I was too young to need to know, I'd still ask questions, unrelenting. Teeta used to laugh when we'd get caught in what he called "an n-pass," like now. He'd laugh and say, "Mika, you sure ain't gone let go of no bone if you have it, huh?" I wasn't. But sometimes I watch Daddy back down from a fight and push down his anger and it puzzles me. This was just like when I was sent to detention for not calling my English teacher, a white lady, "ma'am" just because she "wanted to hear me sing," how Teeta would say it. He always said white folks want to make Black folks perform like we puppets or something, and it started with the yes ma'am, no sir jigs. I didn't say it, so I went to detention after school and over the loudspeaker the front lady called my name to the carpool aisle and my teacher said I could wait for my parent to pick me up from her classroom. Daddy came in huffing, clearly walking too fast down the campus. When he got there, I tried to explain my side of the story at the same time Ms. Finch was saying whatever she was saying, and he shushed me, let Ms. Finch speak over me.

"My rules ask that students respond and acknowledge deference by using 'ma'am.' Don't you agree our young people should be brought up with decency?"

"Yes, ma'am, I agree," Daddy said. He didn't look at me when I gasped.

What a crock of shit.

"I am glad to know you will support me in its enforcement," Ms. Finch said.

"Yes, ma'am, I will," Daddy said.

I wanted to throw up.

When we got to the car, I started back.

"Daddy, I thought—"

He didn't move his hands from the steering wheel and didn't turn to face me, which was how I knew he was in a place in his head he didn't want to be. I mean, NPR won't even on. I used to hate when we'd be driving and Daddy wanted to explain to us how he knew how something worked and he'd turn to meet us in the eyes. Mama would suck her teeth and say, "Major, we get it. Keep your eyes on the road." And he'd face forward and then our eyes would meet in the rearview mirror as he continued explaining whatever it was. But he had kept his eyes on the road this time and fussed at *me*.

"You knew your grandfather couldn't pick you up today and so it would be me between shifts," Daddy said.

"Daddy, I thought you said—" I started again and saw his knuckles protrude more; hands getting tighter around the wheel.

"Mika, baby, sometimes you gotta know when to pick your battle or your war. But today—"

"But Daddy, y'all had told me—"

"It's about *battles*, Mika. Sometimes you lose a battle but can still win the war. You gotta start knowing the difference."

It seemed like every day we was facing a battle with white folks—the gas station proved it. When was the war? I didn't say that, because by now Mama was back sleeping, and Sissy was clicking FWD and RWD on her cassette player trying to find a song to drown us out, and this would be a war with Daddy I didn't want to start. We only had about an hour left of our drive to Florida, and I just counted the mile markers like counting time, by the way Daddy taught me to calculate it. Only about sixty-five markers to go, just waiting until we got there, to Magic Kingdom.

ALL THE COMMOTION AND EXCITEMENT AND MAYBE NEAR-death experiences with white men didn't wear me and Sissy out for Disney World. Maybe she was acting excited because I was excited, but I rolled out of the hotel bed before the sun crept through the curtains and started getting dressed. Mama let me bring my good summer clothes for this trip, the ones we got from Target: a pink-striped shirt, matching shorts, and a matching bucket hat. Sissy had the same outfit except in green.

Our first stop was to see Snow White and her dwarfs. Mama wanted to see them. Then Goofy, of course. I made Sissy promise she'd help me re-create the photo that she got to have with Goofy all by herself, when she was about five or six. It was my favorite photo of her. Smiling. Leaning into Goofy's side. She had on almost the exact outfit I had on to meet him, too. When Daddy gawked at how much they charged us to take a photo with Goofy, Sissy said it was alright, that I could have it, and we kept it moving. Through the park we kept singing Disney songs. He didn't think anyone heard, but I heard Daddy humming the Chipmunks song behind us. We all turned into a chorus when we landed on "Under the Sea" from *The Little Mermaid,* Sissy's favorite.

"The seaweed is always greener / in somebody else's lake."

And almost on cue, here come Sebastian and Flounder. No one wanted to take a picture with Ariel. I looked for Ursula, my secret favorite. Mama says I like her because I'm conniving and scheming. How when I was little I liked to do things in the dark. How I'm sweet one day, evil the next. Two-faced, she called it. Still, I liked Ursula. I felt like I won't ever gonna be Ariel with the great voice, but Ursula was a woman who was dark-skinned, big-boned like what Weesie would call it, and got what she wanted. Even if it was temporary. She still got her desires. Those poor unfortunate souls. All of them.

It was when we got to the Magic Kingdom castle, though, and Cinderella emerged, that Mama and Daddy got all annoying with the camera and used *two* rolls of 35 mm film on us, and Mama convinced a white woman to take some photos for us so we didn't have to pay the fee. And we could be in the photos all together.

Y'all know by then I was over it. We still had so much more to see, and we were standing outside the castle and just taking taking taking pictures. Mama saw my face start to sour before I knew I was making faces and she stopped clicking the camera. Last time this happened when we went to an amusement park, I was so done with it all I frowned through almost half a roll of film. When the proofs came, there wasn't one that didn't have my crinkled-up face in it.

Mama was visibly upset as she took her last photo in front of the castle: "Just wait until you're older. You'll wish you took this more seriously, Mika." I shrugged in front of the camera and asked to keep going through the park.

We were here at the Magic Kingdom. Finally. We won't have time to save up enough change for another trip before Sissy graduates high school. She says she's not going to college but wants to work and make her own money and live on her own and make her own decisions, and sometimes I don't blame her. I get it. One day I heard Mama and Daddy talking about regrets. If they had it to do all over again, they'd have had us closer together. Us being almost five years apart meant it was always hard to find formative trips that both of us wanted and cared about, would remember and be excited for.

But I was excited, that's all that mattered to me. I had my wrist wallet with my eleven dollars' earnings from my friendship-bracelet business, and used most of it to buy a keychain to hold the picture of all of us in front of the castle. Teeta always said I had a soft heart and a hard shell, like how the outside of a pecan is dark and hard and if you crack it just right at just the right time of year, you'll find all the soft meaty insides, the good stuff. He said I was full of—what did he call it? Nostalgia—but I shouldn't let just anyone see. So I don't.

He says when you're nostalgic like me, you never want to experience change. He's right. I have everything I want—good grades, my future, my bike, my Teeta, and weekends at Redwood Court. I know that every time we settle into the good, there's something else just around the river bend. Like clockwork.

The drive back to Columbia from Florida was like the never-ending story. I felt like it was going to be next week before I would see signs for Savannah, which let me know we were close to home, but far enough to still be bored to death. I was writing in my journal about the trip so I could remember every detail to tell Teeta when we got back—the slushie with every color of the rainbow swirled above the globe top with the Mickey-shaped straw, the life-size Cinderella carriage and live horses—and I looked up and saw signs for Two Notch Road, which meant we were in Columbia. Y'all, then the weirdest thing happened. Mama turned down Daddy's mixtape and twisted around to smile at us, but mostly me. It was quick, kind of like at the gas station, so she startled me. I kept my head down kinda like Daddy that day, 'cause I didn't know what to do with it. Sissy was listening to her Sony Walkman with her face pressed against the window but won't looking at anyone really. Mama waved her hands in front of Sissy to bring her earphones down and listen up.

"Girls," she said. Her voice was higher pitched than it had been all week in Florida. Sissy rolled her eyes and audibly sighed when she took off her headphones. I kept writing, even as I tilted my head in Mama's direction.

"Girls, when we get home, go straight to your room."

I definitely rolled my eyes and hit my hand down on my journal pretty loudly at that point. I knew that phrase. Won't I too old for this? Last time Mama told us to go straight to our room, she followed us in with a bush switch she had taken most of the leaves off of except for the top two or three and cut up our legs for the fact that Sissy and I fought so hard at Ms. Sherry's house we ended up rolling around in the back-country Elgin dust and "ruined our freshly relaxed hair." You usually knew when it was coming, though. Mama would be silent the whole ride home, ignoring our fake questions, like "What's that stop sign for?" or "Ain't that where we stopped for cinnamon rolls last time?" or whatever. Her hands gripping the wheel. Music off. Air so thick in the car you felt your back press further into the seat. Her silence let us know it was gonna be hard lashings. She'd make us get on our bed together and lay there and she'd punctuate whatever she was saying with lashes from the switch, which whistled as it whipped through the air before whacking against our thighs. Screaming ain't stop it. Made it worse. Finally, I think once Sasha started getting old enough to withstand the whuppings without screaming and almost like Mama ain't get nothing out of it, she stopped for the most part. Or they became less frequent. Or maybe we stopped fighting so much when we went out. I don't know. I just know that whenever Mama told us to go to our room my defenses go up.

"But we ain't even do nothing, Mama."

Mama laughed at first. Won't nothing funny. She shook her head.

"No, no. Of course not. It's a surprise. Just go straight to your room, OK?" Her voice went up another notch like she was a soprano in Sasha's chorus, like those high notes I play three and four lines above the music staff.

I didn't know what to do with this version of Mama. At all. Or what surprise waited for us when we got home while we were all in Florida together. But when we pulled onto Forestwood Drive, and the car tipped down the hill, and Daddy just let it coast, I smiled when I saw Teeta's truck in the front yard.

That didn't necessarily mean that he was at our house, though. He always parked in our yard, under the silk tree, even if he went to our cousin's house down the hill just past Mr. Henry's and Miss Mary's house. But our lights were on inside—the ones in the playroom and in the front room—and it made me wonder what the surprise was. So I jumped up and asked, "Why Teeta here?"

"He *and* Weesie are here to get the car," Mama said, a small correction. That made sense, but Weesie stay at Redwood Court, so the idea of her here wasn't even on my mind. Mama and Daddy unpacked the trunk, backseat, and camper after they pulled into the driveway and I ran inside, much faster than Sissy, to see what the fuss was.

Of course, Weesie was in the living room on the phone. Never too far away from gossip.

"Hold on, Betty, the grandbabies just getting here. Yes. Yes. I know, they must be. Teeta is in the back finishing up. Yeh, lemme talk to you later tonight when we back. OK. OK. Bye, now." Weesie looked up and motioned for us to give her a hug and kiss, even though we all knew Sasha had stopped kisses and started side hugs by this point. I planted a kiss on Weesie's cheek and gave a quick hug, then ran back toward our room, calling after Teeta to see what he was up to.

Sissy and I both stopped when we reached the threshold of our playroom.

"Where are the toys?" I asked at first. Sissy shook her head. "Look, it's a whole bed in here! Aunt Olive's desk. Pink curtains!"

I looked, but I must not have registered it yet, even though it was weird that Aunt Olive's desk, now my desk, had moved into the playroom.

Sissy checked in the other room, and the stereo that was in the playroom was in our old room. Both rooms had computers—an important fact. Daddy had already given us our own phone line, tired of complaints from every woman in the house over AOL versus Sissy's phone time. Teeta was in our old room, putting the final military corner on the now-single bed.

"Well, well, well. My little Cinderellys are back from Disney, eh?" Teeta said when he saw us standing in the doorway, looking confused.

"Teeta, you did this?" I asked.

He nodded and coughed at the same time. "Yeap! Surprise!"

Sissy walked in our old room to check the stereo with the record player on top, a cassette door, and an eight-track slot. Daddy said don't try to use the eight-track player, and anyways he put the eight-tracks up in the attic, but everything else on the system worked. We had Daddy's vinyl collection, stored in an Icee box, a shoebox of Sasha's mixtapes, and a handful of tapes of Christian music that our aunt gifted or Mama bought on days she was feeling particularly Christian—usually Christmas or Easter. The comforter in what was our old shared room was hunter green, Sissy's favorite color, and there were half curtains in the two—big sisters got two, I suppose—windows, also hunter green. Sissy's computer, which we all knew she won't use, was on a card table. I was the computer whiz kid. Daddy gave her a computer just because. Hopeful, I guess.

"Teeta, where are all of my toys?" I asked again, leaning into my room, the old playroom. My Barbie Dreamhouse was gone. It had been years since I'd used it, but having it brought some level of comfort—that nostalgia Teeta talks about so—and somehow, I had convinced Sissy to keep a night-light going all this time, and I liked the shadows the Dreamhouse cast on the walls. Now it was gone. Some things couldn't be taken out of the house, so they got repurposed: Daddy's large tool and storage box, which was also the TV stand, was still in the room, but now it held my stuffed dolls and a few Barbies. It made sense that the pencil sharpener bolted to the top stayed in my room. I was journaling now, becoming a writer. Ever since I read Anne Frank and Zlata's diaries, I was determined that, should anything happen to me before my time, as they say, there would be a record that I lived, that we all lived, and that I crushed on boys like Roger from my band class, and fought with Mama, just like any regular girl.

Teeta came over, coughing, into my room, "Well, well, well, Mika. You have your own room now. A 'puter, a TV, a shelf for your books. I wanted to surprise you with this! You're surprised, ain't it?" he finished, coughing into his handkerchief. He looked at it and stuffed it into his back pocket. I ran to hug him. I was surprised. My own little corner—a whole kingdom—all of it mine.

At the Cookout

When I asked if they would be there, Mama and Daddy said they weren't going to the cookout this weekend because they already had plans. When I heard them say that, I didn't think anything of it, even though it was weird; the amount of times they had plans before was so low that when I think about it now it was almost like they knew something about the cookout was gonna be off—even though they swear they didn't. We weren't prepared for none of what happened, though.

In the school drop-off line, Daddy said he'd take me over to the Court Friday after band practice and I could come back Sunday night, as long as I made sure to take and do my homework. That's how I knew they were making other plans—I didn't do the asking this time and Daddy had his schedule lined up perfect so I knew it meant I wouldn't have to collect-call his pager and use my code MIKA PICK UP (6452-7425-87) so he could be reminded that he had forgotten about picking me up after school and the office would be closed so I'd have to use the payphone outside.

"If you pack what you want to take by Friday morning, you can leave it in the car so it's ready when I get you, Mika," Daddy said. It was Thursday after dinner and Mama was cleaning up, and I was in the living room with Daddy. I creaked my head slightly so he couldn't see suspicion on my face. What adventure are they planning without me? Last time they pulled this, they dropped me off to Redwood Court and came back with smiles on their faces. I took one look at Mama, then down at her shirt, and saw it. I walked over and picked off the small piece of something on her sweater and sniffed it and looked at both of them with disgust. Shrimp. I asked them point blank if they had gone to Red Lobster without me, and Mama was so surprised I had figured her out. This day felt like that. I just know they're going some-where I want to go—Carowinds? Olive Garden? Charleston to see Grandma Annie? Part of me wanted to act like I didn't want to go to Redwood Court and stay home so I could see what they were planning. I asked if I could stay and play with Crystal next door instead.

"Mika, we won't be home and Sasha has a full work schedule. You can't be home by yourself," Mama called from the kitchen.

So I didn't have a choice.

"Besides, I thought you loved the cookouts? Teeta got frank 'n weenies for you and I'll send you over with some deviled eggs Weesie asked me to make."

Just thinking of the gas smell of the half-stuffed boiled eggs made my face curl up. Wasn't any use fighting whatever they planned to do with me, so I let it go. I did love cookouts. I loved Redwood Court. I loved when it was just me and Teeta, like over summertime when Weesie was still at the salon, and I had the days to govern myself. On the weekends, with Weesie home, it was becoming harder to stay so long—Weesie kept the pale-yellow phone attached to her ear like a permanent earring. All my friends had Weesie's number, too, I made sure of that, but if the phone finally rang at all (which was rarely) it meant Weesie had put it down, and by the time I got through to Allison on the phone, she'd say something about how many times they had tried to call me but it was busy. Thank God Teeta wasn't a phone person. I'd hear him chatting with Deacon Jackson in the mornings before I'd come out for breakfast, but that was it. Once I heard Weesie telling Ruby how I was pouting 'cause I wanted to use the phone and she told me to wait a minute, and Teeta explained to me, loud enough for Weesie to hear in the kitchen, that everyone he needed to talk to lived right on his street, so he would just go out to talk to them *in person* if he had something to say to them. His shoulders rose up and down with his chuckle. I smiled. Weesie stuck her tongue out at him or both of us. Sometimes, I wished Mama and Daddy played around like that, but Teeta said he was serious once like Daddy, and then he said he realized that serious won't the glue that keep you married as many years as he and Weesie—even when things get hard.

"You gotta laugh a little or else what's all this for?" Teeta said.

Weesie looked over and half smiled. Her one eyebrow raised. That was also something weird for Teeta to say, 'cause I'd heard Weesie tell someone on the phone about his "episodes," she called them, but I don't think I've ever seen them. Sometimes he'd stop and breathe real slow with his eyes closed, but mostly all I saw was Teeta sticking his tongue out, or Teeta sweating over a grill, or setting up the Easter Egg hunts for all of the children of Redwood Court, or him calling me "Cinderelly." It was hard to put the two pictures of the same man together, but if I had to try, it would be something like my Topsy Turvy doll Mama got me that had two faces.

"What are y'all's plans?" I asked Mama and Daddy again when Mama joined us in the living room. Daddy kept tinkering with a customer's computer as if I wasn't asking a question, and Mama sucked her teeth because I had.

"We just need a break, Mika," she said. "Just the two of us." I could always count on Mama to give it to me direct, even when I don't get all of what I want. Daddy was a man of few words, unless it was him explaining a complex electrical or engineering process and you had to pretend to listen through the whole thing, paying enough attention for a few seeds of words he dropped to feed back to him, or else you risked him starting all over. But a break from *what* was the thing I was asking. I never got an answer from either of them before I was deposited at Weesie's door after school like a special delivery.

PREPPING FOR COMPANY TO COME OVER TO REDWOOD COURT meant driving up and down Decker Boulevard and Parklane Road—getting groceries from Winn-Dixie, then Piggly Wiggly, then Kroger, stop through Target 'cause it was right there, then the collard stand. Weesie calls it the collard stand because that is the only place she gets her greens since the day she moved to Columbia from Georgia, even though they have other vegetables and some fruits, and boiled peanuts, too—things Weesie picks up from the other stores she drags me to. It never made any sense to me, but we trucked across town: ground chuck and onion and Styrofoam cups from Winn-Dixie; more frank 'n' weenies (on sale), sweet potato patties, and Chinet paper plates from Kroger; and packs of chicken legs and potatoes for the potato salad and chips from Piggly Wiggly. I managed to scoop a composition notebook from Target.

Between the last store and the Court, when I asked what the cookout was for, Weesie turned to me and said, "'Cause it's the weekend." I started humming the O'Jays tune, and if it were Daddy in the car, he'd go, "Ah ha, it's Friday," and I'd echo that line, and he'd turn to me and say, "And I just got paid." But I was with Weesie, and she heard my humming and turned up the volume on Gospel FM.

"Who all coming? Is it a fundraiser?" I asked, mostly to know if my cousins were coming over or not. The way all the personalities mashed up at some of these cookouts, and as the house grandchild, I often had to host—with Weesie hollering after me every few minutes. I'd be at the top of Redwood Court and she'd come yelling out the kitchen door in the carport: "Mika—make sure these chil'ren got drinks. Put the snacks out."

I couldn't tell you how she made her voice travel so far and so clear, all the way to the rounded top of the cul-de-sac, but if I pretended to not hear her, she'd keep going until I answered "OK!" and coupled that with movement after whatever she'd asked me to do. Mama would take my word for it, and I'd have a few moments between order and action. Weesie, though, always said, "Faith without work is dead." I knew it was a Bible reference; the few times I didn't get out of going to church when I was at the Court, it seemed to be the only thing Pastor would be preaching about. So, of course, Weesie would use it against me. She said the faith phrase whenever she asked me to do something and I acknowledged it but didn't move. Then she would say, "Don't make me ask you again," and that's when my friends would become the peanut gallery and snicker until I kicked up the kickstand and headed back to the house.

There'd be so many adults rolling around in the kitchen during this cookout, and Teeta out back at the cinder block grill he stacked by hand, that it didn't make sense for me to add to the chaos by rummaging around looking for a few cans of lemon-lime Chek soda and sherbet for the punch.

"One day you'll appreciate what I'm trying to teach you," Weesie said when I slammed the stack of Styrofoam cups on the island, then threw ice in the punchbowl with such staccato that a few heads turned—and a few cubes jumped out onto the floor.

"Being a good host is next to being a good wife. Your future husband will thank me, too."

I don't know what she was talking about, except showing me how to interrupt folks minding they business. One time, Teeta said Weesie was always middling into things, and the last thing I want to be is a middler, yet there I was, in the middle of things at the cookout while folks fixed their drinks and Weesie dumped Duke's mayo over cubed potatoes. They was talking this 'n' that, then joking and telling me to close my ears like I ain't never been around grown folks talking about grown folks things, and every once in a while I'd look longingly out the side door and see my cousins and friends double-dutching and such, wishing I was out there.

Finally, I escaped the throes of the cookout-prep kitchen and rode back to where my people were. At the top of the cul-de-sac, you could see beyond the stop sign at a better angle. It's how we could tell who lived on Redwood Court and who did not. Even with the cookouts or celebrations, we kids spent so much time figuring out what car was going to whose house for what reason.

White Lincoln: Buddy.

Red pickup: Mr. Taylor.

Tan minivan like Mama's: June.

Rusted buggy: Calvin.

White Toyota Corolla: Ruby.

Cars creeping down the street, of course, were strangers to the Court. We'd watch them creep, creep, then circle the top, pushing us onto someone's lawn, then they'd disappear beyond the stop sign.

When a gray two-door car that sat so low to the ground I wondered how it could make it past anyone's curb came creeping down the road, we all hushed to see better. I guess we all got it from our grandparents, but we just couldn't talk or play hand games *and* see who was in the new car. It was *creeping,* creeping. I looked over at Shana and Janice and they shrugged; they didn't know. The car started to turn into Uncle Quincy and Aunt Jesse's house, and we went back to trying to pop wheelies like we saw Uncle Junior and his friends do when they crossed the threshold just past the stop sign. But we stopped again when the car started to back into Weesie's driveway, and I guess that's how the driver solved the low-car-to-driveway ratio.

But who was it?

"That's a hot car," Shana said, and I nodded my head. Teeta had told Junior not to have his friends who like to enjoy their lives illegally come by anymore, 'cause Teeta didn't want trouble 'round here, and for the most part, it seemed Junior listened. Besides, he'd just left the party, so won't no one trying to come get him. The only other young-people-looking cars (what Weesie called the cars we called *hot*) that usually came by during the cookout were Junior's company, and since Teeta forbade the Trouble Boys, Junior started to send his parade of girlfriends, always older, apparently with cars that kissed the ground like this one and had to back into driveways.

On our bikes, we all inched closer to Weesie's house to get a better view without saying that's what we were doing. So we came down the Court in a zigzag to drawl it out. Then Shana's cousin initiated a race to the stop sign, and we all lost track of who was winning and who was gone lose, because we were goose-necked in front of the ground-low gray car. A woman was still in there. I was riding Sissy's bike because Dee needed to ride mine. (*Yes,* I knew how to zip down the Court by now.) Most times no one challenged me with a race, because on Sissy's bike, I was the only two-wheeler with *ten speeds.* Speed ten meant I pushed harder but went faster. So I shot out in front of the herd, but braked just enough to see the woman who was putting on lipstick in the rearview mirror. It also meant she could see the folks in the carport behind her, and only if they looked in her rearview mirror could they see her. Looked like her hair was a shield of curls down to her shoulders and bangs down to her dark eyes. All I saw when I looked at her was the pictures of Egyptians: dramatic makeup, broad shoulders, hair shields.

Still technically in the race, I heard the *whirr* of wheels gaining on me and pressed on to victory at the stop sign. I called time-out for a water break, and instead of going to the garden hose, I chose to venture back into the middling space inside the house to see who this woman was. The difference now, though, between Weesie calling me in from outside before versus me going in without her call was the adults had settled into whatever space of the event—whatever corner of the front or back yards, grill side or spades side—they'd been.

Weesie had set up a card table on the carport for spades. She was in the middle of the game with the largest cut of watermelon— a host cut—I'd ever seen. I hadn't noticed then, but she hadn't even taken her hair out of her rollers! I paused for a second and looked over Weesie's shoulder while she counted books in her hand: trump, trump, deuce of diamonds, deuce of spades. She was going to clean the table. She cut her eyes at me, and I knew to keep walking and not call out that I knew she had at least seven books, like she and Teeta taught me. Instead, I gave a different observation.

"Weesie, some woman pulled up and just sitting there in the car."

Weesie froze like in Simon Says, then collapsed the cards spread out like a fan, calling out, "Seven books," and the table gasped at her count. She stood up and started to walk toward the car, patting her rollers closer to her head as if it would make a difference, 'cause Weesie was someone who simultaneously cared what she looked like and was carefree. On Sundays, she was "dressed to the nines," she would say, whatever that meant. Nine pieces of clothing? She counted them for me one day: white-heeled shoes, white stockings, slip 'cause she considered even the unseen as important as the seen (God could see *everything*), three-piece skirt suit, pocketbook to match, lace handkerchief to cover her knees when she sat, earrings with just enough shine, and of course, the crown—her hat.

"But, Grandma," I called out from under the bed covers while she finger-primped her curls, just set free from the pink foam and yellow plastic rollers. "Wouldn't you count your hair, too? You always fussing and talking about how your hair adds season to an outfit."

"Needs to add some *spice*," she said and winked at me in the mirror.

So I don't know how she dressed to the nines on Sunday, when she out in the world and such, but on Saturdays she can dress different. The two sides to every coin or some such. Like today, at the cookout, she had on hot pants, house slippers outside, and didn't even bother with her scarf over the rollers.

"Everyone's family today, Mika," she had said earlier when I asked why she won't getting *dressed* dressed. To the nines. Looking around the spades table, thinking of the folks out back with Teeta 'round the grill, my friends, those folks in the kitchen sippin' punch. Yeh, I guess she was right. Everyone was family. So it had been weird to see that car we weren't familiar with back into the driveway. That was the first sign of not-family. Everyone who had ever been to our cookouts knew that to come to the cookout meant you had to squeeze your car every which way across the lawn so as to fit as many as possible. You couldn't block the driveway. It was like the blank block on a slide puzzle. You needed space to move around to figure it all out.

When the echo of a metal chair scraping against the painted concrete of the carport rang out, everyone at the cookout froze in place. Weesie don't *never* get up in the middle of a spades game. If it was something that made her leave mid play, it had to be something. It was like looking at my Barbie house—everyone staged so quiet and still, waiting to be moved by someone else.

At the edge of the carport, but not quite at the car, Weesie's hands went back up by her hair, but not like she was trying to fix it. She crouched low, I guess to try to better see the woman, who was still fixing her face before getting out the car. Weesie's other hand went to her chest, and that's when Uncle Pete looked and squinted, too, and I think he must have seen the face in the side mirror, and I don't know what he saw but it must have been what Weesie saw, 'cause he immediately stood up from the card table and told me to get Teeta. He had turned back quick and then didn't look away from Weesie, just like I didn't look away from

Weesie, but I knew it was me he was talking to, 'cause I was the youngest out front, and the one who could run back to Teeta the fastest.

You ever know when a storm is about to come and it's late summer, like it was at this cookout, so the air is first sticky like bee honey? But when it starts to feel like molasses you know the weather turned. If you weren't sure if the air was honey or molasses, all you had to do was look to the ground at all the winged ants falling out of the sky, like they came from nowhere then swarmed just to let you know something was brewing. When I got out back, Teeta saw the look on my face and how I had shot through the back gate and didn't speak to anybody. He was about to flip a burger patty on the grill when I come up between panting breaths, "Teeta, some woman out front in her car talking to Weesie, and Uncle Pete said come get you."

And I just believed—I just *knew* it was something, because I had started running back out front—just to see—and Teeta won't even on my heels at all. To paint a picture: for this season, he moved the barbecue pit to the far back right corner of the yard, so it was farthest away from the gate. I had gotten to the gate, zinging by still-frozen guests like a pinball knocking through the machine. I turned around and Teeta had only pulled the can of beer away from his mouth and it won't up there when I told him to see about Weesie. Like he knew a storm was hovering just above the place, too. Uncle Pete saw me then and asked me where Teeta was, and I was looking in the backyard, nervous because I felt like I needed to take shelter like it was a tornado drill. Both Weesie's hands were on her hips now, and she was rhythmically lifting her heel fast-like and everyone else was still like they in the Antarctic.

Cousin Greg took it upon himself to walk up to the car and

see with his own eyes and hear with his own ears who this visitor was, since no one was brave enough to do it, and Weesie was stuck in quicksand. He shuffled back and spoke soft like a low boil up against Weesie's ear.

"That young woman saying she someone called Cynthia and says she looking for Teeta, but called him James. Look just like him, too."

You won't believe what happened next. Weesie's head was facing the driver's side of the window, hands on her hips, heel still tapping like how she used to set up to pop me in the mouth 'cause I had said something smart. Then her head turned three times around on her neck like some doll, I swear, and she said, "Someone asking after *James*?" She had said "James" like she didn't know the name or whose body it belonged to. I heard it. By then, her eyes jutted just past my shoulders. At first, I thought she was looking at me like that—her body facing front-ways to the car, her eyes cutting in my direction. But I turned and realized she was looking at Teeta standing behind me. Teeta grunted when that happened.

"James," Weesie said, repeating his government name, and we knew then the weight of what was happening, even if we couldn't put together all the disparate pieces: Uncle Pete standing watch like a hunting dog pinning a rabbit, no one moving except for Ruby letting the air out the house holding the door open, trying to get the scoop for the inside folks; there was the question of Cynthia, the woman in the car, Teeta behind me, and Weesie Care Bear–staring across the way.

I was caught in the crosshairs like how Daddy taught me to look through the barrel of a BB gun. There was a line north to south, then one east to west, and where they met: the crosshairs. Teeta was there, too. I wished I had stayed on my bike up the

Court, away from whatever was looking like was about to happen.

When the car door creaked open, we all, in concerto (I learned that in band), breathed in. Uncle Pete rested on his knuckles, still ready to pounce. I have never seen any of us move through the air—even molasses air—this slow.

"Louise," Teeta said, inching forward. It was the use of her full name that shook everybody at the cookout.

I heard someone whisper, "Who's Cynthia?" Betty leaned her head close to Weesie's to ask.

I know I'm the baby of the family, but I also know when to watch and when to ask questions, even though everybody says I test those lines from time to time. Betty was wrong and should have left that line of inquiry alone, 'cause it was clear Weesie was trying to process it all, all of what was happening and how she was gone respond—in Weesie's way.

Anyways. Teeta was slug-walking from the gate toward the car or Weesie—we don't really know, since it was the same general direction. By the time Teeta turned the corner onto the carport, the door creaked open, but the woman still won't getting out. He got just close enough to Weesie for her to shove him in the shoulders with a slight tap, how you do someone whose fault something is and you want them to know you know. She said something between her teeth, low, like how she talk to me in church after I let my feet swing and knock the back of the pew too many times. I couldn't make it out, but she walked back to the card table and picked up her cigarette case, heel *still* tapping. She wiped her face with the butt of her hand, looked at Uncle Pete and no one else, and said, "Damn," heavy-like, and dropped the lighter down on the card table on top of her hand with seven books. After a beat, Weesie looked around again, catching eyes with everyone—just family, how she said when we were prepping—a bit softer now, her shoulders coming down from her earlobes.

When the woman finally got out of the car after what felt like infinity times infinity-squared seconds, I saw Teeta straighten the crook he keep in his back.

Someone else whispered how she look like she could be part of the family, then added, "She older than Rhina, though," and Weesie sucked the air and her cigarette so loudly we all looked up. She shook her head and started walking towards the house—without excusing herself, like a good host.

Teeta crept up to the carport just as Weesie was climbing the stairs to head inside to the kitchen. We all waited in silence for next instructions. Usually, don't nobody stand around waiting for things at a cookout—food and drinks and laughter just flow like the Nile.

Teeta first looked around like he, too, was waiting for what was permissible next. Looking a little lost, with his hands in his pockets, his shoulders to his ears, so I knew he was worrying even though he tried to make it seem like he won't. Then I heard a loud sigh, and he stepped forward, reached his hand to the top of the creaked-open door as if to help open it, then stood by the door as the woman climbed out of the very low bucket seat, emerging towards the light of the day like a flower blooming.

In the light, she did look like Teeta. More than Mama, who has Weesie's nose and eyes. I'm still in the crosshairs, trying to think about what all of this means, then I watched Weesie try to disappear into the house. She paused mid step and hollered our way, "Don't y'all stop the fun 'cause of me! Somebody make that girl a plate. Greg, hold my hand or play it, whatever," flicking her hands for us to carry on.

Then she looked right at Cynthia.

"Baby, if you could move your car—we need to keep the driveway open." She had curled her face into a smile when she said "baby," but it didn't feel fake or anything. Like how she'd talk to me or Sissy when she couldn't remember our names quick enough, and it was a stand-in for our names, but filled with some type of love, maybe tenderness.

"Y'all, I'll be right back with some ice." Weesie turned back around and let the screen door fall shut behind her, like how she always fussed to us about us not doing ourselves.

When it slapped against the frame, we snapped back to it. With that, the cards started falling to the table again.

All I Know Is Love
Will Save the Day

Daddy told me to fix my face when he said he was gone to Charleston for a week, during the weekday, to work the South Carolina Wildlife Expo with Uncle Griffin, *and* that I had to stay home with Mama and not go to Redwood Court.

I acted like he ain't been doin the expo since before I could remember. He say he been doing it since 1988. One early year I remember he did bring us down for the last few days, and that's when I found out the "Expo" was a big room like a science fair. Real stuffed animals crowded the floor with all the white folks dressed in camo like they in the army, and then us: four black bodies hunched together floating from table to table.

I could tell you, those were some of the days Daddy walked around like he was on *Lifestyles of the Rich and Famous*. One year, they rented him a car because he explained he only had the one after a train caught the back half of his Lincoln Town Car and he couldn't leave us without transportation. Every year they got him a hotel room for the week and let him order room service. I asked him why he don't just stay with Grandma Annie, and he reminded me that after Aunt Olive died, Uncle Griffin moved into her room, so the house was gone be crowded.

"Besides," he started, "you know your mother loves to keep the house like an ice box even in winter, and I get a chance to have *my* room like an oven." I ask why they gotta go through all that fuss all together, and he said because of course no one can set up lights, electric, cable, and a security system as quickly as him, and Uncle Griffin had shook hands with the right white folks to secure the contract with no end date for years. So they went every year to light the art, guns, foxes, and deer heads mounted on walls like trophies, and to set up food stands like at the state fair but with no funnel cakes or caramel apples or cotton candy—just the slimy-chicken taste of fried alligator bites that Daddy had tricked me into eating that time. Or the time he handed us a stick a meat and said it was a Slim Jim, but when I bit into it and it tasted like the dirt in the woods at Sesqui State Park, he chuckled and asked if I liked my first taste of deer. Sissy and I never finished the rest.

Truthfully, I think Daddy liked going because he was an important Black man in downtown Charleston for the week. Every time we turned a corner, all I heard was *Tom! Tom! Tom! Look here, Tom! Tom, I want you to meet so 'n' so.* You ever hear a word so much it starts to sound like a different word? That's how much he was called, with reverence, in the same part of his childhood city that he couldn't—wouldn't dare to—trek to as a child.

"When I was your age, cops would yoke up boys for no reason other than riding their bike south of Broad Street," Daddy used to say anytime he drove us through downtown near the Pineapple Fountain—never stopping. "They'd try to stop us from reaching Waterfront Park and contaminating the little fountain *they* kids get to splash in." This is also when he'd tell us how he had to walk to school while the white kids rode the bus to the same school. The first time he told these stories, I did the math.

"Daddy, won't you born after that? When white folks and Black folks could do things together, though?"

"Charleston must have lost the memo," he said and huffed and shook his head.

I was sad to not go to Charleston, not because I'd miss the expo or seeing Daddy, as he would say, "in his element," but because I'd miss our walk down the tracks, Daddy leading the way, cutting left and right with his machete, telling me to watch for any snakes. I loved looking for ghost crabs scratching sideways back into their holes. Then we'd make our way to the river, and it was so close to the ocean you'd think won't no way white folks knew what they was missing out on when—as Daddy told it— this area was abandoned and only had a few two-room shacks that Black folks could buy. When they got back to South Carolina after years abroad in Italy and Germany, Grandma Annie had demanded they settle in West Ashley with the Blacks, both because she was ready to be "with her people" and, well, because this was the only choice.

"Now, your grandmother says white folks calling for their land back," Daddy would say. We'd watch an old friend slink his way through the brush and cast a net out into the water and pull in a blue-crab feast. I loved the salt breeze on my lips. Daddy reminded me it was February and won't be no crabs or tracks-walking 'cause everything hibernating. So won't be nothing for me to do. Besides, I had school.

"I guess that's how they get away with parading all the dead animals around the city without nature revolting—no one is awake to be offended," he'd chuckle.

It didn't matter the excuses. I dreaded the weeks he'd go and I had to stay with Mama, basically alone. This year, it would be two weeks. Even though we had two cars, Daddy still requested the rental so Sissy could drive herself to work. It wasn't a coincidence that *this* was the week they increased her hours, I bet, she told us as we were milling around that Monday morning, me getting ready for school, Mama for work at La Petite Academy childcare center, Sissy for school and then work, and Daddy for his great exodus.

Mama looked at me. "Then I guess it's just us girlies." I rolled my eyes.

"If Teeta gotta come pick me up, take me to school, then pick me up from school, I don't see why y'all won't let me just stay at Redwood Court."

She sighed. Looked at Daddy. He flattened his lips so much they disappeared, then raised his eyebrow at me. Sissy scooped up her bookbag and practically left a smoke trail behind her on the way out the door. As she was leaving, she said Teeta's truck was rolling down the hill.

"I gotta go to school, I guess." I kissed Daddy goodbye, asked for a pen, and went outside. When I hopped in the truck, Teeta was still scooting the napkins and newspapers off the passenger side of the seat.

"Teeta, I don't know why they just won't let me stay with y'all this week," I started, even before the door closed.

"Why, hello to you, too, Mika!" Teeta said, patting me on the head, which he knew I hated but only did when he was trying to correct me.

"Sorry. Hey, Teeta," I said. I flipped the radio station to the Big

DM 'cause he'd let me, and the drive to school was only five minutes, max, unless we caught the freight train crossing, but we
didn't, because Teeta had gathered me at 8:03 and the train comes
on schedule at 8:10. If we get caught behind its 156-car-plus ca-
boose body, then there goes breakfast, and Daddy—it's always
him I'm late with—has to walk me into the principal's office to
announce and account for my tardy.

"Woo-ha! Got you all in check!" I leaned into Teeta's face to
say the line like Busta in the video. Teeta never drove fast enough
to match the rhythm of the station, but I made do, swaying to the
"ya ya yaa ya ya," which happened right as we were crossing the
railroad tracks.

"Teeta, it don't make no sense for you to drive from Redwood
Court, longer than the drive to take me to school."

"'Cause Rhina has to be at work same time as your school
start," Teeta said. He turned onto the road my middle school was
on and lined up for the carpool lane. Those that rode the bus
from Newcastle and all over Northeast Columbia, like my friends
Janice, Romona, and Destiny, hopped off near the back. There
were a few more cars before they let us exit, Miss Theresa the
crossing guard explained for safety, so I had time to just put it out
there.

"But, Teeta, if I stayed at Redwood Court, I can just ride the
bus from your house," I said. I saw the wheels turning in Teeta's
head and before he could respond, I raised my finger and started
again: "Actually—why is it that I can't ride the bus that pick everyone up right in front of the picnic table in my yard? That I gotta
write Redwood Court as my address for school, anyhow?"

I had asked too many questions for such a short ride and Teeta
was leaning up against the window with his cheek on his fist.

"You gone have to ask your mama these questions," he said.

Then coughed, but it was a wet cough, not a dry one. Daddy says the wet coughs we gotta look out for, 'cause it's the body trying to get rid of things. I could see Teeta swish something in his mouth. He looked around the car for something—a napkin? Handkerchief?—but tapped the steering wheel like he was upset. He lifted his head how I do when I'm taking medicine I don't like. He swallowed, wiped the back of his hand across his lips, then finished what he was saying.

"Your mama the one want you to go to these schools, say they better." When we reached the real drop-off area, he leaned across me to open the door, kissed my forehead, and waved at Miss Theresa, who shut the door behind me.

When I got to the hallway right in front of my homeroom class I realized I left without the balance to my lunch account for this week. If Miss Barbara is there, I'll be fine.

AT THE END OF THE DAY, VALERIE YELLED ACROSS THE CAR-pool lane that my ride was here, and I looked up just as Teeta got to the stoplight on the corner. Right on time. Good, I'm starving. Teeta was sweating today. It was a warm Columbia February that made you think spring gone come early, but it won't warm enough to be sweating in a car when you could adjust the temperature. I asked him if he was alright and he hummed. I side-eyed him, not believing, and remembered his cough that morning. This ride, I don't touch the radio on the way back—he had it tuned to the public radio station—and I was missing Daddy. I couldn't help it.

At home, I was somehow still surprised to roll down the hill at Forestwood Drive and see his rental car was not there. Teeta pulled into the driveway but didn't get out. I asked if he was coming in, and he said nope, Weesie needed him to watch the pot of butterbeans she set up on her lunch break and he dared not let them burn. He hummed and licked his lips so, and even I could taste the smoke-salty paste the beans made over rice. That was one of the reasons I tried any way I could to get to Redwood Court: the food. Especially 'cause Daddy was gone and Miss Barbara won't in today and even though it was Meatloaf Monday at school I only had some water and a pack of crackers for lunch. Whoever took over for Miss Barbara didn't know whatever agreement Daddy had—credit one week, payoff the next or some such—and made me put the prepared tray directly in the trash window because I couldn't pay. Everyone saw it. Everyone. My ears burned at the stares. I didn't even really like meatloaf, but that won't the point. I would have made do. I had to sit the whole of lunch with nothing in front of me. Frances, who always packed her lunch—ham and cheese Lunchables, apple slices, Juicy Juice, and a pack of cream cheese and chive crackers for a snack—slid the crackers over to me. I thanked her and ate three crackers over the forty-five minutes, and then the other three during snack time. When Teeta dropped me off I was hoping to come home to Mama starting dinner like what Teeta said Weesie was doing. Instead, the house was cold like an icebox in February, and I heard the TV playing from her bedroom. No lights were on, but because of the way Daddy kept the trees around the outside of the house it was dark, and I squinted to adjust to the change from bright afternoon light to what seemed like a cave.

I called her name when I walked in, then leaned back out the door to wave to Teeta that I was in OK. Mama moaned back at me. I knew these days—migraine days or sinus days or "on-the-rag days," Daddy called it—when she went from bed to steaming bowl with a towel over her head, or a frozen mask over her eyes, or the wrinkle of a packet of Goody Powders opening. It don't much matter which one, it was only just good luck getting anything from her for the next day or so. You always knew the cloud had passed when you heard the *snch, snch, snch* of a lighter trying to catch and smoke started snaking its way through the house, but that didn't always mean you were in the clear. Daddy called these times "your mama's moods" and usually he'd entertain us until she'd emerge from the cave, fill a re-used plastic KFC to-go cup with ice, and spend half the rest of the evening crushing the cubes between her teeth. The bravest of us would engage in convo and get one-word answers or "uh huh" between crunches; otherwise, we'd ride the mood out—three castaways on a ship until the next day, when she'd be the first one up and playing the Family Christian Radio station and frying eggs or making her buttered cinnamon-sugar toast.

There was no Daddy buffer this afternoon. I crept to the door and stuck my nose through the small open space and purred her name. She was back-flat with one arm across her forehead, the other hanging over the side of the bed.

"Mama, I don't have much homework. Can I see if Crystal can play?" Mama just brought her head down to her chest, nodding yes, and I bolted out the door before she changed her mind. Even though Crystal was two years younger than me, we still got along. It was a bonus that she lived with her grandma, so we'd usually play, then eat. I loved the way her grandma fried chicken and served it with ranch dressing and twice-fried Food Lion crinkle fries, and I swear she started heating the oil and tossing the drumsticks in the ziplock bag filled with flour whenever I knocked on the door. Like the meal was waiting to start until I got there. I've never seen *my* mama do this, and I think Crystal's grandma knows. Weesie says she's too tired to be frying up chicken for us the way we like to eat it, so she convinces Daddy to buy it. Crystal's is the kitchen where I get home-cooked fried chicken, and I hoped Crystal's grandma would start pulling the chicken drumsticks out the fridge as soon as she saw us rolling in the grass. Or else I'd be left to . . . who knows what Mama was planning for us for dinner.

When I got next door, I knocked and knocked. I heard the tap water running in the kitchen, dishes clanking. Someone washing. I waited to see if anyone would stop to answer, but no one had come by the time I counted to six-one-thousand, so I knocked again, this time harder, with more emphasis. The water shut off, and house shoes scraped across the wood plank floors. The door creaked open, and I was expecting Crystal, but it was her grandma with a cigarette hanging out her mouth, house coat barely closed, and a bonnet on her head. Had she been in bed like Mama? Were they synced up? Mama and Sissy talked about this a lot, how whenever they got their blood it came around the same days and so Daddy was stuck buying maxi pads from Walmart what seemed like every other day. I never saw Crystal's grandma like this; most grandmas have dresses they wear for inside and dresses they wear for guests. Even though she fed me in her kitchen and not in her dining room, she mostly treated me like a guest, and so I didn't expect her to come to the door like this. The sun was still out; folks still coming home from work. She pulled the cigarette out of her mouth when she answered the door and gave me the answer to my question before I even asked it.

"Crystal can't come outside tonight, baby," she said and started to close the door. The way she pulled it open, a whiff of air from the kitchen escaped—spaghetti. Garlic bread. I probably looked like the Looney Tunes characters floating through the air behind the scent of something they loved with heart eyes. Her grandma started to close the door on me.

"She can maybe come out later this week if she learn to act right in school," she said and continued to shut the door. "Have a good night, baby," she said, closing the remaining space between us.

So it was gone be me and Mama and the silences of the house. I dragged my feet between the two houses, between the thorny hedge bushes, and slogged my way up the steps, across the front porch. I sat outside and watched our neighbors mill about as they were coming from their schools, their works, their whatever lives, then eventually go inside. I thought about going down to Shontae's house, but I didn't ask Mama about that, and the last thing I needed was for her to come out and see me where I won't suppose to be or to call Crystal's grandma looking for me and I won't there. Miss Mary waved at me from her porch. Asked if Mama was home. I yelled back that she was sleep. We wished each other a good night. I sat counting the cars, fourteen so far, coming down the road. Fireflies started to rise up from the ground like smoke or steam and I watched them come and go in their flashes, making little wishes on each wink: Maybe one day I'll be famous. Maybe one day I'll have a boyfriend. Maybe one day I'll live forever.

I leaned back on the porch, my head closer to the front door, my feet dangling over the three stairs. There was a tinny noise behind me; I thought I heard the TV playing in our kitchen, but the way I left Mama in the bed not too long ago made me believe maybe it was Shontae's Mama in her kitchen with the TV on and the windows open. It had gotten warmer as the night rolled in; one of those weird warm days in February when you forget it's winter and think summer is just around the corner. I was outside with no jacket (don't tell Weesie) and had slipped my shoes off and rubbed my feet back and forth against the clammy cement, to feel something. The sun was going down, and I swear I could feel the energy being pulled to the streetlights, about to turn on. This the thing about winter: even when it's warm, you only get but so much daylight—a second, it seems like, after school. When I heard a voice, I realized it was Mama on the phone, and she was up moving things around in the kitchen. The faint smell of the bottom of the burnt pot she always liked to use made its way to me, and I knew I was in for a long night. Whatever was going on in the kitchen was for me, and me only. Two lone fireflies drifted up from the grass, and I took that as my cue to go inside to wash my hands and face in preparation for dinner.

I KNOW THE SMELL OF COOKED CARROTS ANYWHERE, ANYTIME. You can blindfold me, ask me what the smell is, and if it's the earthy-sweet scent that sticks to the inside of your nose and lingers, even if you sniff to breathe deeper to clear the nostrils, I'll know it's cooked carrots. I hate them, of course. They stick to you like glue. *Everyone* knows I hate them, but I swear that's all Mama knows how to cook. Everyone knows my carrot hatred, just like everyone knows I grind my teeth in real pain whenever metal touches metal, so all the real kitchen cooking utensils are wood or plastic. If Daddy wants me to taste his spaghetti sauce and he has a silver spoon in his hand, he looks me in the eyes while he holds the spoon how me and Sissy practice eating and drinking like the rich, with our pinkies out, and he shows me he can bring a taste of the sauce from the pot to my mouth without making me cringe. Mama and Sissy always roll their eyes like they do when I get the whole "special" sausage, Daddy calls it, on top of my spaghetti plate, and I always just *know* I won something; I always believe it is the luck of the draw.

When I opened the door, my jaw clenched shut. Cooked carrots and the sound of an eating spoon scraping the bottom of a pan. In Sunday school Teeta taught us that hell is just all the bad things of this world on repeat, and I think now, *I am there*. I walked into the kitchen with my fingers in my ears and hummed, and usually that stops the assault, because usually it's Daddy at the stove because he is the chef at Forestwood Drive—but right then it was "just us girlies," as Mama said, and the spoon kept scraping, swirling the cooked carrots.

"You need to fix your face," Mama said, taking her cigarette and ashing it in the ashtray next to the assault pot. I dropped my hands from my ears during the break and pleaded with her.

"Mama—"

She held her hand up, shook it. I stopped mid whine. The spoon resumed scraping, and it sounded louder now, echoing in the empty house. I saw the meat chunks, the ranch seasoning packets. The cut potatoes. Roast—Daddy calls it Mama's Depression Dish, and we laugh and then have to push the pieces of tough beef across our plates until it looks like we finished. Usually she'd quick-prep something to go with it—corn, canned green beans, mashed potatoes, rice—to round out the meal, but I didn't see any other pots up on the stove.

The scraping stopped immediately when I sucked my teeth. She didn't look up at me but reached for the cigarette, near the end of its line, and took a drag.

"Mama, Daddy didn't settle my lunch balance for the week so I couldn't eat lunch today. I'm starving," I explained, hoping she'd understand my prepping her to ask for something, anything, else. I continued, "Mama, and you know I don't eat carrots cooked."

She turned to me. Blinked. You ever wondered if your Teddy Ruxpin could move on its own to look at you with that stare, even though you know he only moves when you put the tape in his back and press play? But one day you thought you counted three blinks without a tape in? The shock and surprise. The way he has all his expression in his eyes? Mama blank-stare-blinked at me three times just like that, and I believed she was unraveling like a tape reel.

"This is what I have cooked for dinner tonight," she said. Straight-faced. Slow like the last dregs of honey from the honey-bear squeeze jar.

"But Mama, you know—" I started again.

"I know this is what I've cooked for us," she said. The carrots were bubbling down to a sticky mess, which meant she had to scrape them again.

"But Mama, you know—" I wanted to say about the noise this time, reaching my hands to my ears. Her eyes got wider. You ever have someone move so fast you blink and then they across the room? Mama was suddenly chest to chest with me, holding my wrists, squeezing and pulling them down from my ears. She seemed so big and so small. We were almost eye to eye. Of course, the noise stopped when she did this, but I was so shocked, I resisted and still had the feeling of scraping in my body, like the echo of the timpani drum, and Mama was about to go off on me for fighting back now.

"Mama," I tried again. Closer to a whimper, surrender. She had yanked my hands so they hit my hips. She wasn't going to hear anything I wanted to say. When her eyes go wide like that when her and Daddy are in a fight over whatever they fight over, all I know is I hear the same words over and over like a broken record. My few words skipped and started, skipped and started the way Daddy's turntable lets you know the song done.

"This the meal I cooked. You hungry, you'll eat it," she said. The times when she put her hands on me were so far apart these days. When I was younger, everyone said I must love my butt getting cut so much as to fight with Mama "over nothing," and Teeta or Daddy would come to my rescue and set Mama off worse until someone would say that's enough and the lit flame would die out and somehow we'd slink away to our corners of the house.

Once, I heard Weesie say to Mama when she was fussing at me, "That's the cost of having daughters," and didn't she warn her about it when she was my age? They love they daddies too much and don't know hurt until they have daughters of they own. Mama looked hurt tonight. I was hurt, too. I twisted my arms and hands to be able to grab hers—still holding my wrists at my waist—and yanked them off. My ears were warming and I felt the anger inside me roll into a boil.

"I hate roast and you know it and you're making me eat it knowing I'm hungry. And I hate you, too!" I yelled, my voice in another register, like the way my flute screams above the rest of the band. Mama stomped around the kitchen like she was going to leave me there alone and retreat to her room. She turned around, waving her hand up and down my body like she was measuring it.

"You're always so hungry, Mika. If you don't want to eat what I've cooked, fine. Prolly good for you, anyway. Why don't you look in the mirror and ask yourself if it would hurt you to skip this one, then?"

She twirled around and disappeared into her room, then slammed the door.

.   .   .

YOU EVER GET SO MAD AT SOMETHING OR SOMEONE, AND I
mean so mad it feels like you about to light into a ball of flames?
Once, as an experiment, Daddy showed me that holding a magnifying glass just so allows you to harness the sun to start a fire. We
practiced on ants: the blot of light would be bright on the concrete until it was just the right distance between the sun's rays and
the ground, the blot zooming in and in until it reached a point
about the same size as the ant. We watched it flail, run around in
circles, zigging back and forth until it sparked into a piece of fire.

Mama had her blot of light shining on me so I couldn't explain it. She lights me up. It's why I didn't want to be alone with
her at Forestwood Drive in the first place. I know, I know, in the
kitchen before Daddy left, I said "No one's even gonna be here"
as my reason to escape to Redwood Court while he was gone,
and Mama heard it and it probably hurt her feelings. But right
now, alone in the kitchen with her, I knew I was right. When I
said it then, Daddy lifted his hand to my arm and flicked it with
his middle finger, so hard and in such succession it sounded like
he was snapping his fingers to remember something he had forgotten. I winced. He had raised his eyebrows in a *mind your mouth*
way, but it was true. Look at it now. I was so mad I dropped to the
floor screaming "I hate you" again and again to her closed door
until my voice grew hoarse.

But no one was home now to save me from the fire. I am
thinking about all the ants I burned for whatever reason—because
I could, because I knew how. I had the right tool and used it in the
right conditions to hurt them. They were just ants, carrying
whatever crumb into whatever tunnel for whatever queen.

When I was younger and threw myself to the floor, usually it was enough—the energy would shift in the house and Daddy would say a general "That's enough" in my direction and it would be the right amount of cool to calm me down.

But Daddy wasn't here now. I tried to say it to myself. Mama won't going to come out. "That's enough," I mumbled, hearing Daddy's voice in my head so much so I felt I was lipping the words he would have said. I waited, but nothing I imagined would put out the flame inside me—a fire that Mama had started with her magnifying glass, harnessing the sun to set me ablaze.

My anger turned to tears now, and then the crying escalated because I was mad I was crying, and all I knew at that point was that I had to do something. Yeh, there was Grandma Annie's voice in my head now, "Mika, an eye for an eye makes everyone blind," but that won't going to cool the heat trapped inside me. I wanted Mama to feel this hurt.

I pulled myself off the floor and slapped my feet down the rest of the hallway, loud enough she surely heard me. I dragged my hand along the wall where she'd hung the framed photo collages when we first moved in, saying the house won't never going to feel like ours until we put photos up. Each frame fell like its own towers of babel. I turned around to see if that would be the action to bring her out of the room.

Unsuccessful, I went into Sissy's room, on the hunt. First daughters get all of the sentimental things; I get hand-me-downs. Mama had taken a ceramic arts class in high school and made lots of little knickknacks precious enough for Weesie's curio. What Mama kept for herself, she gave to Sissy, who she was carrying in her belly while the clay table turned and turned. "I was thinking about you when I made this," Mama said when she found out she was having a girl. She said that with every piece. I didn't even want the little white girl in a yellow dress and bonnet. Or the clown that scared me how the night-light lit shadows across his face. But I did want this jewelry box that Sissy kept practically empty on her dresser. It was as large as a shoe box. White, but pearled like the inside of a seashell. Mama had called it her alabaster box like in the Bible, and we shrugged but assumed that it had meant so much to her that Sissy only put soft things in there like the notes she got from her little boyfriend, money she said she was saving so she could move out as soon as she graduated, and—of course I know, because I look!—not one piece of jewelry. But Mama would come into our room sometimes and dust it off, then say we needed to clean. Once, Sissy put it in the closet at the top because she found evidence of my snooping, and Mama asked her what happened to it. So, a perfect target.

When I snatched open Sissy's room door and grabbed the alabaster box, I felt supercharged with new energy and purpose. Mama had emerged from the room to survey the damage in the hallway just as I was coming to deliver the blow. She started to fuss about the photos, but I couldn't hear, couldn't think; I was a machine with one goal. I threw the jewelry box at her feet. It hit the doorjamb with such force that it shattered into countless pieces.

I could breathe again. The pressure valve, released.

Mama fell to her knees. Just like that—she was standing, and then she was on the floor, scooping with her hands the chalk-white remnants of the jewelry box. And crying. Mama was crying, stringing "nonononono" together like a never-ending chain. I braced myself for whatever was going to be launched in my direction next, but she didn't look up. Just picked up two pieces at a time and tried to see if they would fit back together like a jigsaw puzzle.

This is the thing about seeking revenge that I guess Grandma

Annie was trying to teach me: I won't satisfied. I called out, "Mama," a few times to get a reaction—any, really—to test the level of upset she must be now. But I might as well not have been there. She was alone and whispering her no's and gathering the pieces, stopping occasionally to wipe her eyes, leaving a streak of white dust across her face.

Only one time in my life did Daddy whoop me. I didn't understand it when it happened, and even now I can't tell you what I did, but I remember him going to the magazine rack in the bathroom and snatching a *Men's Health* magazine and rolling it up like a paper towel tube. He made me get on the bed, like Mama does when she 'bout to whoop me, and he hit me three times. I screamed less because it hurt and more because Daddy *hit me*. When he was done, his shoulders slouched and he slinked out the room into the living room. I waited for the television to turn on, which usually meant he was mentally transitioning from one thing to another, but it never turned on. The surprise of it all had knocked the wind out of me so that I was still on the bed trying to catch my breath. At the top of my fifth big breath, I heard the floor creak and looked at the door. It was Daddy. Holding the magazine limp in his hand.

"I'm sorry, baby," he said. I swear I heard him sniff. "I'm sorry."

I just said OK and he turned away. The kitchen trash can creaked open and something dropped in the bin. After a few steps the television clicked on.

Watching Mama on the floor, I thought I knew what Daddy must have felt. The punishment, for him, did not fit the crime. Or something. He swore he would never hit us like his daddy, and he broke that promise and hurt us more. I guess whatever went before that won't worrisome enough anymore such that he came back and apologized *to me,* and given that he was after me with the magazine for whatever trespass, it felt weird to be the one to have to forgive this trespass against me. So this is what the commandment means. Wait 'til I tell Grandma Annie.

I guess it meant that I was to apologize to Mama now, too? My trespass greater than the first. I walked over to her, then got on my knees, crawling to the broken mess between us.

Hearing Mama whimper made my body tingle, and I felt energy rise up in me again—like the universe was shifting because a child had made her mama cry. The upside-downness of it. I was filling up and filling up like a hot air balloon. I'd have to face Sissy, too, about the jewelry box. I'd do that when the time comes. But I found three big pieces that still fit together, clean breaks on all sides. It felt hopeful to see the corner of the box, like it could maybe be put whole again. I showed them to Mama and saw in her hands large pieces of another corner as well. But still: the dust pile on the floor. I looked, then she did, and shook her head.

"You might as well bring a broom to sweep all this up," Mama said. I popped up quickly in an effort to be as agreeable as possible. Either the storm was over or we were in the calm eye of it, and I still had twelve days to go before Daddy was back from Charleston.

"I'm sorry, Mama," I said when I returned. Lowering my head, I focused on trying to move the tiny pieces through the lump of carpet and into the dustpan. I pushed the big pieces. Then just picked them up one by one. While she watched. Still on the floor.

"I'm sorry, Mama," I said again. I sniffed. Locked into my broken record like how this all started.

"You can't just break anything you want, Mika. You can't just think that your feelings are more important than anyone else's," Mama said. I stopped, started to reply, but she beat me to it.

"You can't always have the last word either. That comes with growing up—knowing how to hold your hurt together so you don't hurt someone more."

Mama held her hand out in front of the broom to get me to stop sweeping. She got to her feet, finally, and pulled my chin up so I looked her in the eyes.

"What also comes with growing up is apologizing and meaning it. Especially when you've hurt someone you love. I was hurting when you came in, then you hurt me, and I reacted. I'm sorry, Mika," she said. "Do you forgive me?"

I looked down. I wasn't ready to let it all the way go. She brought my chin up again, even though I resisted.

"Yes" slipped through the slit between my lips; I didn't even open my mouth for the full word to get through. If I'm truthful, I admit it's so hard for me to accept apologies, y'all. It's so hard. But it felt like something Mama need to hear.

"Thank you," Mama said and exhaled, like she was holding on to something also. "Now. This"—she pointed—"this was more than a jewelry box to me. When I made it, I was grieving. I had lost my first child. I kept his burp cloth and knit cap in there until Sissy came and I could give the box a new life."

My mouth dropped open. She placed her pointer finger over my lips to shush me.

His? A brother? Where was he? What happened to him? She saw the questions in my eyes.

"I know. And yes. Before Sissy. Before I met your daddy, I carried a boy in my belly. One day we'll talk about how he got there," she said and looked just beyond me, unlocking our eyes, hers welling up with water. "But today, I'll say that this"—pointing again at the broken pieces—"was the only thing I kept that reminded me of what I had, what I held, and what was lost. He died a few hours after he was born, because I wasn't too much older than you when I had him."

She wiped her face. Her chest lifted quicker and quicker with shallow breaths.

"Now it's like David's gone again," she said, her voice cracking. She leaned against the door jamb and broke down. I let the broom drop to the floor and wrapped my arms—would that make it better?—around her, crying, too.

"I'm sorry, Mama," I said, and I finally meant it. My voice must have changed, or else the context. My shoulders heaved up and down with each staccato breath. Her arms finally reached up around me in an embrace, and my heart slowed back down. She rubbed my back and squeezed.

"I know, baby," she said. "I love you, OK? I love you." Mama kissed me on my forehead and repeated her love for me until the flames inside us both fizzled to embers, then went out.

When You Believe

The summer after I turned twelve, Teeta almost left us. One day, he was sitting in his den, reading his Word, preparing for Sunday School lessons, running through tissue after tissue with his cough. Mama and Daddy came to the house to pick me up, and all three of them—Weesie, Mama, Daddy—passed around a manila folder with a black-and-white image—something that, if I squinted from the den where I was posted up with Teeta, looked like a butterfly: two white wings with two black dots on either side.

Each time Teeta reached for a cigarette to light, Weesie would glare and ask: "When are you going to stop those?" And he would shrug and underline in his Word or highlight a page.

Mama told me to watch out for Teeta smoking. He would take to sneaking sometimes. One time, he was in the hall bathroom for what seemed like a century. I began to worry. Was he dead? I went out to the backyard and moved a bench from the play area, dragging it under the bathroom window. On my tippy toes, I peered in and saw it: Teeta sitting on the toilet lid, puffing on a cigarette. I banged on the window, and he jumped. I jumped. He flushed the cigarette and went back to the couch.

All I knew was that he should stop smoking. Weesie had quit cold turkey, just like that. One day she had her Virginia Slim in her hand while sitting at the island in the kitchen on the phone, and the next day she didn't. "I didn't want Satan to have a hold on me like that," she said. "So, I quit."

Anyways. Everyone whispered around me like I didn't know the whisper of bad news coming. When Aunt Olive died, Mama answered the phone and gasped. I was in my room and heard the click of her ring against the plastic receiver. She called out to me; I came thinking she was going to let me in on the news, but instead she asked me to come in and shut the door—leaving her inside for privacy, I guess, and me outside—but that only made it easier for me to listen, to understand.

She whispered, "Major. You for real? Gone? Just like that? Gone?" and then hung up the phone. I don't know why she needed to keep the truth away from me, because I was too young then to stay at home, which meant I had to go with her to Aunt Jesse's house to tell her the news about her sister. She told me to get dressed, we were going to Weesie's house, but when we pulled into Redwood Court, she made a left at Aunt Jesse's instead of a right at 154. Weesie's royal-blue Chevy Cavalier was in the carport, so she was home, and we never pulled into Aunt Jesse's house, *ever*, when we came to Redwood Court. Uncle Quincy wasn't home—he was out delivering the mail—but Aunt Jesse was. Mama still hadn't told me straight up what news we were delivering to Aunt Jesse—I just ran behind her quick steps to the door.

On the other side, Aunt Jesse was on the phone and the kitchen sink was running. Mama had to knock hard, twice. The door swung open and there was Aunt Jesse's big smile and "Hello." Mama said Daddy called to say Aunt Olive was gone. It was the first time I was direct witness to grief. Aunt Jesse dropped her cordless phone, and its crack on the linoleum floor stays with me to this day, as does the sound of her body falling limp to the ground. *Just like that*—legs sprawling this way and that, like how my Raggedy Ann's and Teddy Ruxpin's legs and arms flapped and flapped when I threw them down the stairs. We hadn't even come inside. Aunt Jesse was so undone. "My baby sister Olive, my baby," she wailed. Mama went down to the floor with her, and I just stood there at first. I looked around at what I could do: shut the screen door, the wooden side door. Turn off the water. Put the phone on the receiver. I had to step over Aunt Jesse's leg and foot to get to her living room to sit and wait. Just sit and listen to Aunt Jesse cry.

So I knew how to handle hard news like anyone else, and I couldn't understand why no one would tell me the deal with Teeta. They treated me like I was a delicate tissue paper, easy to tear. Of course, I was his favorite, and he was my favorite, but I was strong. I had stood there and didn't cry when Aunt Jesse crumbled beneath her sadness when Mama didn't know what else to do. I had also saw the signs of something coming. When Teeta stopped picking me up after school band practice, Daddy just said he had some doctor's appointments. When Daddy was late, or forgot, and finally rounded the corner to the carpool lane an hour after I had finished and the security guard was standing with me in pity, I had asked, finally, when Teeta was returning, because at least he was on time, and Daddy just said, "I don't know." He drove the rest of the way home in silence, NPR on the radio, and waited for me to gather my flute, book bag, and pencil case out the car before he went back to work.

On weekends, I had to beg to go to Redwood Court. Before, Teeta would come early on Saturday mornings down our hill, honking his truck horn. I'd bop to the door to let him in and he'd sit for a spell, have a sweet tea and a Little Debbie snack, then rescue me back to Redwood Court. That spring, he stopped coming, so I had to wait for a break in Daddy's schedule to get a ride from him, or call around looking for Uncle Junior to pick me up. Somehow, I'd make it over, and Teeta would be on the couch in his white undershirt and boxers. There were other clues to let me know something was wrong: Teeta was usually up every morning with the chickens he kept out back, fully dressed for the day with leftover grits, eggs, and sausage for me on a plate in the microwave. If Weesie was home to wake me, my first order of business was always: (1) wash my hands and face; (2) brush my teeth; and (3) get dressed and ready for breakfast. Jerry, the orange tabby that Teeta let me call to pick up from the free classifieds, was already eating his leftover sausage that Weesie threw out the side door onto the carport. This morning, though, Teeta was not dressed, his Bible was closed, and his eyes weren't even looking at the TV.

Still, I watched *Andy Griffith* or *Lassie* with him during the day, WWE in the evening. When he'd cough, his legs and head would lift up off the couch like he was doing sit-ups. He stopped using his handkerchief on account of the blood and mucous. Instead, he kept a red Solo cup by his side and spat into that, then covered it with a napkin. We made sure to keep a box of Kleenex on the coffee table and Weesie added Solo cups to her shopping list.

So my summer was changed. Teeta coughed and coughed. I went from my house to Redwood Court. Mama still had to go to the daycare to work, Daddy had to go to his main job at the satellite hut to make sure the PBS shows ran on schedule, and then to his side job at Church's Chicken. Sissy was a manager at a Boys & Girls Club, but the kids were so bad, she said, I shouldn't go over there and be influenced. Instead, I huddled a middle earth, between Weesie and Teeta's house and elsewhere—until, one day, Mama got a call and she shut the door again. This time, she spoke in such a whisper I could not make out what she was saying, except "I see you." I had no context for what that meant. "I see you at Baptist Memorial Hospital" or "Major, I see you at Baptist." What was she seeing? Why did she have to say it in such a way?

When Aunt Hazel came down from Chicago to stay at Redwood Court without an end date, I knew something in our universe had really shifted. Her daughter, Jazz, didn't come—I guess she was old enough to stay at home by herself—but Aunt Hazel brought a suitcase as big as me, and we had to ask a nice man to lift the luggage into Weesie's trunk. He reached out his hand and Weesie shook it. In the car, Aunt Hazel laughed and said we should have tipped him. Weesie shrugged. Almost exactly the day she arrived, though, was the day Teeta went into the hospital, and so I deciphered Mama's hushed and cryptic messages: Teeta had grown so weak from the most recent course of chemo that he was admitted into Baptist Memorial Hospital in the ICU unit. *I see you.*

No one knew what to do with me. "She shouldn't see Teeta like that," everyone said in their own way. So I was supposed to just stay at 154 and entertain myself—doing what? If I tried to ride my bike or something outside, Mr. Reggie or Ruby would certainly tell Weesie or Teeta when they got home, and that would be the end of that.

Aunt Hazel, who hadn't joined everyone right away due to jet lag, emerged from her nap and shower. Weesie caught a ride with Mama because she didn't feel strong enough to drive; her blue Chevy Cavalier stayed in the carport and her keys on the kitchen island. I gave Aunt Hazel Daddy's number so she could get directions, and she dictated them to me to write down. In my notebook where I wrote my stories and songs, I jotted down: "Two Notch North to Forestwood Drive to Taylor Street." With that, we were off to find Teeta, to see him, to—I don't know what.

That trip I learned that the sun rises in the east and sets in the west, so at 4:00 P.M. in the summer, if it was near our left side, we were going north—the right direction.

When, somehow, Aunt Hazel and I made it to Baptist Hospital the first day, we arrived in the bright-pink waiting room. On the television was *Andy Griffith,* Teeta's show. I smiled and eased down into the chair, waiting for a familiar face to walk through the double doors. First came Weesie. Her eyes were as red as the hard upholstered chairs. She gathered Aunt Hazel, said, "Prepare," and told her to follow. When Weesie saw me close my notebook to go with them, she reached into her pocketbook to hand me some quarters, told me "Get a Coca-Cola," and to wait 'til Daddy or Mama came for me. "They don't let anyone under seventeen in the ICU unit." Those words again. This time, I looked around and saw the signs: Intensive Care Unit. I understood only an inch more.

When Mama came out a while later, I asked for more information.

"Where's my grandpa?" I asked.

"He's back there, trying to get better," she said and took a sip of my Coke, which had lost all its carbonation.

"When can I see him? Can you tell him I love him?" I asked.

Mama took in all of the oxygen of the room.

"Baby," she said, grabbing my hand.

"Baby," she began again, as if she, too, were caught off guard by the moment, and the kind of mothering it required of her. "Your grandfather is very sick." She pointed to her nose. "They have him on a breathing tube. On life support right now." Her eyes, like Weesie's, were the color of beets. "Doctors are doing the best they can, but all we can do is pray. Just pray."

Those words were not foreign to me, because to spend weekends at Redwood Court was to go to church. I had been a junior member of Jehovah's Baptist Church when Teeta was a deacon, and then, after the Big Controversy over the money the congregation paid into for the move to a new church that never manifested into a new church, Weesie brought all of us to Antioch Baptist Church—where vacation Bible study and Sunday school demanded more than singing "Jesus Loves Me" and eating popcorn and cheese puffs. I had to know the Beatitudes, the Sermon on the Mount, 1 and 2 Corinthians before seventh grade. And also how to pray, more than just the Lord's Prayer. How to ask God for healing, how to ask God for the true desires of your heart.

At home, Mama was less religious. Any references to God, prayer, etc., were kept for the moments when they seemed we had no control of the outcome, what we really wanted.

Like when we got stranded on the side of the road because Mama forgot to check the gas before we headed to the country to her best friend's house. We were in Elgin, where no Black folks lived. Mama said we should pray that someone nice would come to help us, not the rednecks. Mama had said once, over the phone to her other friend, Wilma, to pray for Daddy when he had heatstroke, and when he was electrocuted on the job at the satellite hut, and when the white Lincoln Town Car stalled after he dropped me off to school and he thought he could beat the freight train at the tracks and he didn't. We all said we didn't know how he survived, much less walked out on his own two feet from a car that was mangled so much it looked like an origami swan. We prayed.

Now she was telling me to pray that Teeta would: (1) begin to breathe on his own; (2) wake up from his coma; (3) be healed; and (4) come home to us.

In vacation Bible study, I learned that God only really listened when you were always in communication with Him. Ms. Hunter told us that we couldn't just come to Him when we were in trouble, but that we should come to Him always. Even with the good. I never knew Mama to come to God with the good, but sometimes I thanked Him, like when I got a ninety-seven on my pre-algebra test, or when Daddy came on time to pick me up after band practice and I didn't have to wait *too* long for him, or when Weesie made mac and cheese. Maybe God would listen to me, but I wasn't sure he ever really heard Mama. She only spoke His name at times like this.

That summer, though, in the waiting room, because I was too young to make it past the double doors of the ICU wing of the hospital to see my Teeta, I prayed that God would give me just a little more time with him.

I am sure something else happened during my summer vacation, but I tell you, the weeklong wait in the waiting room seemed to be the only thing in the world that took place. It was like I was in the waiting room, and then I was in the classroom in the new school year, seventh grade. But Teeta made it home. He made it home and maybe then we all believed in miracles, in wishes, in prayers. I can't call it, but really, we all believed in something.

Indian Summer:
Lake Wateree

Major

When he got off the ventilator that summer but was still in the hospital and I had come to sit with him, Mr. Mosby looked me straight in the eye and told me, "Don't you let them put that thing down my throat like that again."

I nodded.

Mr. Mosby lifted his finger. "I mean it. Promise me, son," he said.

I nodded again. "Yes, sir." Of course, I don't know what he'd been through, but when he made me look him in the eyes like my daddy did when I was little and promise him that I'd stop Mrs. Mosby and Rhina from tying him indefinitely to a machine, I understood he was teaching me to leave this world on your own terms—a soldier's death. Be your own man. He put his finger down and we sat in silence. The room was quieter without the rhythmic pulse of the breathing machine. Every few minutes, a small chirp and beep and the IV released more fluids.

I was thankful that he was off of the machine, though. I had been practicing all week what I was going to say. When the doctors came out early in his stay and told us to prepare, that it wasn't looking good and I had to be strong for Mrs. Mosby and Rhina, I guess I didn't process it myself. The hospital was not far from my office at the satellite hut, and I stopped by every day during a break. I expected him to be asleep or, as the doctors had once explained, in a medically induced coma, but coming to see him during my break was also a few moments where I wasn't expected anywhere, to answer anything or to do anything—I could just be in peace with Mr. Mosby and have the space to think. I wanted to figure out how to thank him for all the years. I mean, I had spent that week he was on the breathing machine turning it over in my head: Mr. Mosby had called me "son" for more years than my own father was in my life. Mika reminded me one day on the way home from school. She had been asking about family trees and my daddy and all of that for a school assignment.

"If you were the only person to have children, and I'm the youngest, does that mean that I'm the last Tabor?" I nodded and bit my lip, my thinking pose—I had thought, *Where will this go?* She continued: "And you're a junior. Your daddy was also Thomas?" I nodded. When she starts a conversation with questions, I know she is journeying somewhere and eventually we'll get to wherever she's going. I stopped asking why, but I did clarify. "Thomas Senior, your grandfather," I said.

"Is he my grandfather? I never met him," she said.

I bit my lip again, tasting iron. I moved to my cuticles instead.

"I know. He died of a heart attack when I was in high school.

But he's still your grandfather because he was my father," I had said.

I heard Mika wonder out loud what my father would have been called, and I guess he would have still had us call him Sarge like his men did. Kind of like how Mr. Mosby calls me Major. After Daddy retired while he was stationed in Italy, we all came back to Charleston. I remember one day we were in a store and a white man called him "boy." Daddy dropped us off and went back out into the night by himself and came home swaying like a cat-tail on the marsh's edge.

He hit Mama that night and I had to puff my chest.

Daddy laughed at me.

"Son, you too young to take this on," he said, pointing his finger in the middle of his own chest, and walked out again. A few days later our neighbor Mr. Green knocked late and walked him in the door. Daddy had a bandage on his head. We did this coming-home-drunk dance enough times until one day he hit Mama again and I found it in me to reach for the broomstick, and I saw it in his eyes—the click. He was looking at me and then he was looking just past me. He tore through the house, through Mama, and when she was passed out on the floor, he lit a news-paper on fire and dropped it by her face. The house whooshed, maybe with the wind, and it was all aflame. I picked up Mama and dragged her outside. When she came to, Daddy was standing at the fence watching the house burn like he was waiting to see if we would burn right along with it.

"Why did you do this to us?" It was the last question I ever asked him.

"What did I burn that I didn't build?" was his response. It was the last thing he ever said to me.

I never saw my father again.

"Daddy, did you cry when he died?" Mika asked me in the car.

I guess not. So much time had passed since our last conversation, like six years. I was in chemistry class and the principal came to gather me. I was a junior and it was my first year at the white school, and so I always had to be very careful not to do anything to start something. I walked to school (Blacks couldn't ride the bus), played football, and walked home. At the principal's office I kept trying to figure out all of what would warrant this call-in. Anything will trip them up. It was when the principal immediately told me to sit down and didn't look me in the eyes that I knew it was something else.

"Son," he had said. I had never heard a white man use that word in a tender way. "We've got news that your father died. I'm sorry."

We sat there for a minute. I straightened my shirt, said thank you, and went back to class. I don't remember the rest of the day but the next thing I remembered my best friend, Bebe, was riding his bike over the Savannah Highway bridge and found me there at the top, standing there looking down at the marsh. He stood with me for a bit and then put me on his handlebars and we rode home.

"When we found out he was gone, we learned he had run down the coast to Jacksonsville, Florida. Your Grandma Annie reminded us of her cracked ribs and how long it took us to rebuild the house that he burned down, so we knew we weren't going to the funeral. We stayed in Charleston."

Mika turned to me, but I couldn't look at her. Water was gathering in my left eye and I was focusing on shallow breaths and no quick movements. I could feel her trying to see.

"So, you didn't get to say goodbye?"

I cleared my throat. "No. Until our last trip to Florida, I had never even seen his grave."

I guess it was the theatrics of the summer with Mr. Mosby—all of it that had got me tender.

I had shown Rhina and the girls his headstone in the sea of veteran headstones, and then we were smiling with Mickey Mouse. I thought I had resolved my feelings about the night he left us and the years in between. Seeing his name on the tombstone didn't close any open chapters. But when Mika said in the car on the way to Lowe's that—and she had counted on her fingers: "Wow, Daddy, Teeta has been my and Sissy's grandpa longer than you had a daddy"—I realized what she was saying was more than that, even—I had a father in Mr. Mosby, longer than I had a blood father, and now I was losing him, too.

There I was, sitting in the hospital room with Mr. Mosby. What do you say to the man who has called you son in the way a father does and he didn't even raise you from birth? After I promised Mr. Mosby I'd help him leave honorably, he fumbled for the TV remote control, and I reached and flipped stations until he held up his finger. Nurses said he'd probably be too tired for real conversations so don't push him, and that suited me just fine. We watched *Andy Griffith*.

When I woke up because I felt slobber soak my shirt, I wiped my face and looked over at Mr. Mosby. He was watching me sleep, and I apologized, explaining the network had a late news broadcast and I had been at the satellite hut overnight. He shook his head, in his way that said *Don't apologize,* but didn't look back at the screen. My hands started to sweat. So much of our together time was him or Mrs. Mosby famously filling the silences. I never had to learn small talk. Stories. He was asking me to tell him a story, I thought, or else he knew I had come to say—what, exactly?—something, and was trying in his own silent way to get it out of me. I wasn't ready. Would I be? I turned the hospital TV to my network station, and it was the nature special. Local fishermen calling out best South Carolina fishing techniques. Mr. Mosby smiled and looked at me again.

"Remember Ms. Cook's lake?" I said. He nodded. "I had come over to see about Rhina and you grabbed your tackle box and asked me if I could swim and I said yes and then you made me climb into that life raft of a boat and pushed us out to the middle of the lake and asked me again my intentions with Rhina, right as you were getting a catch. That day, it was like whenever you threw the hook in you caught something. It was so fast. Throw in. Catch. Throw in. Catch. And then there was that big one."

He nodded and smiled. His chest was rising fast like he was trying to laugh. I held my hand out. It was OK. I started laughing.

"That big one hooked and you didn't know what to do so you jumped up and suddenly I was trying to juggle, keeping the boat from capsizing by redistributing my weight, trying to say I wanted to marry Rhina, and somehow get you to sit back down."

I moved to the edge of the seat so I could be closer to him.

"I don't know how Mrs. Mosby knew we were there—was it Junior?—but she comes up to the dock just to watch you fall in the lake." My shoulders went up to my ears with laughter. The corner of his mouth curled at the memory.

I looked at the heart number, the oxygen number, the things the nurses taught me to read when I was trying to understand. His vitals were rising too quickly, as I had started to get excited, recalling how he was in the lake, yelling, Mrs. Mosby on the dock, yelling, and I was trying to tell him, *Just stand up!* by doing a gesture like raising the back of a car trunk, and trying to comfort

Mrs. Mosby from the boat. I looked out to where she stood at the lip of the lake and tried to channel to her: *I have him, it's alright, I have him for you.*

"And then I had to jump in the water and stand you up. And we walked back to the shore. Just like that. But you had looked me in the eyes, and you said, 'Thank you, *son.*'"

I shook my head because my chest got tight with the memory.

Mr. Mosby whispered, "We didn't even bring any of those catches back for supper."

I laughed. "Nope, we sure didn't. But I knew you were going to let me marry Rhina when you called me son."

Mika

I learned in school that Indian summer meant a hot day when it was supposed to be cold. In Columbia we get a lot of those, like they're their own season—a string of days when you think you're still in summer because you're outside sweating and you want to be in shorts like your white classmates but Weesie shuts that down fast, saying we have to "dress the season not the weather," whatever that means. I've lived through enough Indian summer days on Redwood Court to know that's prime weather to be dragged out to Lake Wateree. The first sign was when Daddy started to gather tackle and pulled the rods out of the dusty shed. It had been a Daddy/Weesie thing, mostly all I knew about it. Something about Teeta almost drowning. How I knew I would be invited was when the straight poles came out of the shed. I always asked when I was going to graduate to a reel and rod instead of just a rod, but no one ever answered me. If it was just me and Weesie, sometimes she'd let me pull in the empty hook after watching the floater bob lightly up and down. A turtle stealing her bait. But I never got to cast—that was the real fishing part. The straight poles were for shallow-water fishing. One time I caught a real fish, but Weesie said it was gonna be full of eggs since it was at the edge, so she snatched it off the hook so fast I touched my lip like it was hurting. She threw it back. I was so mad. I prayed we wouldn't catch anything that day.

Daddy came inside saying Saturday would be a nice day for fishing and we should all go. I counted the poles: four.

"Sissy supposed to go, too?" I asked, and that really would be a miracle. It was like when Teeta took sick and everyone rushed to get Sissy a car and teach her to drive in order to have another person with a car around the house, but then she went off and got two jobs—even with school—and she disappeared behind the cashier stands of the sub sandwich shop and Mama dragged me there so much I swear it was more so she could see Sissy than it was about the soggy sandwiches, but we got both.

"Somehow, she's off work this weekend," Daddy said, setting the rods down. He wiped his hands on his pants and a faint dust cloud puffed out at his hips. He followed me back inside the side door of the house. I started to ask Mama if she knew we were *all* going fishing this weekend. She was painting her nails with Ricki Lake playing in the background. She lifted her fingers to blow them dry and asked what I had said.

"Daddy says we're going fishing this weekend. Even Sasha."

Mama raised her eyebrows in surprise, but I couldn't tell if the surprise was because "we" also meant *her* or that Sasha was going.

"Even Mr. and Mrs. Mosby," Daddy said. I wasn't facing him, but it sounded like how he says things with a smile. I heard him lean on the washer. If you were gonna get small talk out of him, it was gonna be him standing in the kitchen leaning on the washer. Nowhere else. If he went around the corner into the living room, he'd ask for the remote "right quick" and turn to *Deep Space Nine,* which was somehow always on, and you'd lose him to space. If he came in and didn't lean, he was only doing a pit stop on his way to his work shed.

"I figured, since it might be the last few warm days before it's too cold to be out at the lake, that we'd all go. Especially since Mr. Mosby is getting stronger and can make it. We can bring a folding chair just in case."

Mama stopped blowing on her nails to say she did have a hair appointment but she guessed she would cancel. Something about Mama had shifted after we brought Teeta back from the ICU. She was always the family memory wrangler. Wanting to take pictures when no one else did. Any of the pictures we have she's never been in, because she's holding the camera telling us to smile. All of the trip ideas, Mama's: Disney, King's Dominion, Myrtle Beach. Then, all of a sudden, she didn't care. I had heard Weesie say one day on the phone that she had come to the ICU room and Mama had been squeezed up in the bed with Teeta when he was connected to the breathing machine. Earlier that day the doctor had asked her, how long was she going to carry on letting a machine breathe for him? And Mama had climbed into the bed with Teeta then, put her head on his chest and said, "As long as it takes." Weesie said she believed Mama ain't been the same since it seemed like the doctors won't trying to fix him at all. So now to have Daddy be the one wrangling us all for a family trip was the real unusually warm weather in an otherwise cold season.

Daddy pushed off the washer and leaned toward the door.

"Best time is bright and early, to get a good spot where you know the sun will heat the water later in the day. That's where the fish'll be. So we gotta leave early."

Mama went back to painting her other hand, blowing on the wet paint.

Weesie

Back in Georgia when I was young, Lady taught me that Cherokee summer meant you were in trouble of possibly losing a whole harvest. The fields would heat up too quickly and the plants themselves would think it was summer and not fall and bolt to seed. We'd miss the fruits altogether, because the crops went swiftly to their dormant stage or died off.

When the doctors told us to prepare to say goodbye, and Teeta come up off the breathing machine and almost looked full of life like he did before he went in, I knew not to be fooled by whatever this brief moment of clarity and strength was. Surely, it must be Teeta's final bloom.

Teeta

I won't surprised when Major come to my room, full of words he won't speaking. I've watched men watching men they love die and be bursting with what they never said but should have, and then I watched the silence continue to eat them up, more than the war, more than homesickness, more than unrequited love. Weesie was the one who told me 'bout his father first. He was just a boy—a season or two before he showed up at his sister's house at Redwood Court to take classes at the university. He had the smell of a boy running away and running to something. And I had to see where his head was at when he started sniffing around Rhina.

You can't go into the army, be dropped out of planes over

bodies of water talking 'bout you can't swim. I'm sure when he signed up himself later, he learned that of course I knew how to swim, at least from my Korea days, but I had to do it. See for myself that his acting was true like his words.

Major

I wanted to tell Mr. Mosby thank you for that time he gathered me when I was home from Korea on leave and we talked about his time in the Korean countryside. I told him about the developments along the Zone, how the Koreans embraced us, mostly, and I liked the challenge of trying to pick up single grains of rice with chopsticks and eventually your tailbone gets used to sitting on the floor. And they had sent me home for break before training me for my next post, in Brussels, and he had said, "Like the sprout?" and we laughed. I didn't have Daddy to ask about what it was like serving when we were in Europe, and Mr. Mosby was in war times, but when he asked if I was taking Rhina and Sasha and I said no because she was expecting again, he put his hand on my shoulder and said, "Son, you get out now while you still have a woman and a family who know and love you. No paycheck from the army gone give you that." I had thought, despite my promises to break the patterns, I was turning into Daddy, translating provisions into love. Mr. Mosby was saying he could be my model so I don't have to make my own way. I never thanked him for showing me how else to be the head of the household, and I was coming to the hospital that day to say it, maybe, except then I started talking about that first trip, when I thought he was going to die on me with Mrs. Mosby watching and maybe that meant that I wasn't going to marry Rhina after all. But looking at him, I knew he was tired and he was prepared to ride out the rest of his days, starting that day, and I had to be the wall between the family's emotions and his wishes. But I gave him my word. So it goes.

It took a few months, but Mr. Mosby began to fill out again, and so everyone looked to the slow climb in weight as an indication that maybe the worst of it was over. That he might live. When he was hooked up to the ventilator, we all lost track of the idea that he wasn't eating all that time, fighting to breathe on his own while he also must have been silently starving. We all watched Weesie spoon-feed him grits like Lady ran around after Mika with a pot claiming to be fattening her up. Even though it looked to us like he was reclaiming his faculties, we also sensed it wasn't all on the up-and-up—he didn't go back to his victory garden, we called it. Weeds and ivy started to take over 154. I had asked Reggie to alternate the yard maintenance with me, and when the ivy reached the front door, Ruby started the phone tree; we all knew how important it was that the landscaping keep up, and it was more than for appearances. In addition to looks, an unkempt yard also signaled that maybe there weren't any men around, and yeh, I had all my jobs, but I did know to keep an eye on Redwood Court.

At any rate, the grass would slow down soon, and the weeds, with fall coming. The thing about Columbia, though, was that there are so many Indian summer days that greenery gets tricked in and out of their approaching dormant stages. But this weekend it all would line up: everyone home, the water nice and high so the fish would be jumping.

That's how I had it in me to take us all fishing the weekend it looked like the weather would be warm enough for Mr. Mosby's smaller frame. The two of us never went fishing again after that first time when he called me "son" in the middle of the lake—it

must have looked like a type of baptism: me standing and picking
him up out of the water, and we were changed. I always thought
we'd keep going to the shore to cast a line, but we never did. We
had our moment then, but something moved me to have this moment now. A loop closing in on an opened beginning.

Weesie

I tell Teeta that I'm headed out to get me a basket of crickets since
we all headed out to the big lake and not Ms. Cook's pond. Ms.
Cook's pond scratch an itch, sure, but Lake Wateree got large
striped bass and, like I say, "the bigger the bait, the huger the
catch." Mann taught me that. You hook the crickets just under
they wings so they stay alive longer, and you don't use a heavy
weight on the line, so they just dance across the top of the water,
right into the fishes' mouths. I know Major like his fake worms
looking like candy, and I can't send Teeta out for the run because
he just off that breathing machine and we just brought him home
from the hospital. I'll never forget the way them doctors sent that
death-care nurse over to convince us to let him go, to let him off
that machine, talking about God's will—but I knew my God was
gonna send him home, alive, with me. He did it, but Teeta ain't
left the house, and I don't know if he gone change his mind about
the lake either when the time comes to head out, but I'm gone be
ready with my crickets and I guess I'll get a cup of worms for him
and I'll drag out the stick poles, too. He can drop a hook at the
edge with the girls.

　　When I pulled back into the carport, Reggie met me outside
and waved me down. It look like he was leaving my house, which
I left open in case Teeta needed help. Reggie said Teeta had called

to ask him to come over because he thought he could make it 'cross the hall to the bathroom but he couldn't. Reggie gave me the updates and I thanked him and went inside.

"You should have let me let you stay in our room," I said when I walked in the blue room with a washcloth to wipe him down. Doctors said the chemo would seep out his pores and I shouldn't share a bed and we should help the skin cells slough off or else his pores would clog and his body would turn into a forest of black-heads.

"I thought I had it in me, Weesie, I really thought," he said. I told him don't worry, I know we have good days and bad days. I held his hand out and rested it on my breast while I rolled up his pajama sleeves, and he squeezed a little and I knew he was still in there, my Teeta, even as I knew we had officially started our goodbyes.

"You think you up for Lake Wateree tomorrow?" I asked. I couldn't keep my eyes on him like I used to. I took to looking just over his shoulder and out the window. Calvin was tinkering away on his buggy. June's grands jumping rope in our driveway.

Teeta cleared his throat. "I want to. I know I need to," he said. His voice started to sound froggy again, so I reached for the Styrofoam cup of water and pursed my lips like he won't know what to do. I couldn't help myself. Lady always said it: a man once, but a child twice.

"Major got everything and I just come back from getting my crickets. The girls coming, too. Everybody. Can't remember the last time we all went out together."

"Lady's funeral," Teeta said. Five years ago. He was right. Homegoing's the only time people really find time to be together. I was in a haze of mourning. I forget most times how folk sat around my dining table. Where was I? In the kitchen? At the dining table? In the bed? Teeta said they had to mop me off the floor, just about, when it came time to close the casket and head for Palmetto Cemetery. Sasha had taken my handkerchief and covered my legs and everyone talks about how Mika 'bout disappeared—musta been scared—but we were there, all of us, together.

"Sure was Lady's funeral, huh," I said and set the cup down. Teeta, too, had stopped looking at me. He must have caught his reflection in the TV just at the foot of the bed. Major brought it in from the back house and set it up so he could get *Andy Griffith* any time. Mika was sad about that change because she liked to play out there and have time away—it was all changing, for all of us. I could see the horizon coming into view and Teeta on the other side of it.

"We need to leave early, so I'll make a salmon-and-grits dinner so it'll stick to your bones. Got a Cherokee summer day, so it'll start and end cold, with a little warmth in the middle."

"Kinda like life, huh," Teeta said and lifted the corner of his mouth. "All the hot loving happens in the middle of it." I smiled and missed him so hard just then.

"Let me go fix dinner," I said, leaning in to kiss him on the lips, and he squeezed my hand. Doctors tell you the way to let a body heal is to leave it alone, but what about the hearts of the hurt and the lovers?

Mika

We four packed the van and headed to Redwood Court to pick up Weesie and Teeta. I held the cup of worms in the back seat all the way or else Mama wasn't going to go with us. I put it in a plastic bag, even, and tied it up to show her they won't going to crawl out. I don't know why Daddy packed her a fishing rod with a whole reel the way she carries on about bugs. I don't know why she come to be afraid when everyone around her ain't. Daddy rolled his eyes when her voice went up two octaves above the orchestra like my flute. Sissy had her Sony Discman loaded up before the van even started, and I knew she was listening to that white band she started playing all the time, 'cause she was whispering, *"You're gonna be the one that saves me / cause after all / you're my wonder wall"* and I was ready for Daddy's mixtapes, though with Weesie and Teeta in the car it's just gonna be different.

I love Teeta but it took forever for him to come down the three steps at the kitchen door. Everyone fussed over him like they did my little cousin Destiny, Uncle Junior's daughter, when she first learned to walk—standing a few feet out with their arms open, waiting for Teeta to push the walker and shuffle behind it. Daddy said for us to wait in the car so we can leave on time, but I just knew that if I didn't go to the bathroom now he'd be more mad later, so I squeezed out from behind the second row of seats in the van and floated past them making the fuss with Teeta to go. The kitchen door shut and I knew they really didn't see me, because when I was washing my hands, I heard the van honking from the road. I run out and squeeze back in and Teeta was laughing 'cause Mama was freaking out, not because they left me but because the worms were not being tended to, and they had decided to put Weesie up front with Daddy, so Mama was closer to where the worms were.

On the road it was just like all our road trips: everyone fast asleep except for me and Daddy. I had started counting the mile markers because Daddy had turned the volume down so low all I heard was Mama's snoring every other breath.

When the van drifted onto the grated side lines the third time,

I knew Daddy was falling asleep to the hum of the quiet road. So I started to ask him what was so special about Indian summer and why we were going all the way out to Lake Wateree instead of Ms. Cook's lake.

"More shoreline to choose from, for one," Daddy started, always answering the second question first. "At Ms. Cook's, you only have her dock or you gotta go in a boat." We had passed mile marker twenty-nine, just out of Columbia. We needed forty-one. Daddy was looking in the rearview mirror to talk to me, so I kept looking, too.

"But what's so special about Indian summer? Don't things start to die in the fall?" I asked. I didn't mean to use that word, not now, not with Teeta with us in the car, even if he was asleep. Daddy squinted his eyes in the mirror at me.

"They go into hibernation for the winter, but Indian summer tricks fish into thinking it's not time yet, so they're nice and plump—good eating."

"Yep!" Teeta said, clearing his throat—his constant now. He had to hear me talk about things dying in the fall. "Even come to the shoreline where the water is more shallow, so it's like a hot-water bath compared to the rest of the lake," he said. Daddy nodded in the window. Mile marker thirty-four.

I guess that was supposed to be consolation for me and my cane pole they stick me with, even still, even now that I'm bigger and could hold my own. Mile marker forty-one.

When we got there and parked, I think all of us at the same time realized what was before us: waiting on Teeta and his legs and his walker and the woodsy floor peppered with pinecones, straw, acorns—all the things that would make his ability to get anywhere impossible.

Weesie was holding the cane poles at the edge of the parking

lot, the lake just beyond, and it was like my Bible picture book of
Moses about to part the Red Sea with his staff. Maybe we were
standing there waiting to see if a path would clear. Daddy spoke
first.

"I'll carry Mr. Mosby," he said. "Just make sure there aren't
any pinecones in my way. We can't fish here with all this traffic."
So he swept Teeta up off the pavement, and I remembered all the
times Daddy did that with me—the rush of my body going
against the pull of gravity. He'd do it almost as easily as picking
up anything, really. A sack of potatoes. Laundry. A hammer. He'd
say it was from working the extra shifts at Church's Chicken, that
I weighed something like two bags of the steak potato fries. We
walked single file: Weesie, Sissy—kicking a path clear—Daddy
and Teeta as one, then me and Mama at the back. It felt like this
took longer than the thirty-mile-marker drive, but we found a
clearing with a picnic table, and you could walk right up to the
shore. Almost as soon as we arrived and Daddy set Teeta down in
his fold-out chair and Teeta sighed like he had walked that whole
way himself, the sun came out.

"We just in time for the warming light," Weesie said.

And we started to set up for the day.

Rhina

Major says my hysterics are a distraction; maybe they are. Ma
never made me go fishing, so when was I supposed to be OK with
worms? When he told me his plan, that he wanted us all to go out
to the lake together, he said it so clearly, with such conviction, I
knew there was no way to bow out. We both knew. Daddy had
made it off the machine by our prayers. Each night, I laid prostrate on the floor begging for healing, more time, peace beyond

understanding, faith, and each time the same answer came to me, clear as a voice in the telephone: *Start saying goodbye.* I wasn't ready. Who is ever ready? It was like I had only really gotten him, the real him, when the girls came. Folks always said your parents become someone different—who we wished they were—when the grandchildren come, and it was like Daddy got rounder around the edges and made room for folks on the inside. And now, like his soul was waiting for that transformation alone, he started his departure.

Major didn't say it, but I knew this was a goodbye for him, too. A man like a father in his life leaving him again. Daddy told me how Major sat at the foot of his bed talking to him just about every day in the hospital. The nurses told us to talk to the sick even if they're in a coma, that they can hear us and knew we were there. It's why Teeta asked why we didn't let the girls back there. I mentioned the rule and he sucked his teeth—we know what's best for us and ours, he'd said. "Think about what it has meant to Major all these years to have someone you love die without a goodbye," he went on. "Imagine what it would have done to the girls, 'specially Mika." I had never thought about it like that, so I packed our lunches and a folding chair and blanket for Daddy and went along with the plan.

Even Sasha was into the idea of fishing, and that surprised me. At the shore, we lined up—Major, Mika, Daddy, me, Ma, Sasha. It was our regiment: each of us flanked by those who loved us most. Daddy's girls next to daddy's girls. Sasha and Ma: peas in a pod. One of the days before I could fully opt out of fishing trips for whatever reason or another, Daddy had dragged me somewhere. I didn't even pretend to fish like with a cane pole, I just stood there, looking out into the lake counting turtle heads polka-dotting the surface and helping keep watch of the three floaters he had going. For someone who had felt that fishing was about peace—like the Serenity Prayer, he'd say—it didn't make much sense to bring someone who ain't find as much joy in it as you, but there I was.

"Who else is my baby, baby?" he'd say and lift the right corner of his mouth and wink, and I guess I understood that being with someone, sharing time and space, was as important as anything else.

Of course. Of course. He reset all of his lines. He stood at the shore, one hand in his pocket, and pulled me to his side. I was surprised at first and resisted, then melted into the lean.

"Sometimes," he had said, "I think about one of the last things I want to do before I go." He looked down at me. I watched the floaters out on the lake. "I think it's gotta be fishing with my favorite girls and maybe, if I'm lucky, whatever grands you give me. Yeap."

Then one of his rods started tugging and we both jumped to try to reel in supper. He was winding and watching the line get tight and pull away from us, and then he'd turn a few and pull it closer to shore. Pull away. Pull closer. After some of that, he said he'd let the fish run a bit and faced me. "This must be what Heaven's gonna be like, huh?"

Daddy must have told Major that story, too, or how else were we all here? I mean, Junior wasn't here and maybe that was for the best. When he got pulled over again and the cops took him in this time, Ma wrung her hands all night: *her baby, her baby.* Daddy, exhausted and only just a few sleeps in his own bed instead of the hospital bed, shook his head when Major come to tell us how much it was gonna cost us all to get Junior out. "Should just leave him in there," Daddy huffed. And they did. They had to. Daddy had said no to cashing his pension for it. How was he and Weesie gonna pay the mortgage? And no to Ma on a second house loan, even partial. Lawyer said he could be out in a few months on good behavior if he behaves, so that's our prayer these days. That Junior behaves so we can have him home in time. That's my prayer.

Teeta

Only Mika caught something. A little slug—fish so small it slid right off the hook when she lifted it up grinning ear to ear to show me. I clapped and praised her, but knew we were going home empty-handed. It was too late in the year.

I tried to tell them that fish don't think about the weather, 'cause they know the season. But Major was chomping at the bit, and then Weesie was, and when they sent Mika to tell me we was going out to Lake Wateree, of course I wasn't going to protest, but I didn't have it in me to really fish. I could barely hold a broth spoon to my lips, but you know when the cloud comes over a house folks start seeing what they wanna and acting funny. Look for the warm days in the middle of winter. Like this trip. Like Major wanting to do this trip. Our first time getting to know each other in a father-son type way and we at a lake, and today . . . today we all here. Junior done decided what life he want to have, with or without me, I guess. I can't be mad. I bucked, too, when my daddy got the black lung. That's how I got on the back of the truck to Columbia. I could never tell Major he didn't really want to watch his father die, that being there somehow wasn't better than his being gone. I saw it. A man as tall and bushy as a cypress chopped down to pieces until he fit into a pine box 'bout Mika's size. You don't know what you're saved from sometimes.

Major

When you hold an adult body in your arms, they can get close enough to your ear to say something so quiet no one else can catch it.

The girls and Mrs. Mosby were kicking up the pinecones and small branches; Mika and Sasha were making a game of it, which would have made it hard to hear, but Mr. Mosby leaned into my ear and I lifted my arms a bit to support him. He had said something, but the bounce from my steps kept taking his words, so I slid my feet like skiing.

"Thank you, son," he said. "You must have known I needed to see the water one last time."

I just said, "Yes, sir," like I was back in the army. Not that *this* was what I knew he needed. Not like that. I kept holding on until we got back to the van.

Whatever else is coming for us, what's next, won't be able to take this day. All of us, together.

Part Two

Thirty-first
Annual Chitlin Strut

"We have a roster of every verified blood Bolton who lived or lives in South Carolina, and we're always trying to grow the list," Devine said. She was sitting in Weesie's kitchen, not the living room. When Weesie saw them coming up the driveway, she had drawn the wood-paneled accordion divider, which made the living room all but invisible to the guests, Devine and Loretta. Even though they made claim to being family, their last names were not Bolton, but anyway, Weesie welcomed them inside. Weesie loved and yearned for unannounced guests—ones that she knew—now that Teeta was gone. He was only a few months buried and Weesie still wore her wedding rings, and like a similar habit, despite her favorite person in the family having passed away, Mika still agreed to spend her school breaks and free time at Redwood Court.

These older Black women, maybe a few years older than Weesie, had arrived like door-to-door insurance salesmen. On Forest-wood Drive, it was young blond men in crisp white shirts who came to her door. If Rhina was home, they'd get a chance to speak. If Major was home, the door would remain closed.

At Redwood Court, Weesie's assessment of the business—and, honestly, which door the visitor approached—determined the subsequent interaction. Strangers came to the front. Folks who knew better came through the carport to the kitchen door.

Weesie looked at the pamphlet Loretta was opening up on the island. Her visitors had been more frequent since Teeta's death: mostly old friends he used to sit with, wanting to show their love for him by stopping by the house. Mika, who was nearby in the den to see about these visitors now, spent those post-Thanksgiving break mornings and afternoons in the backyard that Teeta had curated for his grands' leisure and comfort. He had erected a bench swing set, a jungle gym with a slide, double-seat carriage swing, see-saw swing, and a gymnast bar. Each day, Mika practiced going from one end of the jungle gym to the other without touching the ground. It was practice for training in case she ever got called to be in a game show like *Legends of the Hidden Temple,* which she used to watch only at Redwood Court because Rhina forbade her to watch a show with a talking stone face called Olmec who urged game players to "unlock ghosts and skeletons" by running through an obstacle course. Mika knew that the kids who lost had too little upper-body strength to swing them from monkey bar to monkey bar over the foam lava pit to the finish line. If they fell into the pit, the kid contestants had to start over until their time ran out.

Mika had been practicing for the final moment—to make it to the end of the jungle gym and hit the buzzer to win—when she looked up and saw a car she didn't recognize in the driveway. Because she had already done two rounds across the jungle gym and sweat was beginning to form at her brow, she decided to go inside to investigate—which could double as a chance to take a break and get some of the sugar-free Kool-Aid Weesie kept just for her. Always red.

Entering through the back porch and den, she heard a woman's voice—raspy, the way Teeta's was starting to sound before they started chemotherapy.

"This your granddaughter? She pretty! She so dark, though. Who's the Bolton parent?" Devine asked.

"My mama," Mika said and took a sip of the red drink and wiped her mouth with the back of her hand. So much had changed for Mika at Redwood Court, but many things remained constant: access to a fridge that seemed to be specially filled to her tastes—with the big crunchy pickles, not the soggy ones, with Duke's mayonnaise and the square-cut ham, and orange juice pouches that she liked to sneak into the freezer to make freeze pops. No one had seen Junior in a minute, and so most of the days were just the two of them, her and Weesie. Now it was like Weesie went to the grocery store just for Mika, the cupboard at the bottom of the china cabinet stuffed with Little Debbie sweets: Star Crunch, Zebra Cakes, Oatmeal Creme Pies. New routines in place, what remained a breakfast mainstay was always, *always* grits, sausage patties, and eggs. Perfectly salted and peppered.

In the cupboard was one last jar of the Sanka, which Teeta had taught Mika how to make when no one was looking. Weesie didn't know—no one did—that she used to drink coffee with him: heated the water, scooped the instant coffee grounds into the cup, and added one spoon of sugar. Weesie would have no other reason to buy Sanka, so Mika moved it to the back of the spice cupboard and drank it sparingly, in the afternoons. She would have made it on a day like today, but Weesie had these guests who were in the kitchen drinking lemonade and Diet Coke. Weesie had only two chairs at the island, and it was clear she wasn't going to invite them to the dining table, where they could all sit. Or the den. She stood.

"We have another cousin," Loretta said. Mika looked them over again. She had never seen these women before. They were family? "Daisy. She's from Tampa but she's in town this week, and she just officially joined the family and wants to meet more of us. She has a grandson, Donnell, 'bout your girl's age—what, middle school?"

"Eighth grade," Mika specified.

"How did you say you found us?" Weesie interjected before Mika could offer up any more information.

"Well, we'd been studying genes for about two decades when we learned that the Boltons owned the most slaves in South Carolina, right up the road in Ridgeway. They invested in one big purchase and had the most Africans from the same town over on the continent, you know. Which means the chances of those called Bolton being blood relatives and not plantation relatives —'cause you know that's not our real name, we just claim it—is higher than most. Even had the president authorize that claim 'bout five years ago. So, we set out to find more blood. In all our years, because we have so little time to tell our story anywhere else but when we going up to glory, Devine and I spend Sundays reading the obituaries in the paper, looking for mention of the name Bolton."

Weesie sipped her sugar-free lemonade. Mika migrated back to the den—far enough away as to not be seen as intruding, but close enough to hear.

"Teeta," Weesie said and brought her hand to her chest. Devine pulled out a few newspaper clippings.

"Teeta?" she asked, seeking clarification.

"James, my husband."

Devine pointed to a newspaper clipping. "Says here that you are Louise Bolton Mosby of Thomson, Georgia, of the late Georgia Mae 'Lady' and Johnny 'Mann' Bolton of Augusta. Funny you tell so much of your story here, for your husband's obituary, but I guess it was good for us, to find you." She looked to Loretta. "Right?" Loretta nodded.

It *was* odd, she knew, but when Major sat Weesie down to write the obituary, Weesie understood she had to start this as the blueprint so that when it was her time, they would know what to do. Teeta's obituary had a lot of branches on his family tree to work out. Including what to do about Cynthia. Rhina and Weesie went back and forth and back and forth. Won't no use crying over what Teeta did before they were married, but it stung to have to think about it while mourning. Rhina didn't want her to do it, write that woman's name in the obituary, for reasons only daddy's girls would fight for, especially since Cynthia would be listed as first daughter. But Weesie knew it was her one last time to set the record straight. She instructed Major to write that three children survived him, "one Cynthia Corley of Horry County" and "two under holy matrimony." That was where she wrote Junior and Rhina's names. Of herself and her children, she listed every given name, believing that generations from now, her descendants would be able to find their way back to her, like a roadmap. She laughed to herself now, thinking about how quickly the roadmap worked. And for whom.

"So, once we got those names, we went back to our records and found we have a Georgia Mae Bolton, later a Georgia Mae

Montgomery, then a Georgia Mae Briggs, but didn't know which of those were married names or blood. We saw she had some children and found your name. This was years ago, but it wasn't really confirmed for us that the two were the same until we saw your husband's obituary. Then I looked you up in the yellow pages. We decided to finally call on you to tell you about how you're related to quite possibly the largest Black family in the history of America and, if you ever choose, could join us on one of our trips to our motherland. We were able to trace back to the exact tribe over there. How many Black folks can say that?"

She pulled out a map of Africa. Mika wanted to get up and see; they had not called out the name, only pointed to the left side of the continent, where it rounded out a corner of the Atlantic Ocean.

Weesie squinted, but the two other women didn't know her eyes were bad and could not read the small print of the map. So she was silent.

"Usually people think they're from Ghana, that's the easy answer to *where are you from?* But we know the truth. We know we were snatched from"—Devine circled the area with her finger— "Nigeria."

The women waited for a vocal response. Anything. They were beaming at the reveal, that they could answer what for many of us was unanswerable—the essential African American question: *Where do you come from?* Mika thought about that seemingly innocent school project she was assigned back when Teeta was alive, when she was tasked to bring in an artifact from a place where her family could be traced. "Don't you want to know where we come from?" she had asked then, pressing Teeta with questions he didn't have the answers for, ones maybe too big to address straight on. Now here were these two strangers knocking on Weesie's door, supposedly filling in the gaps. But Mika realized that her feelings knowing this new piece of information— this tie to Nigeria—were about as anticlimactic as Teeta's response had been when Mika had asked him for what he knew. What did he say then? That we'll never really get to know? That he believed we emerged from the dust like Adam and Eve—created in God's own image? That seemed about as plausible to Mika now as understanding what to do with the idea that the country her people apparently came from was Nigeria. It only opened the road to more questions. Some that had answers, sure—about diaspora, middle passage, slavery, and the rest. But other, more complicated ones, too: If Nigeria, who were her people there? What were their names? What were their stories? She laughed thinking about how Major might take the line of reasoning: Is there an alternate-universe Mika there, with a Sasha and a Weesie, and maybe—still alive—a Teeta? Mika tried to consider the full weight of making such a claim about her family's origins, and how, for these two women, the idea of pointing a finger to a country in Africa seemed to weigh so much more than the making of the Bolton line, the line Weesie knew and had started collecting her own artifacts for, here, in America.

Mika looked to Weesie for ways to accept what news had come from these two women in her kitchen. Weesie seemed nonplussed, certainly not as enthusiastic as Loretta and Devine.

To be fair, though, Weesie *did* acknowledge her African roots each February, along with the rest of the world: her church had African American history activities, and congregants were encouraged to wear bright-colored dashikis made from kente cloth to one Sunday service a year. Weesie and Betty loved this because they got to wear all those African prints with the bright yellows and oranges and reds, sometimes blues. They got to feel more connected to something bigger than Columbia.

And Mika had recited that poem one February Sunday—per Weesie's request—which was meant to be a celebration of even the hardships of Black life, with all the erasures, the unknowns, the questions.

"We made it all up," Mika whispered to herself, rewriting the lines. It was all anybody could do with what they were given, considering the circumstances. That's what Teeta was saying, she thought. We make it up where we don't know, we move it along. We pass it down. Maybe it is enough.

"You said you had another cousin here?" Weesie asked. She had picked up the black pamphlet with a gold-outlined picture of Africa and the name BOLTON in all caps.

"Yes. Daisy. She's not unlike you. Recently widowed. Two children. Grandchildren. One grand she takes care of. 'Cept she lives in Tampa. Came here on a home-journey trip; we call it trying to find her *real roots,* when and where they started in America. She'll be here until the middle of next week. Though she's verified a Bolton, we haven't cleared her invitation to the annual family reunion, which is a shame, because it's in Columbia this year," Loretta said, holding her cup between both hands like she needed something to steady her.

Mika still sat in the den, watching Weesie with these strange women. She studied them like in science class with Mrs. Dorn, when Mika had to go out and collect insects. Devine was short and round and reminded Mika of roly-polys—the way her arms moved when she spoke, it was as if she had more than two. She couldn't understand how Weesie didn't tire of her exasperating animation. Loretta was taller, lanky. With her arms perched on the edge of the island, her hands gripping the glass with both hands, and her neck bent, Loretta looked like a praying mantis, Mika thought.

Weesie turned and got the washcloth from the sink. She wiped the counter twice—Mika counted—and then the stove, so her back was to Loretta and Devine while they explained the next steps of the joining-the-family process.

"We need to make sure you have the right relatives, and usually we confirm that through papers. Do you have any birth or death certificates for other Boltons?"

Weesie stopped wiping the stovetop and was silent for a moment, as though considering. Born in the one-room house her grandmother Sarah was a slave in, Lady didn't have any papers. Weesie heard that her great-grandfather had been recorded in the church registration (as "Saved property of") when he was baptized, but the story is that the book burned up when the Klan came back and tried to reclaim the small parcels of land that were leased out after the war and saw the small clapboard church and thought it was a negro one. They got it wrong. Turned out that was the only way the poorer white landowners kept their legal documentation of who belonged to who, and when the church burned, many of the negroes had taken it as a sign to "'joy their freedom," and that's how Mann Bolton was later told that he was the first of the Georgia Boltons of the Bolton Plantation born of a "free" man and a "free" woman. The public story is that the first free person was his father, Luther Bolton, who was born in 1866, a year after slavery ended, but he wasn't born knowing he was free. Weesie didn't tell her guests these facts, because they came to her door assuming she ain't know anything, really. So she kept on letting them think that, to see what all they had on her family. When they asked if she had any proper documentation about who she was, she only had the words, the stories.

"Well, no, I don't have no certificates or nothing, but—" She moved towards the living room, pulled back the wood-paneled accordion screen that separated the kitchen from the living room, where she kept the family heirlooms, and closed the screen quickly behind her. Mika saw Loretta, who was the closest to the room's entrance, lean over the island, trying to peep in. Just as quickly as she slipped in, Weesie emerged with two plaques.

"This is Pete Bolton, my brother. The funeral home gives these plaques to blood family of the deceased. Of course they gave one to his wife, Viola, but he was my only brother, I explained, and they made one for me, too. He died not long ago from hard lung. He came back from the navy, where he worked on the coal ships feeding the engine fires. Eventually he got burned—a coal ember caught in his rolled-up pants. Third degree and all. White bandages from legs to neck. But that ain't kill him, no. The smoke from being cooped up in the belly of those ships all those years did."

She handed the women the wooden plaque with the gold-plated front. Mika, when the house was quiet, went into the living room and memorized things. She had seen this plaque several times and knew that the women were reading the Lord's Prayer. To the right of the scripture was a candle with a battery-powered flame. It was long burned out, and Weesie had not replaced it.

Weesie wiped her face with her free hand while the two women held the plaque and inspected it like some primary-source document.

Because Weesie believed in loyalty, she encouraged everyone to send their gone to Oakwood Funeral Home. At the rate her loves were falling, she had become a regular customer, and the

owner was a close enough friend to have attended the funerals—
mourning with the rest of the family as if he were kin.

"This is my granddaddy Luther Bolton," Weesie said, bringing out another plaque, this one older. "He lived to be almost a
hundred."

Loretta's and Devine's mouths dropped almost simultaneously. Devine reached for the plaque first, but Loretta's arms unfolded in such a way that Devine had no chance.

"This is Luther? As in *the* Luther Bolton, born in 1866 in
Thomson, when we still didn't really know we were free?" Devine
asked, reaching towards Loretta, who still hadn't turned over the
plaque.

"Well, technically." Weesie cleared her throat. "As I know, or
was told, his family knew, but where was they going to go? So
much blood, work, death in those fields. On that land. It was
home. Outside of those fields, well, the whites was waiting for us
to walk out into the open, so, damned if you do, right? Damned
if you do." Weesie shook her head and collected the plaques.
"Even though we claimed the Bolton name in Thomson, Georgia, we knew. We always knew we came through Ridgeway,
South Carolina, where the plantation was. Then, when money
was tight, the Boltons split up all the families. But us Boltons kept
the name so we could find each other later, I guess like now. So
that's how we end up with that name and end up there."

Loretta looked at Devine while Weesie disappeared behind
the wood-paneled divider to replace the plaques. Mika was done
with her Kool-Aid but didn't want to venture into the kitchen
while Weesie was gone, so she grabbed the nearest thing to her—
the coffee table photo album, which held the faces and names
and circumstances for each stilled moment of people she knew
and didn't, people who continued to walk the earth and those

who did not. She was about a quarter of the way through the mindless flipping when she landed on a cookout photo—her godmother, side-eyeing the camera, holding a hot dog frank without the bun, charred black as night. Next to her, in a car seat on the ground, was Mika's cousin. Next to them was Uncle Pete, who married Viola, that Virginia girl, and had all the children of the family. So many that they called her Mamas, because, well, she acted like everybody's mama. Mamas and Weesie fought over Uncle Pete's attention. When he died, and then when Teeta died, you wouldn't even know the two weren't blood sisters.

Weesie returned from the living room and began to slowly wash her hands, humming "Going Up Yonder" as she scrubbed under her nails. That was her universal signal for readying the transition from holding company to preparing supper.

Loretta and Devine took the prolonged moments with Weesie's back turned as the correct signal and began to wipe their mouths with paper towels.

"Welp," Devine started. "I think you've helped us understand what we hoped we'd come here to find, and that's more kin." She said this while opening her pocketbook, which was as wide as a satchel. It covered the whole of her lap. Mika chuckled; Devine dug around as if she were trying to pull the last crab claw from the bottom of the pot. Finally, her face lit up; she removed a large composition book. From where Mika sat, it looked as though the spine was held together by brown packing tape. Devine looked up, saw Mika's eyes there, and moved her hand to the left edge to disguise or hide it. She turned to Loretta and nodded for her to continue. It was clear the two had had these conversations many times, and they moved now like a sideshow act at one of the small-town fairs next to the flea market Weesie dragged Mika to on weekends.

"So, like we was saying earlier, we have—*you* have—a cousin, Daisy, up from Tampa, with a grandson 'bout as old as your girl over there. We'd like for y'all to meet; it's much easier to find your way into such a big clan as ours by having a match, and we never imagined a match like this, see?" Loretta pointed to the open pages of the composition book. Mika couldn't see it, she so wished she had a real reason to be in the kitchen at just that moment.

"She a tiny thing," Weesie said, looking at what must have been a picture of Daisy.

"This here her grandson. She took him in on account of his father being caught up," Devine said. She didn't need to say much more. She looked at Mika and lifted her chin.

"Oh, Mika just comes over for school breaks and weekends. My daughter and son-in-law both work too many jobs and too many long hours, and besides, we have the whole cul-de-sac that she can play in, so she come here." Weesie felt the need to clear that assumption up.

"Oh," Devine said. She seemed disappointed. "Well, anyways, we have your name and address, obviously. If you don't mind, could you list your immediate family, living and gone—full names—and any other grands? Also, your phone number? If you're interested, we were thinking of taking Daisy and the grandson down to the Chitlin Strut Saturday over in Salley. You could meet us, bring your girl. Least she'll have someone her own age to talk to and play with."

"I'll need to check my calendar," Weesie said while writing in the book. "Please give my number to Daisy anyhow, though. I'd love to meet her, and I'm sure Mika would love to meet more blood her age. She only has a sister five years older than her, and the next cousin is four years younger. She used to live under Teeta's shadow—that's how she got all that stuff out back—but now I guess she's stuck with me. Now it's just us," Weesie said.

Mika added "chickens" under her breath. Weesie's favorite phrase: "Just us chickens." She turned to Mika and winked.

Mika continued flipping through the photo album. She had completely forgotten that Weesie had a picture of Teeta's last birthday party, with the cake from Kroger instead of a home-made one—the sign of Weesie's cumulated exhaustion—and right where Mika stopped flipping was a photo of Weesie stand-ing next to Teeta's open casket, with every Easter lily in the Co-lumbia metropolitan area flanking her side. Mika never saw this photo taken, but Weesie was in street clothes, so she'd probably asked to see Teeta before the wake. Like when Grandma Georgia Mae died, Weesie had gone over the night before to wash her hair. Anyways, Mika had no idea what anybody had worn to the wake, because as soon as she arrived and saw Teeta in the casket, she asked to be taken home. She decided it was best not to go to the funeral the next day and avoided all photos of the event. But Weesie documented *everything,* and here was the proof. Mika gasped and slammed the book shut, then creaked the album open again just to see—to see if, in the casket, his face looked how she remembered it alive. The mustache, split in the middle. The big bushy eyebrows that grew back fuller after chemo. The curly hair that pushed back in the shape of a horseshoe on the top of his head. She looked and looked, and studied the flowers, the way Weesie smiled with her hand resting on the edge of the casket, the same way she rested her hand on the edge of the table after single-handedly finishing Sunday dinner. Her face looked similar: ragged. Soul-tired. Slight smile, or else corners of the mouth fac-ing up. Squinting eyes.

Anyways. When Mika looked up, the kitchen was empty of

the two guests, and Weesie was now scrubbing and peeling sweet potatoes for the Sunday candied yams.

"If you want to come out with me on Saturday, we'll need to get you some clean clothes from home and maybe snacks for the ride."

Weesie paused her scrubbing and shook her head.

"Lord, what if they real? I mean for real." Weesie started scrubbing again. "I wonder why they ain't started with any other Boltons in Columbia. Maybe I'll call Mamas after supper to see if she knows anything. Or even what this Chitlin Strut is or how we'll get there. Maybe she'll want to go."

Mika nodded her head and, with their company gone now, reached for the remote control and flipped on the television looking for any distraction and bit of background noise.

EVEN BEFORE TEETA DIED, MIKA HAD TURNED OVER HER Saturday mornings to Weesie. They both loved a yard sale hunt, so on Friday nights, Weesie would pull out the classifieds and they would map their early morning scavenging. Mika enjoyed those mornings (and the occasional flea market trip) because her allowance went much further than at the mall or even the dollar store. Once, she found a brand-new pack of notebooks—six of them!—for seventy-five cents, but when she asked the woman to break her five-dollar bill, the woman said, "Kid, do you have a quarter? I'll take a quarter," so Mika got all those notebooks without blowing her allowance.

She asked Major for her weekly allowance to take with her to the Chitlin Strut.

"The what?" Major said it in a way that made it sound more like a statement than a question.

Mika shrugged her shoulders. "Grandma wants me to go with her out to the country to this thing, the Chitlin Strut, to meet some new cousins of ours."

Major was always tinkering with some electronic device in the living room. This made Rhina mad, that her flowered velveteen couch with wood armrests was always covered with a speaker here, needle-nose pliers there. When he wasn't working making sure the public television broadcasts went out uninterrupted, he was doing somebody's handiwork—last year he changed the engine on their neighbor Mr. Henry's car after hitching it to his back bumper and dragging it to Forestwood Drive. Mika and her mother had dumped salt and baking soda on the carport to try and dry up the oil stains for weeks after. This year it was computers, and Major thought he'd make a real go at it—a whole business of building and selling them, building networks. He was trying to convince Mika, ever under his wing up until about now, that she should learn how to build a website, because that would be the future, he said; but she was in eighth grade, and while she wasn't free enough to go to the mall by herself or with her girlfriends and their boyfriends, she was too old to still be called a daddy's girl and sought her distance by going to Redwood Court. At Redwood Court, as long as she made her bed and took out the trash and vacuumed the occasional room, she was free. Some days, Weesie would run an errand and leave her home, and that's when she'd sneak-ride her bike past the stop sign at the end of the cul-de-sac.

She waited for her father to look up from the innards of the computer he was working on, what he called a "motherboard."

"I just need a few dollars to eat while I'm out. Grandma says I might have a cousin my age. Donnell. He's from Tampa. We don't really know how we're all related, but she wants to meet them Saturday."

"Why this place?" Major asked. Mika knew better than to come to her father without all the anticipated questions answered. This type of interrogation was usually reserved for when she wanted to go out with friends and their parents. Who are they? I need to speak to them. When will y'all get back? Who's driving y'all? Who else is going? And so on. Maybe the fact that she had mentioned a boy, who may or may not be blood-related but who was her age, had prompted this particular line of questioning.

"I don't know. Two women stopped by; said they were family. Knew of Great-Granddaddy Luther and stuff. Weesie was listening and entertaining them. They said it was too late for us to join the annual reunion this year but that we could meet a few relatives who wanted to go out to see the Chitlin Strut, so that's why. Grandma doesn't want to go alone."

There it was. The rub. Everyone was hyperaware that Weesie thrived most in the company of others. It was why the first thing she did after putting on her housecoat in the morning was open her door and make her round of calls. If folks weren't sitting around her island in the kitchen, she was sitting in her tall chair with the phone cradled between her ear and shoulders, somehow now even more than before. Mika also lost a companion in Teeta when he died, so they had found new common ground. Mika's parents were sensitive to this, of course—they allowed most things around this tender Big Thing. Especially this first year. Major put down his screwdriver and reached into his front pocket for his cash clip. Mika looked quickly as he hurried past the twenty-dollar bill towards the singles, and counted as he took some out. Three. She didn't see a five in the spread, so either he was going to send her off into the wilderness and unknown with only three dollars or he was going to sacrifice a ten or a twenty. This was her chance.

"I could give Weesie some for gas," she offered, though she knew that would not be the case. Major paused with a ten-dollar bill between his fingers.

"OK. Ten dollars for you, for the weekend and the week. Ten dollars for your grandmother," he said, and he went back towards the twenty and pried it from the clip.

Mika grabbed it quickly and put it in the pink wrist pouch she used to keep her money close at hand. She tried not to look too eager.

"Grandma will come over and pick me up first thing. She asked if you could look up the directions for us."

"Sure. But I still don't know where it is exactly," Major said. He turned away from the cut-open computer and faced the screen of his functioning computer.

"AOL, I guess? Look up 'Chitlin Strut,'" Mika ventured.

MIKA AND WEESIE HAD BEEN AT THE DESIGNATED MEETING place for over an hour. They didn't see anyone who looked like Loretta or Devine, or anyone who looked like they, too, were searching for kin.

The Chitlin Strut, Mika had learned (Weesie asked her to take a quick loop to see if she saw anyone and come straight back), was like a mini version of the South Carolina State Fair without the exciting rides, like the Saucer, which spun teacup-shaped seats in a tilting circle. By turning the wheel in the middle of the cup, you could spin yourself 'round and 'round. Because she had been master of the tire swings at her daycare, Mika knew that you had to find a focal point as you turned and to keep your eyes there or else you'd lose whatever was in your stomach. The Chitlin Strut didn't have the Zipper either, which she was finally old and tall enough to ride. The Zipper was an elongated Ferris wheel with cages you climbed into and the attendant locked. As the cage reached the top of its track, you'd flip backward and tumble until you reached the bottom. If you pushed your weight around like down through your toes and let inertia and gravity do their thing, you could flip 'round and 'round the full circumference, over and over until the ride stopped. The Chitlin Strut didn't even have candied apples with caramel and peanuts, or elephant ears with powdered sugar, or baked apples. Mika had wanted that extra money from Major so she could get the fried dough as wide as plates and just the right amount of salt to keep the sweetness at bay.

But no. Just row after sporadic row of small tents with red awnings, the ever-present waft of used-up cooking oil, and the stench of pork innards. It really was all about chitlins. It was like being trapped outside in an open field in a flea market that smelled like Weesie's kitchen the night before Thanksgiving, after she'd washed and washed and cleaned the intestines of a pig to serve the next day over rice.

All that work to coax the extra money from her dad for this adventure; now she didn't even know what to spend it on.

The ride over had been no fun either. Major had tracked down the location—not without effort—and looked up the directions to Salley, South Carolina. He laughed, warning them that it was going to be far away and small, because any place named after a person (much less a white woman) was going to be situated miles and many minutes away from any main road. Mika learned this from her trips to Georgia to see her great-great-aunt Nora Lee, who was eighty and still skinning goats on her front porch, and who would go out to her chicken coop with a handful of feed to coerce a hen to her hand and then snatch it up by its neck and wring it around and around above her head like helicopter blades until it stopped hollering.

On the first loop around the grounds of the Chitlin Strut, Mika saw no signs of Daisy or Donnell—though Mika wasn't even sure what they looked like, because she hadn't gotten a chance to look at the photo in Weesie's kitchen. While she was walking and looking for faces that might be family, Mika staked out each vendor stall to see if anything was worth her little dollars. There was Miss Jessy's Fried Chitlins, Freddie's Best Chitlins, June's Chitlin Plates. There was one stall that spelled out "chitterling," and even though Mika dared not touch the dish on a normal day, she knew that only white folks spelled "chitlins" that way, and Weesie said they didn't know how to clean them right, so don't never take any chitlins from folks who put the -er and g on it. One stand was selling popcorn and nachos. Another had hot dog franks and fries. Right smack in the middle of the sun, and with no tent cover whatsoever, was a single pie-and-cake lady. She had no sign or signal that she was an official vendor. If Mika was to buy any sort of sweet thing, this might be her only chance, she thought. Over by the stage, someone announced a hog-calling contest at two-thirty in the afternoon, after the Junior Ladies' Chitlin Strut beauty pageant.

A tall young man the color of baked sweet potato skins— brown with an undertone of gold—stood under one of the few trees in the whole place, holding a boat of fries and a soda, trying to balance them. He wore a backwards baseball cap and a black button-down shirt and cargo pants with bleached-white

Adidas. Mika wondered how he kept them so white, given the mud-packed parking lot. When she walked past, craning her neck, she hoped he would look up, and thought to look for signs of kinship. Maybe it would be in the eyes. Maybe Loretta and Devine had shown Daisy and Donnell a picture, but he didn't look to be searching for anyone, really, only studying his fries and soda.

Did Loretta and Devine show Daisy and Donnell a photo of Mika and Weesie? Were there any photos of the two of them together? It was always Mika and Teeta, Weesie and Teeta, but never the combo Mika and Weesie. One of them was always behind the camera. If they didn't have a photo, though, there'd be a chance for Donnell to associate her with kin just by looking at her. Mika was the dark sheep of her mother's clan. Because of those differences, Sasha and Uncle Junior used to tease that Mika had been adopted so often that she almost believed it.

"Look," Sasha would say, "who do you look like around here? Ain't nobody as dark as you." Rhina would tell girlfriends and new friends, "Yeah, girl. When she was a baby, her hair laid flat on her head, and she was so dark, people asked if she was East Indian," and then, "So many people asked me if she was mine." What her mother thought was a compliment only further proved Sasha's point. Mika never heard what came next, if anything, or else she couldn't remember if her mother had ever said unequivocally that Mika had come from her own womb. Major would try to address it by saying he was *absolutely sure* Mika was his because he was there when she was born, but couldn't say the same for Sasha. He'd smile and wink. She'd feel a little better about it, but so often it fell flat and wasn't satisfying.

Mika started to walk over to the boy standing under the one shade tree to be sure, because why else would she suffer the long, hot drive down the road to Salley to be stranded in the middle of the countryside with nothing but chitlins—and now, the loud calls of the folks competing in the hog-yelling contest?

Mika wanted it to be Donnell, though maybe she didn't. He was cute. Something moved in her, then she felt shame. He was supposed to be blood. When she looked hard enough, he looked like Roger, her band class crush. She liked him because it seemed the other girls were fine with corralling him into the friend category, and she definitely knew what that was like. He was too nice and smart and didn't take his shirt off when they went to Michelle's apartment-complex pool. He didn't smoke, and once, Mika dropped a pen in front of him at the Chick-fil-A stand during lunch, and he stopped what he was doing, wherever he was going, and reached down to give it back to her. But she could never date him, because he was friends with Michelle's exboyfriend, and now they weren't supposed to even communicate with each other anymore—and besides, her parents would kill her if she even hinted at the idea of a boyfriend.

Mika decided against confronting the young boy under the tree and asking if he was family. She laughed as she realized that she was walking around mentally asking "Are you my cousin?" like that children's book about a baby bird.

Mika picked up a Diet Sprite for Weesie and then an alreadymelting red slushie for herself before returning to the waiting spot, hoping that someone would have found their way to Weesie by now. But when Mika made it back to where she'd last seen Weesie, no one was there. In the background, an announcement: "Y'all stay tuned for the thirty-first annual Junior Ladies' Chitlin Strut beauty pageant, coming right up!"

Mika looked around, holding the two drinks, and slurped the soggy slushie.

Across the way, the young-boy-maybe-cousin was gone, too. She strained to find him again but did not see him anywhere.

The ice was melting in the clear cup, and the drink was by now just red syrup. Mika thought to do another round—this place was not big enough to lose someone, right?—but decided against that urge because she wanted to reunite with Weesie and get out of here with as few delays as possible. She moved to a picnic table a few feet away. Maybe, at one point during the day, it was covered with shade, but now it had full sun. As she moved towards it, she heard her mother's voice talking about not needing to get "much darker" than she already was (but how could she avoid it?) and hesitated at the thought of posting up for who knew how long in the heat. But her choices were to stand or to sit for however long. Knowing Weesie, it could be *years* before she found her way to Mika.

Mika watched the Diet Sprite bubbles drift to the top of the cup as Weesie's drink lost its carbonation and ice. She traced the wood grains of the table and wished she'd had the foresight to at least bring her journal and pen. Something to do.

A cloud passed over, granting a quick reprieve from the sun's blaze. Mika looked up to see its shape and caught a glimpse of Weesie, walking alone, with a takeout container in her hand.

She joined Mika at the table and answered the silent look. "My sugar was getting low, and I needed to eat a little something," Weesie said.

Mika nodded and pushed the cup towards her.

"This water?" Weesie asked.

"Diet Sprite. It *had* ice," Mika said, hoping Weesie would hear the attitude in the way she drew out "had" a few extra quarter beats—so much so that it almost had vibrato. Weesie either missed or ignored it.

"I guess they ain't make it out here. We shoulda known better. Guess I'll call around in the morning to see what happened. We said one P.M. near the front. It's 'bout to turn four, and I haven't seen no sign of them two ladies nor Daisy and Donnell. I guess you ain't seen them neither?"

Mika shook her head, then thought to tell her about the boy under the tree. But what use was it? She hadn't confirmed if it was him. And by now it looked as if he was long gone. She hadn't seen the two women who were in the kitchen earlier this week, though if she thought about it, what did family even look like? How does anyone really know?

Weesie picked up a napkin-wrapped thing from her plate and handed it over.

"Let's eat a little something before we head back," Weesie said.

Mika unwrapped the hot dog franks, savoring their salty, hot firmness after the sweetness of the slushie.

"I tried a plate of Big Ben's Chitlins. They looked to be the cleanest. They ain't mine, but it'll do," Weesie said, mouth full of rice and pork.

"Huh," Weesie started again after a beat of silence. "All these years I been living and cleaning these damn things, ain't no one ever want to eat 'em. Now you gone tell me they got a whole fair for 'em? A whole fair."

Weesie drank the Diet Sprite, and Mika swore she heard her smack her lips. Weesie laughed to herself. "A whole fair. A. Chitlin. Strut. Teeta would die if he knew about this." She closed her takeout container and got up from the picnic table. Weesie waved her hands in the direction of the car. Mika followed the waft of the chitlin plate in her hands.

Rollin' with My Homies

L ast night on the six o'clock news there was—what was it called? An experience? An expedition? No. Something else. The news anchors said they wanted the Columbia residents to know that the county sheriff was taking seriously his responsibility to "serve and protect" the lawful citizens of this city from the growing rampant crime out near the Columbia Mall and downtown areas—where, the county sheriff pointed, the low-income houses were, right next to the university, and that in the residential area just behind the mall there was evidence of new gang activity.

Weesie said the news anchor always knows how to ruin a Friday night, huh?

The county sheriff said that the new gang wore long white shirts and white bandanas, looped through either the back right belt loop if they were higher up on the gang rungs, or the back left if they were just jumped in. Those looking to be prospects wore a black bandana around their wrist. The sheriff didn't say "jumped in"; Weesie did, when she was recounting the exposé— that's the word—to Ruby who, since she was home in time to call Weesie, must have narrowly escaped being stuck at church late preparing for their special praise dance performance.

Antioch Baptist Church is marking its twenty-first anniversary of the opening of the building Weesie worships in. The church went through at least three iterations and locations around Columbia before it landed here, closer to Redwood Court. A sign, Weesie said once, that she was meant to be a part of the congregation. This year, Weesie is leading the planning committee for the Pastor's Appreciation Luncheon and even though we all don't go to church like that ('cept for Easter), Weesie made us promise to be there to support her. She even wrangled Sissy into coming along, and these days, since she moved out of the house after high school graduation, that's no small feat. Of course, that means our hair has to be crisp as a brand-new dollar bill and as shiny as a penny, so we both got to go to the hair dresser. Weesie is fine doing our hair up right on the day, and wants to ensure quality control, but she prefers the hairdresser to do the heavy lifting of the whole ordeal beforehand: washing, combing out, drying the hair, greasing the scalp.

Weesie wants me to go to church with her this week; says she needs a photographer for the praise team practice runs, and so Daddy dropped me off after school. It's funny, I love Redwood Court, but when I was smaller, there was a time when I hated to spend the night. I always felt abandoned by Mama and Daddy. As much fun as I would have at the Court, I liked sleeping in my own bed, and when Teeta gave me my own room on Forestwood Drive when we came back from Florida, it made it even harder to

leave. Especially since he's been gone. Now any time I'm over at
Redwood Court, all I hear is Weesie on the phone. Even when the
television is on and we was 'sposed to be watching the news together, she'd get up and make a call.

"Yeh, it's me, Weesie. You caught the news? Yeh. It's a miracle
you home by now. They dance your feet off? Yeh, I'm thinking
'bout gettin' some salts, soaking. So, listen. They saying 'bout
them gang boys that the county police will hold random searches
across town, and that they won't be easy on perpetrators. Yeh. I
know. You right. It's like someone circled a map and said, 'Where
Black folks live, that's where we'll search.'"

Weesie was sitting at the island ashing her cigarette, one leg
dangling, the other leg propped up on the foot bar. She had
stopped smoking in solidarity with Teeta back then, but I know it,
too: good things don't last always when you grieving. I watched
as she lit cigarette after cigarette on the phone with Ruby, worrying after Uncle Junior and his white shirts and long shorts,
which took on a whole new meaning now. One time, when he
grabbed his belt loops to pull up his pants over his butt, I saw a
flash of a white cloth like a bandana dangling on his left side. I
don't know if anyone else saw it. He caught my eye catching the
flash of bandana and tried to say it was part of the new job uniform: the white shirts, bandana to cover the face for the smell.
The poultry-processing plant wanted all of the folks who stood
on the line quartering chickens for Winn-Dixie to wear white so
they could monitor the work better. Especially, Uncle Junior said,
because everyone who worked on the line was Black, so if you
walked in wearing white shirts it was easy to know where you
belonged.

But it was after the accident where the machine couldn't tell
the difference between a chicken thigh and Uncle Junior's arm

and it kept twisting and grabbing, trying to separate bone from joint, skin from bone, and he couldn't never find steady work—it was after *that* he kept wearing white, even when he was on medical leave.

"Ruby, just, they say it's a new gang show up almost out of nowhere, like weeds," Weesie said, shaking her foot so it was tapping against the stool base.

"Newcastle Gangstahs," Weesie said. I wonder if it was really spelled like how Weesie said it, without the *-er*. Instead of writing it on the screen, the six o'clock news showed the tag, a block-style *N* and a block-style *G*. It looked like the drawings me and my girls do to decorate notes passed in class—the chain-link *S* that starts with six straight lines, and so on. It was Uncle Junior who showed me how to do it. He liked to doodle. Wanted to be a tattoo artist one day, he told me, so people would live with his drawings forever. If the soft cast from the chicken plant accident won't on his arm (doctors said he'd have to protect the skin growing back for months), he would have tattooed his own arm by now. Worked the pictures in between the scars, made them art. He said the scars looked like mountains and valleys; like how the horizon look on the way out to Georgia where Weesie was from. Instead, someone else tagged the cast with his initials, and from the back seat of the car, when he lifted his arm just so, you could see the belly of a letter. Looked like a box with a tail. Probably a *G*, but because the white shirts were two sizes too big (as Weesie said, "I don't know why I'm buying XXL for a medium-sized boy"), the upper part of his cast was almost always strategically covered.

I think that's why Weesie won't fully connecting the tag on the screen with what I later saw in the car when Uncle Junior came super-late to pick me and Sissy up from the hairdresser that weekend. I mean, it was long past when we were pulled from under the heat that set our curls. If Sissy's car hadn't broke down, and if Daddy had fixed it like he said he would instead of letting it sit in the driveway, we could have been rollin' down the street hours ago. But now we're both at the mercy of the folks around us with cars. Whenever they find the time to scoop us up.

A silver Ford Explorer eventually rolled up and started honking and honking. But when we looked outside to see if it was for us, we sat back down, sighing. Neither of us knew anyone with that car. Uncle Junior stormed in a few minutes later and huffed at us to let's go, he's been waiting, and Sissy and I looked at each other with the same confused expression.

When we got outside, he led us towards the Explorer, but we didn't ask any questions. Lately, Uncle Junior been showing up with new trinkets here and there. Daddy would raise his eyebrows at whatever new thing. Mama would whisper to him, "Fix your face." I haven't heard Weesie make anything out of the fact that he won't working but coming around with expensive new toys, which is funny because if it were anyone else she woulda been digging around trying to get to the bottom of it. Sissy walked up to the car and ran her hand along the side like she Vanna White, presenting it to me. She did what none of us had the balls to do, but they had that relationship—more like brother and sister than uncle and niece—and asked him point-blank where he won the new ride.

She stuck her finger in her mouth, then touched the roof of the car and made a sizzle sound. "It's too hot a ride for someone without a job."

Uncle Junior just pointed to the inside of the car, instructing us to get in. You can tell the bond they have is tight, because he wouldn't have stood for that jab from anyone else. Sissy does that a lot, though. She's like a SweeTart—make you so sticky with whatever nice thing she's done, then cut you across the cheek with her words. Or erect a brick wall of silence 'cause she's ignoring you while listening to whatever music she's got in her headphones. Today she was syrup-sweet to me, with a tang in her voice toward Uncle Junior.

Sissy asked him again. The story he told us about the Explorer was that it was his new lady's, she let him use it. But I saw it: won't no evidence of a woman being in this car, almost ever. No tissues in the console. No air freshener hanging from the rearview mirror. No lotion or body spray. Seat flat and pushed all the way back, like it was never made to be anywhere else.

When Teeta was alive, he always fussed whenever he got in a car after Uncle Junior drove it. "Damnit, Junior rolling my seat all the way back," he'd growl, scrambling for the seat bar. "Least he could do is put it right. But he wont to lean back like he in a lawn chair at the beach." Teeta would knock around at his side until the seat was so close to the steering wheel I wondered how he breathed.

But Uncle Junior, since he was so far back and insisted on one-handed driving (with the windows down—even though we complained 'cause we had just got our hair done), his arm stretched so that it pulled the white T-shirt off his cast arm, and I thought I saw it then. Sissy, in the front seat, heard me gasp and asked what was wrong. Honest to God I didn't know I even made a sound. On any given day Uncle Junior call me a tattletale, so I didn't want to be accused of anything, and besides, at first I didn't know what I saw, so I shook my head *nothing* and turned to look out the window. All the windows down 'cept mine got my bangs sticking up like antennae. The wind caught Uncle Junior's shirt again and puffed it up like he was in a Missy Elliott video, not standing the rain.

When the sleeve puffed out from the wind through the window—'cause we were passing by Sparkle Car Wash on Two Notch and Uncle Junior saw some of his boys and lifted his arm— there it was, clear as day, *NG*, the same way it had popped up on the television screen at Redwood Court and had Weesie spiraling like waiting for a war invasion. He was joining up? The news said that the initiation process of this next-generation gang was tougher than what they have gathered of existing groups. They did the special because the codes of the past seemed to be differ- ent, and I heard it in Weesie's voice on the phone, just last night, talking about how them boys had tripped up an old woman with a walker at Walmart and then jumped her like she was a "grown- ass man." That's what Weesie said. She agreed with Ruby that it could have been them, and now I can't help but think how Uncle Junior could fix his hand to the face of a woman his mama's age just so he could belong somewhere. As if he didn't belong any- where before.

Outside the window I didn't roll down, Columbia flashed by like those early motion pictures I learned about—how still im- ages caught in quick succession and played back nonstop was the earliest version of the moving image. Studying that at the county library is how I won the junior history award, and now every- where I look is just thousands of still images stitched together like one of Grandma Annie's quilts. I flex my neck to keep up with each passing image of Columbia from the back seat: there is the dialysis center where Teeta worked as a night cleaner, the mental health hospital where he operated on the dead as a mortuary as- sistant, Oakwood Funeral home where I saw his body last at the wake the night before the funeral.

I ask Uncle Junior where we are going, shouldn't it be to Red- wood Court? He and Sissy are flipping back and forth between two radio stations, kinda like how me and Sissy used to fight over what station we were gonna land on with the one television in the playroom. She'd go to MTV, I'd choose Disney. Her and Uncle Junior are going back and forth across some divide like the birdie in badminton. He presses the button for the hip-hop station, she presses the button for classic rock. Isn't it ironic? This fantastic voyage. I ask from the back seat where we're going and Sissy says I'm asking like I have somewhere to be, and Uncle Junior just says we're cruising through town for a bit, and that he has to "make a few stops." At the stop light he turns up the radio on his station so loud the bass taps against my lower back. I swear I see the windows shake.

I don't know where we are going, but I look for signs: behind the trees here, on Hardscrabble Road, I see the white saucer bodies of the satellites at Daddy's satellite hut, one of four I've visited with him; but this one, tucked in the woods just behind the gas station, is the one he'd have to go to in the middle of the night if the signal for the public television station went down. He always walked around with his chest puffed out—it was him, single-handedly, that made sure every kid in South Carolina got to watch *Sesame Street,* or *Mister Rogers' Neighborhood.* And he was self-taught! He always talked about the importance of working with your hands, how engineers will save the world, and he was one. He knew how to turn the knobs and push the buttons to receive the transmission from the satellite out in space to the satellite on the ground and, he'd snap his fingers, and *just like that,* it would be online. Once, he got paged 911 after picking me up from Redwood Court and I had to tag along, but I couldn't get out of the car. That hut was like the heart of the city, so the voltage was highest and the space too small for me and him. It was the same hut where he came home with rags tied around his knuckles and smelled like barbecue. He was fine, he said. Fine. He had been electrocuted, but when he came to, he realized he could drive, so he picked himself up off the floor and came home.

I look up and see Uncle Junior pulling into the gas station, saying he stopping 'cause the light came on. I still had some change that I didn't use at the hairdresser's snack bar, so I said I was gonna go in, too. He said no, wait in the car. I asked him to get me a Cherry Coke. He nodded but didn't say he would. I saw him dap hands with a few of the folks sitting outside, then watched his head bob up and down the aisle and then at the counter. He pointed behind the register, probably for some Black & Milds, then fisted the paper bag and headed back.

I'm sipping my Cherry Coke he bought me. I smile because even though I am sure Sissy wishes she had her car today, I like the fact that it feels like old times, in the before—the three amigos, Teeta called us—journeying. There goes the bank where Mama cashes her daycare checks and where me and Sissy used to lean real hard in the back seat hoping the teller would send lollipops back through the tube with Mama's money. Now we passing by the movie theater that always had the good Black movies, just across from the mall. I knew we were moving toward Redwood Court finally when I saw that. It was one of the variations on a way home that Teeta had showed us all those years of playing the how-you-know-where-you-going stop-sign game. It was eight different ways you could take from the movies to 154.

I snap out of calculating how long we have until we're at the Court when Sissy changes the radio station again.

"It's like ra-a-ii-aaan on your wedding day!" she leaned out the window to sing. We used to do this on the long drives to Florida or Charleston or Washington, D.C. Our heads facing the wind, blowing our cheeks up like balloons; our hands windsurfing to whatever song landed on Daddy's playlist.

At a stoplight Uncle Junior, hilariously, tried to lean over Sissy to roll up the window, using his bad arm and all. I guess that's how much he wanted it to stop. He was twisted up like the game: putting one hand over her mouth and trying with his other hand to both hold the steering wheel and quickly change the station back to his style. Sissy mushed *him* in the face, then turned around to me with a make-believe microphone in her hand and her mouth wide open to finish, *"A free riiiiide when you're al-ready late."*

Sometimes, I'm embarrassed to admit, I join Sissy in these moments. What did Ms. Fritz call it? Earworm? The thing that gets stuck in your head. I picked up my own fake mic and leaned my head between them, letting the line linger in the air between us: *"it figures—"*

We screamed that line into Uncle Junior's ears. He threw his head back and laugh-grunted, how you do when you're annoyed but also laughing at something, then he flipped back to his original station, Biggie playing, and adjusted the dials so that I felt the *thump-thump thump-thump* in the center of my back again, but this time it was more like a heartbeat.

You Don't Know
What Love Is

The account manager at QuickPay Bonds on Decker Boulevard—the one who had approved the bail bond loan on Redwood Court—warned Weesie that as part of this new loan request, if she didn't make payments on time, she could be in jeopardy of losing the house.

She and Teeta had worked all those jobs all those years to pay off the house and had increased its value, thank God. When the grandchildren started coming, Teeta sought to do some other improvements and transformed the patio porch into a den. The expansion gave Weesie more room to breathe—and literally more rooms. She had a proper living room, where she could accept proper company and show off her powder-blue walls and curio filled to the brim with her keepsakes and inheritances: Rhina's lock of baby hair, Junior's first pair of Stride Rites cast in bronze, clay ashtrays from three years of Sasha's art classes, the plastic figurines (painted black) that adorned her and Teeta's wedding cake. Teeta's glasses. Lady's Bible, and so on. In the living room, she could properly display her accumulated decades of Easter lilies: sent after her mama, Lady, died of sugar and old age; sent after her brother, Pete, died; sent after Weesie's stepdaddy, Big Daddy Briggs, left; and most recently, sent after Weesie stood over the gaping hole at Palmetto Cemetery and tossed the final rose over Teeta's casket.

Whenever it was that Weesie brought herself to allow anyone into the living room, even to just look at her 1920s gold antique sitting chairs and chaise lounge, or even to set a drink on her marble-and-wood coffee table, visitors would marvel at the jungle of plant life sprawling below the bay window. Weesie never revealed the secret to her thriving house plants: the radio on the floor, playing Gospel FM most hours of the day. Teeta had taught her that talking to plants was the secret to their everlasting lives. Weesie figured daily praises and prayers to the Lord would be the best talk therapy. She was right. There were Easter lilies older than her grands, 'bout old as Junior.

If she were in the kitchen clipping coupons or between calls when "Going Up Yonder" came on, Weesie would drop everything, slip into her sanctuary, and practice her Silver Shepherds Praise Dance routine, the one she and Betty and the ladies had choreographed last spring especially for this song. She moved her hips and arms side to side like a hula dancer, then raised her hands, ready to receive the Holy Ghost.

> *I'm goin' up yonder (goin' up yonder)*
> *To be with my Lord*

Some days—she didn't know how—she wound up prostrate on the floor. It had been on those days, she'd replace "Lord" with

"James" (Teeta had too many syllables) and was so overcome with grief that half the day would pass before she brought herself to her feet again.

Weesie was on her knees in the living room, in front of her Easter lilies, when the phone rang.

"You've received a call from the South Carolina Midlands Correctional Facility from: *mamatheysaybailaintgonethroughyet*. If you would like to accept the charges, please press one."

Weesie sighed. Five years ago, when she retired, just a few years after Teeta hung up his State Hospital mortuary assistant lab coat, they had planned out their whole retired lives: fishing at Ms. Cook's lake in the day, weekend trips to Green Sea up in Horry County to see Teeta's family, and over to Thomson to see Weesie's; summers with the grands, and holidays with her nieces and nephews and all their children. Weesie and Teeta had dreamed their little abode on Redwood Court would be forever flooded—bodies floating in and out, the grill forever grilling. All the bikes would be pulled out from the shed and she'd sit under the carport playing spades or eating watermelon while spokes whirred up and down the cul-de-sac.

Instead, Junior's baby mama, who was several years older—and, Weesie would say if you asked her, and often even when you didn't, "old enough to have known better than to get knocked up by a twenty-three-year-old baby boy"—took to revenge when he didn't propose and so filed for child support against Junior. Said the formula cost too much. Weesie asked won't the girl breast-feeding, though? Then said the cost of childcare was going to break her bank. Rhina offered up a spot to the baby at her daycare so long as food was provided, but that won't enough.

Wasn't that something? Her baby boy locked up because of the expense of babies. Junior hadn't been the same since Teeta died. Where Weesie gave her grief to God, the way she started telling it, Junior gave his grief to the streets. Between stints inside, Junior had caught his arm in the machine at the poultry farm, a job Teeta had helped him get. Stunned by the pain, Junior froze and the machine kept grinding and grinding. It caught his shirt first then the fat flesh of his forearm. The all-cash settlement from the poultry farm was large enough for them all not to put up too much of a fuss, but when you count for hospitals, doctors, rehab therapy, loss of wages . . . whenever it would be that Junior was ready to go back to work, he was set so far back in bills his new career became taking up residence with women who wanted to take care of someone. That's how he met Antoinette. He moved in, and not long after, she was pregnant with Destiny. And not long after that, Junior was back at Weesie's with a court date and another late bill he couldn't work to pay off.

Under the advisement of the gentleman at QuickPay Bonds, Weesie had emptied out her bank of that month's pension payment to process the lien that would be put on the house, so Junior could come home until his court date. She thought it a coincidence that as soon as she announced the amount of her monthly pension payments when asked about assets, that was the *exact* balance she had to put down to activate the bail for Junior's release.

But the nice gentleman had said it would only take forty-eight hours to process, or twenty-four hours if she paid a premium, which she did, and he'd said, "Your boy will be sitting at the dinner table before you sign and drive home."

Weesie wished she'd known better and had brought Major with her, for a type of insurance. She felt in her gut that the gentleman was getting over on her, but she couldn't point out how.

"If you want to lower your payments, you can extend the

mortgage loan back out to thirty years," he said, words sticky as blackstrap molasses. Weesie really only understood "lower your payments" and so went with that option. Major—the college man of the family, even though he dropped out after the wedding, soon after Rhina announced she was pregnant with Sasha— had the most schooling and wits about him of anyone Weesie knew. He always used bookish words, words you had to sit with to see if you understood. Maybe if he'd been there when she was signing the papers and making the first payment, twenty-four hours would have really meant twenty-four hours and not two weeks, and maybe the payments would have been more affordable and not redistributed over the next thirty years. He would have worked it out. Her next month's pension payment hadn't even reached her account when she called the gentleman at the bond office, who had said he would clear the original hold to release the bail, and *that* would most certainly bring Junior home.

Except now Junior was calling collect to see about his bail, and Weesie just didn't have enough to pay for another call. It was the third time that day. Another time, when Junior was locked up overnight for being in the wrong car with the wrong boys at the wrong place, he had called, and Weesie had held her hand over the receiver to tell Rhina she was so tired of that boy running up her phone bill before pressing one. When the call connected, all Junior said was, "Fine. I won't call you anymore." And hung up. That was when Weesie learned both that the collect caller could hear you over the recorded message and that even mere seconds of a collect call from jail would cost you close to twenty dollars— more than her minimum monthly department store credit card payment. She thought to press one this time, then looked over to her fridge. The pink envelope announcing *FINAL NOTICE* reminded her that the sewage was just five days from being cut off—yes, Major said he'd pay it for her, but Weesie was sad to think about all that he did for her, especially now.

So Weesie inhaled large enough to say what she needed to say quickly and in one breath, "StillwaitingtohearfromQuickPay. TryFriday. LoveyouJunior," and hung up the phone without pressing one.

THREE THINGS BROKE WEESIE'S HEART WHEN JUNIOR FINALLY made it out of jail: First, it became clear that she would have to come out of retirement 'cause of the loan payments on Redwood Court. They took all of her monthly pension. Second, she no longer had a house paid in full like she and Teeta had worked so hard for all those years. And now, finally, Junior couldn't come back home to live with her because she had applied for and had just been approved to be a foster parent for the extra income and had to certify—notary public and all—that no known felon or person who had spent any amount of time in jail lived on the premises where a foster child would be taking up residence.

One more thing: Weesie had to turn the room where Teeta lived out his last cancerous days into a semipermanent guest room.

Dutifully, Major came over after church to clean out the closet. Weesie saved a few of Teeta's powder-blue and baby-pink polo shirts, with the worn-down front pockets where he kept his pen and reading glasses. The rest went into black garbage bags to be set on the curb. It was Sunday, and the garbage men would be through the Court the next morning. So she didn't have *too* much more time to look too hard at the final things Teeta touched before they were whisked away with the food scraps.

Major dragged out the bedside chamber pot that Teeta used

for maybe one week. Too weak to cross the narrow hallway to the bathroom, Teeta progressed rather quickly to adult diapers. Insurance didn't send hospice right away, so everyone still had hope he'd gather some strength from somewhere, like when God got him out of ICU and off the breathing tube before they just knew he was set to leave them that summer.

Teeta had lasted seven months longer than anyone thought possible—even the doctors.

When he did die, as much as Weesie felt she wanted to, or that it was "the right thing to do," she couldn't bring herself to bury him with his wedding band or his glasses. When the ring wound up missing from her curio the day Junior came home with a rott-weiler and a shiny Members Only jacket, she'd wish she had sent the items with Teeta to the hereafter.

Anyways. Major and Weesie had cleaned the room's two dressers and two small nightstands. Major took the twenty-dollar bill Weesie gave him to the Salvation Army and brought back a nineteen-inch television and a small lamp. When he drove up, Junior was standing in the carport smoking a cigarette.

Junior nodded. Major rolled down the window of his tan Ford minivan.

"Can you help me take these things inside for Ms. Mosby?" Major asked.

Junior looked just past the van to who knows where, cupped the Newport in his hand, and took a long pull while holding the butt of it between his index and thumb. He nodded again, then exhaled a quick stream of smoke and flicked the cigarette, still lit, between 154 and Mr. Reggie's house.

As he approached the van, Junior gestured back to the house. "I just got back and now Ma saying I can't come home. Ain't that some shit?"

He snatched up his eyes to catch Major's. "Sorry about that, man," Junior apologized. He didn't know why. Just like he didn't know where was home or what to do about it until his court date.

Major shook his head but also said nothing. On his way to Redwood Court, he'd stopped over to Forestwood Drive and picked up some old linens that could go on the bed for the new arrival. The social worker had advised them that most likely Weesie would get foster placements who were months away from aging out of the system, and who should begin to think about being independent. Looking at her list, the social worker said it was expected that Weesie would get matched with an older Black male—it was harder to find a loving family for them, and the housing need was the greatest.

Major and Junior maneuvered around the back side of the van, gathering miscellany in hopes of making only one trip. When the van doors shut, Weesie peeped out the screen door, stretching the cable coils to their limits while cradling the phone between her ear and shoulder.

"Hold on, Ruby, I didn't hear no car roll up. I just need to see who Junior is out there talking to. I thought one of those new trouble boys had come by. I tell Junior I don't need them gangstas or whatever they call each other coming 'round, 'specially not now." She leaned further out the side door, like if she leaned enough she could see down the Court. "At any moment the social worker will be here to drop the foster boy off."

Weesie stretched the cord as far as it could go, which only allowed her head and chest to lean out of the house, but it was enough to see what was going on.

"Yeh," Weesie said. "Yeh. It's nice, you know. A big difference already. They sent a first check, like an advance. I bought a new fan. Hold on, Ruby. Hold on. I see Major's here with the stuff I asked him to pick up."

Weesie held the receiver to her chest and called out, "When you brang that stuff in, set it up in the blue room, where Teeta was. Junior, don't go messing up nothing, 'cause they telling me the foster boy coming by soon. If the woman asks, you *used* to live here. Major and Rhina will let you set up a space on their living room floor until you get settled on your own."

Major looked at Junior over the TV they were both carrying and nodded.

IT SEEMED THE OLDER MIKA GOT, EACH TIME SHE WENT OVER to her grandmother's house something had shifted. It started when Teeta stopped picking her up from school, then he took sick to the room she slept in, and just like that he was gone.

Mika didn't know what to expect when she went over to Weesie's house these days, once she heard that Junior would be staying at Forestwood Drive and a new boy would be coming to stay at Redwood Court—like some kind of upside-down Freaky Friday. Instead of insisting she not go to visit at all, Major had Mika promise to lock the door to what used to be Junior's room when she turned in for the night.

Cedric was seventeen and black as Weesie's prized cast iron pan that had been passed down so many generations she lost count. Both glistened about the same. Greased up with oil. He came with a fresh perm on his head—what Weesie called a "conch"—so he could use one of those small black combs that always broke whenever Mika tried to use it against her own tight coils. Cedric kept it in the back pocket of his too-big shorts.

"I took one look at that boy's clothes," Weesie said on the phone, probably to Ruby, "and decided that this weekend I'm gone have his behind up in Belk's."

Mika thought she might like to go and mouthed *Can I go?* in Weesie's direction. She shook her head and continued speaking to Ruby.

"I just couldn't have no boy with me walking around with shirts like girls' dresses and short pants looking like cool-outs."

Weesie had seen this type of dress before—wasn't it Junior?— and that was what worried her. A bit ago, an elder woman who lived alone three streets over was approached by boys she didn't know while she was trying to make her way from the car to the porch. Her neighbor across the street had just come out to put his trash bin to the curb and asked if everything was alright, and the boys ran off into the dark. That was after they got the snack lady. These all was new developments, and it seemed like nothing was going to stop them.

When Teeta was alive, Weesie had no cause for concern, but Calvin, across the street and one house down, had come over the other day to announce a warning: not long after the exposé on the six o'clock news he'd woken up in the middle of the night when he heard glass break. Of course, since then everyone in Newcastle had their guards up, on the lookout. Calvin said some-one broke into his car for his CD adapter and Sony Discman. They rummaged through his CDs but didn't take any, but they did scratch a few with their initials—just enough that he couldn't get through any song on the playlist without it skipping. Calvin said he knew who it might have been because he'd seen young men in white walking up and down Redwood Court when Junior was away, and he knew no one had any boys that age— grandchildren or otherwise—around here. "They were wearing

those pants like what women wear," Calvin noted. "White bandanas hanging from they behinds. White shirts."

Mika asked one more time to go to Belk's with Weesie and
Cedric. She wanted to finally get that black patent leather shoulder bag Weesie had promised. When Weesie said no and not to
ask her again, Mika decided it was a small gift: she could ride her
bike in peace for a few hours, what with all the fuss lately around
the house.

Weesie and Cedric crawled towards the end of the cul-de-sac
in the royal-blue Chevy Cavalier, both windows down, calling out
to anyone outside.

"This my new boy, Cedric," Weesie said to Uncle Quincy, who
was outside and leaning against his mailbox, watching the parade. "Wanted y'all to meet. He'll be staying with me a while. I'm
looking to get him a job if you know anyone hiring, so as to keep
him busy this summer. Maybe Hardee's. You know what they say
'bout idle hands."

Weesie smiled and winked at Cedric. He focused on the work
of twirling the small black comb in his hands.

"We on our way to Belk's for some pants. Keep an eye out for
Mika? She riding around here somewhere," Weesie called out,
having rolled down the street past Uncle Quincy, who raised his
hand in goodbye and agreement.

Mika looked on from the curb of 154 Redwood Court. Weesie and Cedric cruised by Calvin and Betty's house, Ruby's house,
the scary lady's house, the house of the woman who kept the
mangy dog in the front yard, and so on down the Court until they
were out of sight.

Earthshine Mountain

I t was on the overnight class trip to Earthshine Mountain that Mika debuted her singing voice in front of her classmates, and where she believed she finally found a best friend—on the spot, just about—in Gloria Jean. During the day, the class performed trust falls, climbed rope walls, and hiked for what felt like centuries with just a compass, a canteen, and a few feet of rope. That night, all twelve girls squeezed into the cabin loft instead of splitting between upstairs and downstairs, with some in the four beds and the rest on the floor. Mika brokered that deal because she knew she wasn't popular enough to get top-floor dibs, but also, she didn't want anyone else to get the beds. So when the girls stood looking at the four beds to their twelve teen bodies and sleeping bags, Mika stepped forward and offered, "What if we pile our bags on the beds and we all take to the floor?"

Just before that suggestion, Jennifer had stepped forward and dropped her bag on the bed. Of course, Jennifer thought she was going to get to sleep there—that's how white girls who had everything thought. It seemed like no one was going to stop her, and Missy moved in next to attempt to claim a second bed. Again, that white-girl-who-gets-whatever-she-wants move. The girls in the back, the ones who never expected to get anything, started to go downstairs where the chaperones were. Mika was somewhere in the middle, in fact, on the stairs, and faced the decision of wanting to sleep upstairs with the girls who only paid her attention when there was a group pairing and they needed a final head—not necessarily because the girls were claiming the space, but because for once she wanted to savor the spoils of what she was going to fight for. For the most part, Mika was agreeable.

The girls heard Mika's suggestion and stopped unpacking downstairs. The upstairs girls looked around. Jennifer and Missy had already unpacked their sleeping bags on the beds and began gathering their shower packs to further claim the bathroom.

While she got her somewhat-easy nature from Major (Rhina would disagree), Mika did get stuff from Rhina, too: stubbornness on principle, taking care of the little people, relentless protectiveness. Whenever it showed up in her or in Rhina, it was a surprise to Mika. That time in Florida—or was it Washington, D.C.?—when the old white lady tried to take the spot Major was lining up the van to park in and Rhina stuck her head out the window and said, "You know you saw us here first!" Major tried to say it was OK, but Rhina said emphatically, "No. We were here and this white bitch wants what's not hers," then looked back at Mika and Sasha and told them not to repeat what she had said. Don't do as she do. Or something. But Mika took it as a challenge.

"Y'all don't have to be *bitches* about this," Mika said, feeling the word inflate her chest. She had never used it before in front of people, but sometimes you have to choose the right word for the right moment.

Missy gasped. "Take that back."

Mika shook her head. She wasn't going to take it back, even if it did make her uncomfortable having said it. That was the Major in her. She tried to talk around the sting of the word suspended in the loft.

"We're supposed to be building together as a team out here in the mountains," she offered, gesturing around the room. She wasn't sure how much she really believed it, but it was more about the other folks believing what she said.

"We're only here for one night. Who cares who sleeps where?" a voice offered. Mika couldn't catch who it was.

"Exactly," Mika said, her heart pulsing in her ears and throat, then returned her glare to Missy and Jennifer. "That's why we could all have this experience you're trying to steal from us by not letting everyone bunk up here."

When she looked around it dawned on her that all the girls going downstairs were Black, or not white, and all the ones who pushed them out, or stayed to enjoy the rewards, were white. "Everything is black and white," Rhina had said to Major, who tried to pick his battles with Rhina that day in the parking lot and say maybe it wasn't racism, that the woman slinking into their spot must have not seen them.

Mika swallowed to push down whatever was trying to make its way to her head. She understood her parents more just now. So, this was the heart of conflict. Still standing on the first stair, she moved up the step to try to be on the loft landing and swore one of Missy or Jennifer's girls moved as if to block her. Mika took after Rhina in the height department but was solid like all of the women in Major's family, which meant that when puberty started making its full course through her body, she swiftly went from a children's large to a women's medium and sometimes even a large. Whenever Sasha flipped through the Delia's clothing catalog, Mika could only dream. One day. Sometimes, when she was lucky, Weesie took her to Penny's or Belk's, but only for special occasions, like Teeta's funeral. For the most part her clothes were immediate hand-me-downs from Sasha, or from thrifting. That is all to say Mika made up for what she felt was inadequacy in the physical and the social sphere by wits and smarts, a quick mouth. And leveraged her body sometimes to make a point. She stood firm, unphased by the girls acting like they were trying to intimidate her.

"There's twelve of us here and only four beds, y'all. And we all want to sleep in the loft together. Three girls can't fit in a twin bed."

Jennifer started to respond, but Mika kept going.

"If they intended for us to use the beds, they would have told us to bring linen instead of sleeping bags and our own pillows, but that won't on your little checklist, huh?" Mika smiled, not because of the jab but how she slipped and sounded like Weesie whenever her heart rate went up. Most days, kids her age, usually the neighborhood kids on Forestwood Drive, said she sounded like a white girl and meant it as an insult. Major and Rhina were constantly correcting her—they never wanted folks to think she wasn't smart or some such. But as soon as she went into autopilot, she sounded like Weesie: velvet words with punches. Saying it exactly how she said it was almost an undressing, but in a good way. She wanted the girls to see her. "Won't on the little list, huh." Someone, not one of the Black girls, laughed but tried to hide it. She knew. She dug her heels in.

"I mean, didn't think y'all would be rushing in here to sleep on no beds looking like that."

The girls behind her, the downstairs girls, snickered.

"Looks like someone pissed all over the beds 'cause they were so scared for they mama out here in the woods," Mika said. She wanted to snicker herself, and at the same time started to feel charged up, a new energy coursing through her. Maybe, for a half second, she thought she took it too far. Maybe everyone was tired by then. Maybe Missy and Jennifer didn't want to be seen bullying classmates for piss-stained twin mattresses. Maybe they remembered why Ms. Fritz brought them all the way to another state three hours away, out in the middle of the woods, to compromise and team-build. Just earlier, Mika held her hand out and caught Jennifer during the trust fall. And Mika was paired with Roger for the ropes course, which meant they held hands tiptoeing the fifty yards of rope thirty feet above everyone's heads to get from one tree platform to the next. They were the first to go, and probably the most scared—no one had done it before. After she got down, Mika had rooted for everyone's successful passage and for them not to fall. Now Mika just wanted peace, to sleep in the loft, and for her heart to climb out of her ears and throat. That was it.

"You said it yourself. It's just one night," Mika said. Then Gloria, inching back up the stairs, launched the salvo.

"Maybe we can play a game," Gloria said. Mika moved up to the loft, pushing past Missy and Jennifer—making sure to nudge them with her shoulders—and put her things down. The downstairs girls followed suit like ants in a line to the picnic. Everyone and their belongings on the loft, the two groups faced off like a set board of chess. Gloria had come out from nowhere and strategically positioned herself to the front, like a knight. Major taught Mika this move on the chessboard: take control in the center of the drama, and early. Mika opened the floor, taking two steps forward, and asked, "What game?"

Already the loft dynamics were starting to mimic the school cafeteria popularity contests back home. Mika floated between band kids and Black kids. She often sat between the Black girls who talked fast with their hands and made googly eyes at Roger, who sometimes sat at the band table, too, doing his prealgebra homework. He played baritone and did football—his coaches let him do both—so he had to have a calm section of the caf to do his work and sometimes he'd look up to count in his head and would catch Mika's eye and she'd look away.

There were three tables that had the Black kids. A handful of girls played M*A*S*H and recapped reruns of *A Different World*. Sasha didn't watch it, and so that meant Mika didn't either, and sitting with that group would immediately validate any "acting white" claims made against her. At another table were the couples—and, well, Roger had only touched her hand at the Chick-fil-A stand when she dropped her pencil, and even if you counted the ropes course, Mika was still convinced that he'd never go for her. So she was left to the third Black table, which had Black folks from chorus like Gloria, whatever miscellany, and Michelle, who wasn't even Black but wasn't white and because her dad was in the army and before she came to Columbia, she was stationed somewhere where a lot of Black folks lived, and if you didn't see her face and tried to figure out what Asian country she was from but only heard her talk, you'd think she was Black, so she could stay. One of the moves when Michelle was young meant that she was held back and not eligible for the gifted-and-talented program, and so wasn't on the trip, but Mika saw her and Gloria hanging together, mostly singing Fugees songs. Mika always hummed along but never officially joined them in the lyrics.

She sat with Deidre and talked about books or poetry; they had found the Black books section of the library and started a two-person book club.

So, at Earthshine Mountain, when Gloria engaged the chess-board by suggesting *all the girls* play a game, everyone was ready to hear what it was and Mika was thankful that the spotlight she'd felt, the heat, moved off of her.

Here came Missy and Jennifer, though. "What now?"

Mika took a deep breath to start back up, but Gloria put up her hand and rolled her eyes. She was facing Mika, but Mika knew it won't for her. Gloria started again.

"Y'all remember that show *Star Search*? We could have a con-test on the best group performance. We need groups who are going to perform, and some judges."

The judges' spots were all snatched up before Mika could take one. That meant she had to sing. But who would play the music?

"We'll have to hold the headsets out like a mini speaker. If you turn the volume all the way up, we should be able to make it out."

On the other side of the loft, the white side, there were more than enough cassette players or Discmans for the number of girls. Everyone separated into groups and they rattled off their choices; Mika heard one group whispering the words and knew what song they wanted to do, because Sasha played it in her car whenever they drove anywhere, and MTV wouldn't stop playing the video of the white girl with the black glasses roaming through an empty building like she was looking for someone to love her.

> *You say*
> *I only hear what I want to.*

Another set of girls stomped their feet and put their hands to their chests, then stretched their arms out to imaginary fans.

Tell me why. Ain't nothing but a heartache.

And then there was some Spice Girls and Britney Spears. And so forth. On Mika and Gloria's side there were only three options, what with the number of Walkmans or Discmans, and suddenly Mika was glad that Sasha had taken her to Circuit City right before this trip so she could pick out two CDs to start her own collection after Sasha bought her a portable CD player for her birthday.

It wasn't a Discman like Sasha's, sure, but Mika now had something all her own, which was an improvement on the third- and fourth-generation dubs of Major's mixed tapes for road trips—seventies Motown sprinkled with Billy Joel, Queen, Whitney Houston, and Celine Dion. Mika couldn't imagine offering "It's All Coming Back to Me Now" as the song for the contest, even though she actually loved it and heard some girls across the way practicing other Celine titles, pretending to be Rose from *Titanic*.

When she was at Circuit City, Mika didn't want to buy a CD that duplicated anything in Sasha's collection, even though half of it was what Uncle Junior called "that white-boy music" and the other half was Tupac and Biggie. "How Do U Want It" and "It Was All a Dream." The only times Sasha played those were definitely not in the house but while driving Mika around certain parts of town with her windows down, nodding her head a little harder if guys pulled up beside her at a stoplight. Lisa Loeb: nowhere to be found. Mika's exposure to the full spectrum of songs was limited to stolen moments flipping through BET music videos. Rhina had a sixth sense for bass, no matter how low you had the stereo. She'd float from out of nowhere and demand whoever was in violation turn the music off. Mika and Sasha would sit so close to the TV, with the sound so low it might as well have been on silent. And here Rhina would appear the second a song as innocent as "I'll Be Missing You" featuring Faith Evans came on, right at the bridge, and Rhina would wave her arms, huffing and fussing, telling the girls to turn it off or they'd lose TV for a week.

Sasha first picked up Whitney, the great equalizer. Rhina OK'd her because she was never in a music video in her underwear, and she was saved by the old white man in *The Bodyguard*. Major always included "I'm Your Baby Tonight," "I'm Every Woman," "My Name Is Not Susan," and "I Have Nothing" on every single mixtape for the car, no matter what, so Rhina knew Whitney by now.

Gloria had brought her gospel demo, because she was practicing for an audition with her sister—they were trying to get a recording deal. Half the girls on their side groaned. Gloria knew they couldn't win at all if they were going to be singing songs about Jesus. Other than that, she had the Fugees, and that excited Mika. "Strumming my pain with his fingers," she started, to see who else knew it. Only Gloria: "One time! One time!"

At this point, Mika knew only Gloria knew the words, and the other girls looked at them when they finished the phrase. They sang together: "Killing me softly with his song."

Gloria kept going on the word "song," and it went on like it would last forever, with vibrato and all that. Missy had turned to ask if they were ready, but they weren't, because to participate they needed a song all four of them could sing. Like on *Star Search*, every person had a part, and not everyone knew this song.

Gloria asked what Mika had with her. Of course she'd brought her new Whitney Houston, but she never heard any of the kids in the caf sing any of her songs, really. So she didn't mention Whitney. But when Sasha had set her loose in the rows and rows of CDs in Circuit City, Mika picked up the latest Mariah Carey album, *Butterfly,* and was excited because of the crossovers: Puff Daddy on the boat singing about "honey." Bone Thugs-n-Harmony rapping about "breakdowns"—all groups Rhina would have hated, but Mariah's syrupy voice brought it all together.

Mika pulled out the plastic case from her JanSport and offered it up. All four girls gasped in excitement. She'd struck gold.

Gloria took the liner notes out to go through the songs with the crew and waved her hands vertically as she sang, like a choir director. They'd shake their heads at song after song that might not work for the four of them: too much Mariah. Too sad. Too many octave jumps that only Gloria could reach, and this was supposed to be a group effort like that Black-girl group Girls Tyme from a few years ago. They landed on "Breakdown," and Gloria tried to skip over it, but everyone else said it could work.

Mika offered to start off; she didn't even need the liner notes. "You called yesterday / to basically say" and she held her hand up to her ear like she was in a recording studio. Added a touch of vibrato for spice. After Mika started the opening verse, Gloria joined in, doing her singing arm-raise.

Mika smirked because it really won't that serious, but she loved that Gloria was taking it seriously. The rest of the crew were waiting for direction, so Mika took the reins. "OK, we can all do 'Break break down / Steady breaking me on down.'"

Gloria added, "Y'all can do that like a round. It can be the music that me and Mika sing over."

The girls practiced the rounds, the lyrics, the hand movements. Across the way, girls were practicing, but not as animated. Gloria walked over to the judges, who were waiting for something to happen and gave them the rules: one to four stars. Then calculate the average for the winner.

"What if there's a tie?" one of the Earthshine Mountain Star Search judges asked. Gloria said that all of the girls would vote to break the tie. Jennifer offered that maybe they could use the chaperone to break the tie, and a voice from downstairs said, "Y'all should really be asleep right now." And they all looked at each other and giggled and walked into a tighter circle so as to speak and sing softer.

"Let's just go," Mika said, feeling anxious now that she was actually going to sing in front of people again, wanting to get it over with and wanting of course to win.

Missy's group went. As usual, Mika knew the song from Sasha—and liked it, even—but had to pretend to be annoyed like the other Black girls. "You're gonna be the one that saves me," Mika hummed with them. Missy lifted up her arms and wiggled her fingers jazz-hands style while she brought them back down. "And after all, you're my waterfall."

Those weren't the right words, and it was crazy to think that you could get the lyrics wrong when the right word was in the title of the song, but Mika knew if she corrected Missy, she'd show her girls that she knew the song. Hopefully the judges would catch the wrong word. Another group went, doing "Stay," and it was alright, but there's only so much you can do with a group of girls singing a song usually sung by one person.

Gloria and Mika and their dancers / rhythm keepers went next, choreography just like they'd practiced. Everyone even bounced at the knees like Bone Thugz, but *no one* tried that rap part. When they were finishing up, Gloria, with her director hands, put her arms out and started crouching low like pushing clothes down into the laundry basket, and the girls got quieter and quieter: "Break break down / steady breaking me on down," until they stopped.

THE NEXT MORNING ON THE BUS RIDE BACK TO COLUMBIA, with the glow of victory puffing out her chest, Mika initiated a seat change by asking Gloria if they could sit together. When they had boarded the bus in the Big Lots parking lot, Mika had been more interested in making sure she got a window seat than who she sat with, which was a big mistake, because she ended up sitting with a girl who sounded like Beaker from the Muppets when she spoke. It annoyed Mika mostly because she felt only white girls could get away with existing in a constant state of seeming helplessness. And Major always pointed his finger at Mika if she spoke under her breath.

"Say it with your whole chest or don't say it, Mika," he'd say and tap his finger right at the clavicle, where there was no fat and no muscle to absorb the strength of his push. Just nerves, skin, and bone. She learned to speak up.

When Beaker sat next to Mika and all she heard was *Meep-meepmeepmeep* and they had to leave so early the sun wasn't even up yet, Mika sighed audibly and cradled her head in the pillow leaning against the window and pretended to sleep the whole way.

Mika knew that folks tended to fall back in line with the first seat choice, creatures of habit. So when it was time to load up to head home, faced with sitting next to the Muppet for three hours again, Mika decided that giving up her window pillow rest might be worth it. Besides, Gloria had helped her spearhead and lead the winning *Star Search* competition—a full 4 stars for Mariah Carey and Bone Thugz-N-Harmony to the 3.5 stars for Oasis, and a 2.5 for the Lisa Loeb rendition—a good choice, but just . . . anyways, she had in Gloria a new friend now, and Gloria looked around when Mika asked, then smiled and moved over to share the seat.

The rest of the way back, they shared one earphone from the headset and sang "Oo la la laa / it's the way that we rock when we doing our thing!" waving their hands to the bass and the beat.

Call a Spade a Spade

I always wondered what white girls were up to with all the Saturdays they get to have in their lives. Me, I have to give two Saturdays a month to the hairdresser. *Because we can't have no girls of ours going around with nappy heads in this world, Mika.* Weesie and Grandma Annie being hairdressers don't help my case when I ask why I have to worry about my hair being done so much. "Cleanliness is next to godliness," or some version of that, they'd offer. I keep myself clean! "It's not the same, Mika," Weesie'd say.

But it's so much time. Today, between folks who showed up late for their appointments and Sherren taking her time, it was two hours before a drop a water hit my head. Then she'd set the dryer for extra heat and two cycles, then the styling, then waiting for someone to pick me up, and by the time I got into the car it was pink sky leaning into night. I had read all of the crinkly *Jet* magazines—the same ones I read weeks ago. Probably last year.

Or in fourth grade. Already flipped through all the style books and decided what style I'd get when I'd have to come back. I yawned when Weesie moved the Walmart circular from the front seat to let me sit.

"You yawning like you put in a full day at the office, like you know what work is," she chuckled.

I lifted my fingers one at a time, starting at when I got out of Daddy's car in the parking lot that morning.

"I feel like I did, Weesie! Almost seven hours!" I said, reaching into the car console for a pack of crackers. I held the peanut butter cracker up to her and hummed; she took it. Then waved her hand, saying I could finish the rest. Between North Main Street and Redwood Court, I devoured them like it was the last meal I'd ever have. Just as I was scraping the cracker dust and peanut butter remnants off the roof of my mouth, we pulled into Redwood Court, and I knew I'd make it before I choked from any dry-cracker-mouth. I unbuckled my seatbelt right as we passed Ruby's house, and Weesie cleared her throat.

"Before you run in and drink all my cokecola, remember we have Daisy coming to town tomorrow and I want to have a spades game, so think of us tomorrow and leave us some, 'kay?" she said, putting the car in park. It rolled back into the break as I was jumping out with my key, ready.

When Teeta was with us, the door was never locked, because one of them or Junior was bound to be home. Now, between Cedric and Junior's new friends who hang around the house, Weesie had the key guy come and add a deadbolt. Daddy laughed when he realized it was the same key as the lock in the knob, like, what was that really gone do, Mrs. Mosby? She said, point-blank: "Optics are everything." So, because someone was always picking me up from somewhere and most likely dropping me to Redwood Court, everyone decided it just made sense that I had a key. I figured it was mostly so they could drop me if no one was home and they could ask Ruby or Reggie to keep an eye, or Uncle Quincy, which is easier to do than on Forestwood Drive.

When Weesie got in the house and dropped a hundred Winn-Dixie bags on the floor, asking me to put everything up, and I sighed loudly, she goes, "There you go again, actin' like you've been working your whole life." I reminded Weesie how Mama had me do chores for the daycare and sometimes Antoinette asked me to watch Destiny and I did travel with Daddy for his computer business. She shook her head.

"Chile," Weesie said, tapping her cigarette case on the kitchen island. "Excuse me, miss!" I raised my eyebrows. She shrugged. There we were, another n-pass.

"Daisy the one we 'sposed to meet at that place out in the country that one day?" I asked, lifting the packaged sweet potato patties—and my eyebrows, asking where she wanted them put up; she pointed to the freezer. I knew where the sugar-free Kool-Aid and Debbie cakes went.

"That chitlin thang. Yeh. She called later to say she was coming back to Columbia to do some more work on her genealogy stuff, since them two women was sayin' we all connected. She asked if she could stay here with me, so I say yeh."

"I'm 'sposed to call her Cousin Daisy now?" I ask, still feeling a way about how we dragged ourselves all out through the cotton fields, sweated to death when we got there, and all we had to show was some soggy fries I kept like I was really gone eat when we left, and Weesie smelling like her Thanksgiving Eve kitchen—the chitlin funk—only fried.

I asked if Donnell was coming, if I was finally gone meet him, and she said he was with his daddy for the first time in years, so

Cousin Daisy—yes, that's her name *to me*—booked some time away. Something about everybody needing a break. I mumbled, "What about me?" under my breath, hoping the crinkling store-brand chips bag would drown it out.

"You, Miss Missy, can do whatever you want tomorrow once the company get settled and the spades game get going," Weesie started. She pulled from the Virginia Slims I swore she said she was quitting and smirked. "You can do our bike route if you want, too."

Weesie really felt she was giving me consolation. After Teeta left us, she had gotten a bike. Mama said it was probably her way of connecting with me. She said she guess Weesie needed to get her blood flowing sometimes 'cause she was getting out of breath for the dance routines at church. Everyone blamed the sugar, no one blamed the cigarettes. With Weesie, I went past the stop sign, all around the other cul-de-sacs of Newcastle. I stood on my pedals and practiced flying, my hands out in the air like I had wings. Weesie would wobble, hands gripping the bars, still trying to pedal down the hill. I'd say something about letting it go, ride it, we can't control gravity, and she'd shush me, so we'd ride in silence until we got back to the house. No one else my age with a bike in the Court can go past the stop sign, so saying I can bike out alone is not the joyride Weesie thinks it is, but Teeta taught me to find happiness where you can get it, no matter how small. So I smile and think, I'll head out once the first hand is dealt and everyone has what they need.

"Y'ALL MEET DAISY. SHE FROM FLORIDA," WEESIE SAID, SHUF-fling a deck of cards so worn in they bend into the bridge and slide right into place, purring. I want to learn how to shuffle like

Weesie. She says the trick is the cards gotta be *used up*. Gotta be greasy, bent corners. You season 'em like your good cooking pan.

Cousin Daisy pushed her glasses higher up her nose for the third time and licked her lips. "Nice to meet you all. Happy to be here." Her words were crisp like the linen Weesie ironed before putting it into the closet.

I'm moving the wicker basket of chips across the table, trying to find the perfect spot so folks can serve themselves without reaching and so the game can be played uninterrupted. Right before the first deal, Daisy arrived in a Blue Ribbon taxi from the airport and we dragged her bags inside. It was too much for such a short stay, but we didn't say it. We still had a few more prep things to do before the rest of the folks came, so we went right back to work. (Weesie's best friend Essie, who operates the Blue Ribbon Taxi company, called a special dispatch for Weesie 'cause she just didn't know how she was going all the way out to West Columbia, Winn-Dixie, North Main for me, and prepping, and have her hair together in time when the company come.)

"Your ride okay?" Weesie asked. She was placing the last of the watermelon she had cut into smiles on the serving tray. A puddle of juice and a few specks of seeds lingered on the counter. I saw them. Weesie saw I saw and raised her eyebrows at me and I got up to clean it. A perfect host cleans as she goes.

Miss Ruby in the flesh and not on the phone was seated, sipping the company punch. This was a treat for her, too. Betty, who acts as much as my grandma as Weesie does, asked me for a piece of paper and motioned to my journal. I reluctantly go to the back of the notebook and pick a clean sheet and write US VS. THEM at the top, draw a line, and slide it to Weesie. They can have a sheet a paper, but she won't gone get my good pen for them to use.

I swear Weesie shuffled ten times. She was about to go another round before Cousin Daisy saved us, clearing her throat.

"How y'all play? Ace takes all?"

The air stopped, I promise you. Even though the air was moving, 'cause I had flipped on the ceiling fan. Ruby looked at Weesie. She had stopped mid bridge shuffle.

"Daisy from Florida, y'all," Weesie reminded, calling the dogs
off. Then turned to Daisy. "Here, we play joker, joker—"

"Two a diamonds, two a spades," Betty finished, fanning her
cards out in front of her like opening a book.

Cousin Daisy pushed up her glasses again, though they won't
very far down her nose this time. You could see her doing the
new calculations in her head, writing numbers in the air. More
possibilities to win or lose.

Weesie was dealing left 'round, stopped with her, went right.
Every sixth card she flipped it over. Hummed. I saw a king of
spades, a two of diamonds, a four of clubs—Betty sucked her
teeth—and the little joker landed in front of Weesie. She chuckled. Tapped the table. I knew from watching all these years, rack-
ing books on the table with Teeta, that when a dealer makes two
taps with the remaining deck of cards it's a signal to pay attention. As Weesie's guest, Cousin Daisy was de facto Weesie's part-
ner, but Cousin Daisy was so concentrated on the fan of cards in
front of her face, she missed Weesie's cue. Ruby said that's what
Weesie gets. Everyone laughed except Cousin Daisy.

I was sitting next to but just behind Weesie, to give her room
to breathe. When they decided that I was old enough to be
brought into the game, I first earned a seat at the table for taking
score, so even though Weesie said I could do whatever I wanted I
also know she expected me to be there, writing who trumped
what, helping her see who reneged, and making sure the "US"

side of the paper stayed on top. She stepped on my toe, and when I looked her in the eye, she pointed across the table at Cousin Daisy and I packed up the score sheet, my notebook, my company punch, and went to sit to Cousin Daisy's right side—to help. Weesie winked at me and set back in her chair. "We counted four books," I said, and Weesie, having whatever she had, said, "I guess we opening with a pound—write that down, baby—but we can keep going. Daisy, usually if you can take ten books at the jump like what we say we got, that means we won." Cousin Daisy nodded.

Ruby and Betty looked again at their card fans before relenting. Ruby shook her head.

"I guess we going board, then," Betty said.

"Welp, if we get pound, we'll keep playing first to five hundred," Weesie said, and her eyes smiled as the first card out the gate was an ace of diamonds.

I NEVER RODE MY BIKE. WEESIE WOULDN'T LET ME LEAVE ONCE she understood what kind of handicap Cousin Daisy had, what with her not ever playing with any jokers or wilds. We were winning, though. I know I am too young to sit center side with my own hand like I'm a player, but no one knew what kind of spades Cousin Daisy played down in Tampa—and everyone knew the host can't lose—so Weesie had me, I guess, by proxy. That basically was like Teeta was playing with her, because it was always his hands I sat behind and watched as he taught me, silently, tapping on the card he was going to play before it was his turn. I'd follow the round of hearts falling, watch his hand with no hearts, then I'd whisper, "Spade?" He'd shake his finger, point to the table. Weesie had the highest heart, so he tapped the jack of clubs. Won't that a good card? Not here. I pointed to the two of spades—I knew he could trump it all and control the table with what he had left, but he'd shake his finger again, seen only by me, meaning no. Not yet. Weesie would then scoop the book she won and play hearts again. She'd wink at Teeta.

"Now we move," he'd say, loud enough for the table to hear, and everyone would sigh. Teeta slammed a spade down. Everyone sat back, and he'd run the next three to four books while Weesie would remind us that's her man, this her house, don't come to play if you can't play, asking opponents if they had anything better than whatever they put down—the soundtrack to a good game.

But Cousin Daisy was silent. Book after book fell to Weesie, and I could see Cousin Daisy just couldn't keep up with the pace or the pressure. I would tap the end of my pen at the cards and she'd drop them to the center. No one said anything. I guess that's what friends do, know when you need something like a win in spades so they let you have it.

Cousin Daisy cleared her throat. "Why do y'all call it a trump? Why not call a spade a spade?" she asked while Ruby shuffled, though definitely not like Weesie—no one could. Even Teeta did what Weesie called splitting the layer cake: moved a chunk of cards from the middle to the top or bottom until he set it in front of whoever was to his left to cut it. Then he'd say, "Cut the cake!" Ruby was shuffling almost like that, but messier and slower. Betty made a guttural noise at Cousin Daisy's question. Weesie lifted her card-free hand and waved it for emphasis, in the way she does when she starts talking like she's back in the classroom, even though that was centuries ago.

"I mean, that's like, my name is Louise, but those who know me in a very real way call me Weesie. Those who call me Louise,

they only think of me in the very specific context they met me—
prolly business, in which I would have said, 'I'm Louise,' so, yeh,
the same person, but Weesie got more seasoning, I guess. More
people in a bigger context, a bigger way, know me as Weesie, and
that changes how we play together."

Weesie dug her fork into the huge chunk of watermelon on
the plate to her left.

"'Spose I guess a spade no different than the others if you
don't consider how you play them, how they cut. When they cut,
they become a trump."

In another life, if those exist, I think Weesie would have been
a choreographer for how she put down a trump that spliced the
air just so it whistled, and she won the book.

"Maybe think about it this way: That little three of spades,
won't nothing in my hand 'til y'all played something I ain't have,
then it transformed"—she snapped her fingers—"just like that."

We went on like this, me playing for Cousin Daisy, teaching
her Weesie's cues, the ways to wield the spade like a trump, until
finally we inched toward the five hundred mark—of course, in
our favor.

I KNOW I START SO MANY STORIES LIKE THIS, BUT WHEN TEETA
was with us, these games would go on so long that my eyes would
start watering with exhaustion, and he'd tap me to tell me to
write down how many books they won. Someone at the table
would say something about how the youngins can't hang no
more these days, so now I make it my point to suck it up and
straighten my spine and swallow my yawns. 'Cause we started
with one hundred points, the game with Cousin Daisy went
quickly. We all understood that Weesie just needed her taste so

we could call it quits before the sun might find us here. When it was over, Weesie packed up the cards and offered that we should transition outside and sit in the yard next to the concrete firepit/grill that Teeta built. She asked me to find the Skin So Soft for the mosquitos; we grabbed a portable card table and everyone set themselves up like Mama's Montessori semicircle storytime. At this point we'd usually have the sound of silver cans of beer fizzing open, but tonight was ladies' night—so it was just the *clink* of ice melting fast in the Columbia summer evening and too-sweet tea.

Almost as soon as we settled outside, the streetlights ticked on, so it was officially too dark for me to pull my bike from the shed. I leaned into the metal folding chair and crossed my legs at the ankles, like I'm one of the ladies tonight.

"Friday night news struck again," Betty started. "Three courts over, out by the Jehovah's Witness church, Ms. Linda got held up by them boys."

The fire was lit, but sometimes I couldn't make out who was talking, where the voices came from.

"Say she had set up her snack stand like she always do after school when the kids hungry. She was inside and someone knock, asking 'bout pickled pig feet. She was saying she was out when she heard the *click* of a pistol."

Several gasps. I asked if she got shot.

"No, baby, she ain't. We went 'round to make sure she was OK. Shaken up. They made her clean out her cash envelope."

"We can do a kitty if we need to." That was Weesie. She always initiated the calls for support. "I'll send Mika around tomorrow."

"Won't that cash she made selling those Kool-Aid lickups for her son bail?"

"And to pay for the collect calls."

"I know that sting like hell. Last month, Junior rang in a hundred dollars in calls."

I never thought about how much it cost me to press "one" to speak to Uncle Junior. That's why Weesie kept saying we should write. Why we can't accept every call. Why Daddy count from his money clip slower whenever I ask to go to Redwood Court. They all get those bills.

"Yeh. Don't know why she don't empty her cash drawer every day. They got it all. Yanked her up against the house in the carport. She said the gun and they mouths was so close to her face she could smell the vinegar from the dill pickles they must have eaten."

"They just babies thinking they men."

All hums from the ladies; more ice clinking in the glasses Weesie allowed us to bring outside.

"My boy fell into that a few years ago; that's how I got custody of Donnell," Cousin Daisy said. "I told Donnell—he's Donnell the second—that if he didn't watch out, his son would be running the streets like him—was that the legacy he wanted?"

"Sometimes, when them pink envelopes sweep through the mail, when I peel my knee-high tights off my swollen ankles soons as I get home from the second job sittin' next to a old white lady who forgot not to call me a nigger while I'm wiping her ass, I wonder if we got room to think 'bout legacies, the way we livin'," Dot said.

The fire crackled, and wind swept through the flames so it lifted into the sky like an Amen chorus.

"Yeh. Them pink slips. But then, I remember the good times and I think we living 'bout as fine as we can be, ain't it? At least in our own corner of the world?" It was getting too dark to see but it had to be Weesie who said this; she loved that phrase and used it to describe Redwood Court often. "Yeh sure, we go out into them white people's world for the day, and we get through it, I guess, but we get to come back here, our homes, our worlds, at night."

"Is it our corner of the world or a ghetto that white folks want to corral us into like them concentration camps?" That was Cousin Daisy.

I was starting to get the rhythm of who was speaking what, and when, and after the way we played spades, I didn't take Cousin Daisy for one of those "Black Power types." That's what Daddy called them and always, always did bunny ears with his fingers when he said it: "Black Power types who want to blame 'whitey'"—he did bunny ear fingers there, too—"about what they won't take responsibility for." Around the fire pit there was a longer silence—usually the lady banter was back-to-back, woven together like a tapestry.

But the space between Cousin Daisy maybe calling Redwood Court "the ghetto" and anyone else speaking got wider and wider. Just the faint *clink* of tiny pieces of ice swirling in the glasses.

I cleared my throat.

"Cousin Daisy, is it a ghetto because only Black folks live here?" I asked, leaning in so close to the fire my cheeks started to warm. "Didn't that word mean something else before?"

Weesie poked the fire and flames flashed up again. "Somehow we come to adopt that word when we want to use it as an insult."

I *had* heard the word ghetto used before, of course. Teeta had used it to describe the rows of brick houses where folks lived close together without a chain-link fence, trash on the ground, their laundry flapping in the wind in the front yard, and no porch.

I never saw any people outside of the houses so I didn't know if it was Black folks or what living like that. Girls at school used "ghetto" as a way to separate where they lived from whoever it was they were trying to attack at that moment, or to talk badly about something, usually broken or not name-brand, in the possession of someone who had to carry around a free-or-reduced lunch card. I believe we would qualify for that term now that I think about it, but Daddy went in weekly to pay the balance on my lunch card and make good with the cafeteria ladies, so I just always walked on by with my tray. Never mind the fact that I was eating school lunch at all and not buying Chick-fil-A sandwiches or a slice of Domino's pizza, like the girls who used the word "ghetto." Black Ashley used it a lot. Once she said it about a dress my aunt Phoebe Ann made for me, thinking it must have come from a thrift store because a thread was loose and she had used an old red-and-white table cloth. I loved it.

"That dress is so ghetto, Mika, did your parents make you wear that or you picked it out?" she said and sipped on her Capri Sun. She reached behind my neck, and I shrugged, because it tickled, and smirked—not because I was laughing at my own expense but because reflexes will do that to you at the worst times. She pulled a thread and it kept going and going and going and the lace collar started to dangle from the neckline.

"It won't even stay in one piece!" she squealed and pulled more before I caught her hand and squeezed hard, added nail.

I told the table where it was from, that it was specially handmade for me, and that it was *not* ghetto. Black Ashley rolled her eyes and floated to another table.

The fire was kicking in now, burning the larger logs at the bottom, so I could see the faces better. Cousin Daisy fixed her glasses and cleared her throat.

"I don't mean this place as an insult, not in that way, Louise," she started. Someone with a shadowed face, I think Miss Betty, corrected her.

"Weesie."

"Yes. I mean it like, kind of like earlier during the game. Y'all call a spade a trump. You change its name, its meaning. You understand a thing differently when it's called something else, maybe closer to what it's about or what it's doing. If I call my neighborhood in Tampa a suburb, with its cinder block houses and brown lawns ruined by the petroleum runoff from just up the road, folks think I live with white folks, picket fences, two cars, and a dog. The American dream. But we know we don't get paradise here."

"I do. Teeta made sure of it," Weesie said. "When we had our chance to purchase, to get out of how we were living and spread our little wings, we did."

"Of course you feel it is special—it is!—we get to be children of Jim Crow raising children of *Brown v. Board,* living in what feels like three-bedroom mansions, with indoor plumbing and running water. A dream. But white folks would call this the ghetto."

"We don't have to call it that, though."

"I think we do," Cousin Daisy retorted. "I think we do. It changes the relationship we have with our understanding of what has been *allowed* to us."

"You mean like asking permission? Or like we didn't choose?" I asked.

Weesie sucked her teeth at me. "Sth. Mika, what I say about questioning your elders? Don't go being such a damn smartmouth." Weesie only loved to show off my smarts when it suited her—some performance or award, she was center-front row, having dragged Ruby or Betty or Essie over with her. But off script, she said sometimes I was like a landmine, determined to blow up any peace if someone stepped wrong and said something to set me off.

"I don't mean no insult," Cousin Daisy said, starting back up again. "My little ghetto look as cute and manicured as this, but I know for sure that white folks made sure that was where I was to live, and put all the creature comforts around me so as to keep me from venturing too much over to their side of town. My little ghetto is complete with a police station right off to the side of the entrance; there's only two entrances, and they lined with brick nameplates, just like Newcastle. I mean, I felt at home riding into the neighborhood, and also I understood that they keep us all the same, no matter where we are in the world. It's kind of like what I been studying, the plantations they say our people came from, the ones that make us all 'cousins.'"

I didn't see the bunny ears, but how she said "cousins," it had the inflection like Daddy when he used bunny ears.

"You know they figured out that if they *allowed* us to do things normally—marry, have a family, call they work 'jobs,' so on—that folks wouldn't run away? That's how they kept the violence down. The masters set up little circles of houses like cul-de-sacs on the plantations so that if something were to go wrong, it wasn't anything to surround the houses and smoke the trouble out. All by design."

"Now this a slave plantation?" Ruby asked.

"I mean, sometimes it feel like it, don't it? Was reading about this plantation just outside of Charleston, it was its own town it was so big in its day. The town and plantation don't exist no more but in its heyday the master, Marshell, figured out he ain't had to grow crops. He did what other enslavers were doing and let us marry and have jobs and even let some go into town to do day labor, knowing that they'd come home and work the land they lived on because it didn't feel like they was slaves. He refused to call a spade a spade, and by doing it, calling them folks part of his family, and so on, folks got comfortable and settled in so much so that when the violence came to them it was so hard to see it won't an individual failing of whoever was killed—mostly men—but the system, designed for this outcome."

Weesie got up and poured more tea into everyone's glass. Passed around the wicker basket of chip crumbs. Then pushed me toward the house asking me to fill it. I didn't move, I wanted to hear the rest of the story.

"They started killing the men off, and the women were so set in they ways in their little plantation ghettos that they didn't leave. The babies kept coming, even though won't none of their men around. You know what I mean. He'd still go down to the Charleston Market and make his profits. Just rounded them up like pigs to sell or slaughter."

"So this"—Cousin Daisy made a circle in the air—"is a design to get us comfortable again. Look at us. Several of us widowed. Losing our sons."

Weesie let out a deep breath. "Well, you right about that, cousin. Several of us on the Court widowed too early."

Cousin Daisy nodded. "Losing our men, our sons, to the streets or the states or the cemeteries. I didn't think I came here to say all this, but it's so striking how, miles away, we living the same lives and didn't even know it. Here I was wringing my hands like why won't *my* son do right, why did *I* have to lose my husband? Thinking it's a singular struggle, but it ain't. We don't name what it is, and the name keep changing and changing and changing—so much so we think we get our own neighborhoods and stores and call it progress."

The ladies sighed. Was it agreement or resignation? Weesie pushed me back to the house to play hostess or whatever it was that I was doing—waiting on? I filled the chips, grabbed some cookies for me and whoever else, and balanced a fresh bucket of ice. I was worried that after this uncomfortable grown-folk talk we were going to have to suffer through the rest of Cousin Daisy's visit acting nice and proper. Or worse, that she'd leave upset and I would never get to meet my new cousin Donnell. When we were walking outside after the game and I asked her if Donnell would come with her next time she visited and she said we should come to Tampa, I got so excited. But the way Weesie was talkin' now, after what Cousin Daisy was talkin', about Redwood Court was a ghetto and all, I was worried that it won't gone happen.

I don't know how Cousin Daisy did it, or what territory they had to cross to get there while I was gone, but when I came back everyone was laughing, leaning back in their chairs, slapping their knees, gasping for breath.

"Teeta would have loved to know you, cousin," Weesie said. "He woulda said you were a smart-ass who can't play spades a lick to save your life, but he woulda loved extending his family with you in it."

"I been in it. We been in it all this time," Cousin Daisy said and sipped her tea.

Silent Nights

The closer we crawl to the end of the year, the more weary I get. Everybody playing that song, you know it, talking about partying "like it's nineteen ninety-nine."

Some folks saying that we celebrating what could be the end of the world. They call it the Y2K. Whatever that means. Daddy says it's something about how when folks made all the digital things, the norm was to use the last two digits to mark the year. Didn't imagine back then a future where a year started with a two. Which is weird, 'cause I remember reading *2001: A Space Odyssey* in my gifted-and-talented class and in that book they thought we'd be living in outer space by 2001. We not nowhere near there.

Supposedly, on January 1, computers won't know nothing about 00, meaning the year 2000. For all the computers know it could be 1700, 1800, or 1900. I always wanted to be a time traveler and go back in time and ask some questions, but I didn't think I'd live through it. Or write something like: *This is the last holiday season of the twentieth century.*

Weesie has said that phrase a few times on the phone to whoever will listen: "the last holiday . . ." and then trail off, kind of the way she had started counting the last of things when it was clear that Teeta would die. I suspect Betty or Dot or Essie on the other end are finishing the statement "of the twentieth century," but from where I sit, Weesie is marking end times, too.

It started when Uncle Junior went back to jail after Weesie had put a second mortgage on the house to get him out "the last time," and when the phone rang and Weesie sighed and hung up I knew it was Uncle Junior. Daddy had said it would only be a matter of time, that the only system made by the government to "support" Black men was the army, otherwise they just kick them out and wait for them to walk back in.

When the phone rang again, Weesie picked up the receiver and said, "We'll write you, Junior. We'll write."

She turned to me after she hung up and asked in a voice that sounded like a Weesie I never want to hear again—desperate— "Please, baby girl. Please. You write so good. You're the writer of the family. Can you write your Uncle Junior for me? For us?"

I asked her, "Like a pen pal?" And her face turned into a question mark.

"Well, I'm not sure if he can write us back, but I'd like it so he can have some Redwood Court news and stories and love with him, especially now."

The holidays. This last one of the century will be the second one without Teeta, and it still hasn't found its own rhythm. Back then, we were all together—from so many branches of the family tree—like Teeta was the center star we orbited. I guess we all thought it was Weesie, and Teeta was the bonus—or maybe it was the gravitational pull of the two of them, a binary star formation, like how I learned in science class.

One afternoon, I came in after the early sun had set and pulled out my favorite stationery. I tried to imagine what it would be like in there—was it like on TV? Orange suits, gray walls, lots of time sitting around waiting. Bad food. When we started writing our pen pals in school, our teacher told us to feel free to describe the world where we were and to ask a lot of questions—"That way, when our pen pal sat at her desk to write back, it will be exactly like she's writing to you, because she is."

"Dear Uncle Junior," I started. "Remember when Christmas for us started the day after Thanksgiving? You'd help Teeta bring down the tree from the attic, and all the lights and ornaments. Me and Sissy would spend Black Friday untangling the tree lights, finding the best place for the ornaments to dangle on each bent limb. Teeta would pull the outside decorations from the back shed to go up around the front of the house—white strings of lights like icicles, red bows hung under the windows like 154 was wrapped up like a present."

I was supposed to be writing for the family, for Weesie, but I couldn't imagine what she'd really want to say. So I was just making a record of this last holiday of the twentieth century. To write that story, though, so that I could show him what had changed— so he could really see it—I had to tell the story of how this holiday felt off in more ways than one. I had to travel back in time.

"Y'all had started the trend. Dressing up the houses. Then Reggie got the icicle lights. Then Ruby. Remember when you turned on to our cul-de-sac, it felt like we were inside a Christmas tree? I loved it. I miss it, Uncle Junior. Weesie said this year she won't fussing with the big tree."

When Thanksgiving came and went and no one went to the attic or to the back shed, we all sat around waiting for the next instructions. We woulda been moving all the furniture in her no-sit living room, opening the curtains so the tree could be seen from the road. Last year it was the first Christmas after Teeta and I guess we all tried to hold everything together like it was the same, just him missing. This year, Weesie got one of those baby trees like you find in Eckerd's drug store that comes set with lights and ornaments already on them. I was cheated of the ritual of dressing the tree with generations of ornaments, wrapping the lights 'round and 'round, all the way to the top.

"There won't no angel for you to put atop the tree, even if you were here."

I imagined that to be consolation.

"What was your favorite part of the holidays? My very favorite part, and what I know I will miss this year because of the little tree that's on a side table, is that when we'd finally finish our thousand trips to the mall and the drugstore for tape and wrapping paper, and you know we'd have to go back to Belk's, White's, Rich's, and so on, begging for more gift boxes 'cause Weesie was gonna split a pack of socks three ways between you, Daddy, and Teeta, but the clerk won't gonna give us more than one box— when we finally finished that dance and it was the last few days before all the commotion, I loved to go into the living room, turn the tree lights on singing mode, and lay under it like I was somebody's present and listen to the eight bars of 'Silent Night' play over and over."

One of the years, Weesie came looking for me, then woke the whole house up thinking I was snatched in the middle of the night. Uncle Junior was the one who found me sleeping in the living room under the tree. This year, we didn't move any furniture. There were no outside lights. Sitting in the chair next to the tree, I imagined lights blinking, and music playing. All is calm. All is bright.

"Uncle Junior, I know we get older and everybody says things like 'things change when people die,' but sometimes I wish we hadn't lost this part of the before times, with Teeta. I know you're not dead either, but this last time they dragged you back there, Weesie took it hard. The DSS lady came to see what was the commotion and gave Weesie a warning, saying you won't 'sposed to be there, 'cause Cedric was living there now. We all stressed out 'cause we thought Weesie was gonna lose the check, which she extra needed on account of the second mortgage and all. As soon as they packed you in the back of that police car and you rode past that stop sign, Weesie just whispered, 'My baby,' and sat for a while at the kitchen island. We all thought it was messed up they came for you on Thanksgiving. Daddy said it was probably because they knew you'd be there. That we'd all be there."

What else to say except that this Christmas season is weird? Daddy saying it gone get worse. His words. When they came to get Uncle Junior we sat there in shock, food still piled up on our plates, and it seemed the thing that jolted us back to life was Daddy's beeper going off. He jumped up and went off to work. He told us later that part of the thing, about his beeper going off when he was 'sposed to be on break, was that everyone was scared of this Y2K thing taking place in a couple of days. Mama calling it the apocalypse. Daddy was on call 24/7 until January second to see if the world was really gonna end. Mama says, "Of course it is. Been ready for Jesus." Riding with her one day I heard on the Christian radio station that we should prepare now and give our hearts to Him. That's all Mama saying, especially when Junior went back in and she compared it to the Rapture.

"Some of us were left behind," Mama said, shaking her head and spreading her arms out at us. Weesie got more upset.

"A damn shame how they do us," Weesie started. "I don't have Teeta; least I could have was all my babies with me."

I folded up some of my stationery to send along with my letter. I tell him to use it case he can't get his own paper to write back.

"Maybe you could write us all back, that would be a nice present for Weesie," I write. I was debating what else to say in the letter, but I thought, if I was away from my family during the holiday season, I'd want to know everything. "Yesterday we went to Penny's to start this year's shopping. I asked to go to B. Dalton bookstore so I could get some stationery for this letter then we got caught up in KB Toys for Destiny, then we went to Dillard's because Weesie needed her perfume—'Red Doh'—did you laugh like me when I write it how she says it? Dillard's the only place that carries it, but you know it's on the other side of the whole mall, and so we dragged all the presents she charged on her department store cards across the peach tile floor, and I tried to tell Weesie we should come back another day 'cause it was getting late."

As soon as we got in Dillard's, the store gate started to come down partway. All these years and she still ignores the very obvious signs. We all been shopping with Weesie enough to know that that means the mall is about to close. Gather your things. Head straight to your car. She says the Red Door perfume counter is right here. Says, "We'll be fine." We had to find a clerk, then wait for her card to process, and as the clerk was pulling out the receipts we looked up and the gate was all the way down.

The lights went off for a minute. Not just a flicker warning like at the skating ring, when you know it is nearing the end of the last song for the night. In the darkness, someone yelled, "It's Y2K!"

We all thought it. Won't admit it now that the lights came back on. We went to the gate to see if the security guard would let us out so we could walk the shorter route to the car through the inside of the mall. He didn't. So me and Weesie had to exit where we were, through the Dillard's parking lot, and start our walk all the way around the perimeter of the mall at night.

"My feet and hands hurt just telling you about it now, Uncle Junior. I was holding Destiny's Tickle Me Elmo, which felt like it was starting to weigh fifty pounds. Weesie was dragging her feet more and more. You know how she get when she in her element. Forget to eat. I counted the hours since we ate some leftovers for lunch. Or at least, I ate. She had a sweet potato and a cold breakfast sausage while standing near the stove. Too many hours had passed. Her sugar was dragging her feet, and probably about to drop more. I asked her to hurry up in case someone try to come up to us and cause trouble since we were just an old lady and a high schooler with presents for Christmas. Was Weesie always like this, excited for Christmas? Who went shopping with her all hours of the night before Sissy, then me?"

I was stuck dragging a whole day's worth of Christmas shopping up and around the mall. I tried to walk faster to find the car, and every few steps I turned around to make sure Weesie was OK. Still moving her feet. Around the corner there were still way more cars than I expected to see, so I missed Weesie's car at first. When I turned back to her she was swaying like a weed grass and I heard her call out, "Teeta." I walked back to try and hold all the presents and hold her arm, too. She was clammy and wet like you get when you have too many layers on and you take one off, but it's still cold outside. She looked at me but she didn't. It was like she was alert and out of it at the same time. I go, "Teeta?" to make sure I heard her right and she nods, "By the car."

I know it can't be Teeta out there, really, but I look anyways. There *was* a shadow figure near our car, and it was the shadow figure walking toward it that made me realize it was Weesie's car. When we got to the car, it was gone.

"If I tell you something, Uncle Junior, you promise not to tell anyone? Even when you get out? Weesie sat in the car and didn't move. Then she got out of the car and walked around to my side, leaning on the car the whole way like how Ms. Jackson still do. I rolled my window down. Her eyes were half open like she was sleepwalking. She handed me the keys, and I just looked at her like she was the ghost. Weesie said, 'I need you to get us home before my sugar bottom out,' and she leaned against the car. I hopped out the car so fast and pushed her in, put a seatbelt on her and got behind the wheel. Did you know that whenever we left Grandma Annie's house in Charleston and drove back to Columbia, she always prayed for traveling mercies and drew the sign of the cross, marking her forehead, chest, shoulder, shoulder? Father, Son, Holy Ghost. I did just that and started Weesie's car."

Somehow we got home safe, and I ran inside and brought out some orange juice for Weesie to come out from under the sugar crash. I promised I wouldn't tell anyone that she let me drive the car home, but then in the next breath she asked me to write a letter to Uncle Junior, so here I am. She probably expected me to say it. To tell the story.

"Uncle Junior, we love you and miss you, and we're saving up for a long collect call on Christmas Day. Weesie says if you call, we'll accept it. We'll all be there."

First Blood

I n my family, outside of Daddy going all the way to Korea, I'm
going to be the first of us to get to fly on a plane. Well, me and
Weesie. I am scared and excited all at once: it's hard to think that
something as light as air can hold a whole plane with all of us and
our things on it. All I see when I think about our journey is that
Columbia-bound flight a few years ago, coming in to land on a
clear and sunny day and then the news said, out of nowhere a
crosswind came and swatted the whole plane and everyone on it
out of the sky. By the time the news crew got there, what was left
of it was metal stripped like pieces of spaghetti on the runway.
Teeta had prayed for the lost souls when we all read the front-
page news story.

　　To try to make me feel better when I bring it up in preparation
for my flight, Daddy says matter-of-factly that the number of
people who die in plane crashes is significantly lower than the

number of folks who die in car crashes, and so all those years we drove to Florida were more dangerous than this "quick trip" Weesie and I were going to take.

Why didn't we ever fly? Daddy says he likes the feeling of the road beneath the car tires more than sky. It doesn't make me feel any better about the safety of the flying vs. driving when, at the boarding gate, Daddy, who had come back to see us off, gets up from the row of seats and goes to a kiosk. He's reading hard, because I saw his finger go along in a line across the screen before he starts to press buttons. I tell Weesie I'll be right back so we could get to our seats. I want to see what Daddy is doing. He is pulling his army-fatigue-print wallet out of his pocket when I walk up and see *Whole Life Insurance* on the screen. He jumps when I call out to him to ask what this is, and he goes, "Just in case, I guess." In case of what? "Y'all don't come back," he says. I don't know much, but I know that it feels weird to think you could just go up to a screen like a gumball machine and get insurance on just anybody's whole life like you're expecting a loss, and we're just supposed to hop on the plane like we believe nothing will go wrong.

I'm sure all those folks who were returning home or going to see their loved ones were celebrating a safe flight, runway in their view, and then just like that, gone. I don't want to go like that when my time comes. We don't get a choice, I know, but if I could choose, I guess I'd like an expected departure, maybe like Teeta, rather than an unexpected one, like Aunt Olive: going to teach class like any other day and then—gone. I think Weesie believes she'll live forever; she doesn't worry about this—the dangers, the sudden disappearance if we fall out of the sky or what. Instead, I look back from the life insurance vending machine and see Weesie has disappeared from where I left her. I find her at one of the newsstands, at the register getting a ham sandwich and ginger ale, without our bags. Daddy comes over to pay for the sandwich and I go to the bags. This'll be a great trip, already I can feel it. By now we only have a few more minutes left, and Daddy is just sitting, looking at us, not saying much. When I ask, "What?" He says he was "just looking at his baby girl, going on her first flight." I remind him I'm fifteen, in the ninth grade now. "Big girl," he chuckles.

Weesie chimes in that this is her first flight, too. "I was waiting for me and Teeta to be able to travel together in retirement, but we never made it," she says. Daddy shakes his head.

As me and Weesie are finally boarding for the flight, I look back from the gate after the desk woman tears off a piece of my ticket and wave at Daddy. He is holding his right hand up like he is about to wave and then forms his hand into the Star Trek gesture and smiles. I am the only one in the family besides him that can split my fingers in the middle without pushing them with my second hand. I raise my own hand and salute: "Live long and prosper." I turn and follow Weesie to our seats.

Mostly I am cool about it all, until I see we are seated literally on the wings of the plane. Out the window, you can see the engines and their vortex roar gearing up for the journey. I tell Weesie maybe we should ask someone to let us switch seats. She smiles, shakes her head, and says she actually asked for these seats.

"Teeta taught me that all that flying he had to do, you know, even in the cargo planes with no seats, the safest and smoothest ride was over the wings."

He was telling her how to let go of her fear of the sky, and now it is like he was telling me, too. I sit down and buckle my seatbelt, pulling the strap so tight across my lap that it is hard to breathe.

I can't help but think of Grandma Annie standing on the front porch on Sycamore Avenue as we were strapping into our car to head back up the road from Charleston to Columbia. Her hand drawing crosses. Her lips saying the Lord's Prayer. Weesie's eyes are closed, preparing for a nap and not prayer, because her hands aren't clasped, so I ask her if she could pray for mercy travels. She smiles. "Traveling mercies?" I shrugged. We hold hands and I whisper the Lord's Prayer, and at the crescendo, the part that goes, "For thine is the kingdom and power and glory forever and ever, amen," the engines kick into gear and I feel the ground push away from us. We are in the sky.

Weesie keeps looking over me and out the window, and I keep looking away from the window and eventually ask if she wants to switch seats. When the flight attendant announces that we are over Georgia, Weesie waves and I see in her a little girl, younger than me. Outside the window, farmland parcels cut the land like a patchwork quilt. I don't exactly know what I am looking for— like you'd be able to see the conditions under which the plane might fall from the sky—but I just keep thinking of Grandma Annie's night watches, how she'd say if you were quiet enough, you'll get the Word to you—like it would appear out of nowhere, like a fax just starts spitting out pages and pages of information. Like I'd look out the window at the sky and the ground and the heads of the clouds and then it would be revealed to me what is to become of us.

The stewardess is by the row in front of us when, unannounced, the plane drops from under our seats and feels like it is going down the steep hill of a roller coaster (the worst part, if you ask me, and I like roller coasters). I look out the window: nothing. I look at the stewardess and even she seems unsettled, gripping the sides of the serving cart.

"We gone be alright?" Weesie asks what we all must have been thinking. Folks are asking for napkins because their drinks have spilled. The stewardess nods, swallows, and just asks us: "Peanuts or pretzels?" I choose peanuts. And then: "What would you like to drink?" I ask for a Pepsi, and Weesie gets ice for the ginger ale she bought at the gate. I look out the window again and the atmosphere is turning dark, a storm, must be. The plane drops again and then rumbles like cars do when they get too close to the side of the road. On the speaker the captain says, "Folks, we're experiencing some weather. Hang tight. We'll be at your destination shortly."

Weesie looks at me and grabs my hand. I squeeze. You can hear the short gasps of air from other passengers—they must be thinking of that metal spaghetti on the runway, too.

I THOUGHT COLUMBIA WAS HOT AND HUMID, LIKE WALKING through soup, and you think you as a Columbian suffer alone in this, until you exit the refrigerator-cold air of the airport at Tampa into the steamer. It is so thick I want to push it out of our faces like a curtain.

Cousin Daisy pulls up right where she told us to meet her. She jumps out of the car to hug and kiss, linger, ask about the flight, and—still shell-shocked—we just say there was some "weather." Cousin Daisy nods as if she knows, licks her finger and holds it up like she had been struck by an idea.

"Yeah, the gulf's been churning and acting up a bit. Might be storms the whole time you're here."

Cousin Daisy turns around and knocks on the passenger window.

"Why aren't they bags in the car by now, Donnell? Come on,

they won't let us stay in the pickup lane forever." She turns back to us, rolling her eyes after Donnell. "Teenagers. Can't get them to do anything these days."

But I don't want to seem helpless and offer that I can carry our bags. I had even lifted them into the overhead compartment on the plane, so I start to move to grab them lest Weesie agree with Cousin Daisy. Cousin Daisy swats at my hand like she's my grandma. I check to see if Weesie sees it. She does. She doesn't save me.

"I'm trying to raise him up right," she says, squinting at me, "I guess you, too. If a man is around, let him do it."

Even though it runs counter to what Daddy has been teaching me ("Don't need to rely on a man for anything when you're as smart and strong as you are"), I push the luggage towards Donnell and say thanks under my breath. Weesie climbs into the front seat and me and Donnell are in the back, acting like strangers. We practically are, though; not sure if we are even really blood related.

When Cousin Daisy came back to Columbia, I finally decided it was time to call Donnell. She gave me his number, and when I called, I asked him if he had America Online or AIM Instant Message. He said no and said Cousin Daisy didn't trust the wide web technology enough to bring it into the house. How did you do homework? I asked. At the library or a friend's. He gave me his friend's AIM, but I only connected maybe five times total; every other time it was just Brian, always yelling in all caps: DONNELL'S NOT HERE WUZ UP W U? So I just logged off.

In reality I don't even know if me and Donnell like each other or would get along, and yet here I am on my spring break in another part of the world. If I think about it, it isn't much different from when Mama and her best friend Kaye threw me and Shelly into a room 'cause we were fighting, and they ordered us to fight it out until we made up. It basically worked—we used that time to determine that we didn't need to be friends just 'cause our moms were, and as long as we didn't fight, we didn't have to pretend to like each other.

So here I am in the back seat in Tampa next to Donnell, wondering if it's just because me and Donnell are "blood" that we have to be friendly. I have a whole week to work it out. Already it is off to a weird start, though; instead of talking to Donnell, I start clearing the fog from the window so you can see Tampa passing by. Something Sissy woulda done to me. I understand it now. It is easier than trying to think of what to say to someone you don't barely know. He is pressing buttons on his Walkman two at a time, so I know he isn't even listening to anything either. Just messing.

From the front two seats Cousin Daisy and Weesie discuss what we will be up to for the week. I have already been to Busch Gardens and Tampa Bay years ago so I don't need that. Cousin Daisy wants to show Weesie the family plot where other Boltons made their final resting place, and her childhood home, and of course, shopping, etc.

"What about me?" I ask. Cousin Daisy is too short and her rearview mirror angled too low for me to catch her eyes like I could catch Daddy's when he'd be driving and trying to tell me something.

"Oh," Daisy says, almost annoyed at the thought of me asking her something directly. "Well, Mika, Donny's in school this week, so you'll have to hang with us old ladies until he gets off the bus."

Only then do I start to process what that means—how no one,

not even Donnell when I did catch him on Brian's AIM, told me all this.

Weesie accepts the invitation for me. "Oh, Mika's used to it, hanging with us old folks. She was stitched to Teeta's right side before he left us. I know I'm a sad replacement but we starting to get along good enough, the two of us, ain't we, Mika?" Weesie turns and winks. That is mostly true. It was rocky at first, transitioning to a world without Teeta. Me and Weesie just like different things—Teeta enjoyed sitting with me in silence, the soft hum of his black-and-white television in the background. When it was time to be social, he prepared me: "Let's go for a ride," he'd say, and we would ride through town stopping at the lumber yard to catch up with the lumber millers, stopping by Walmart for a Diet Coke and a twenty-five-cent pack of gum just to get in Alexa's checkout line to say hello and laugh and ask about the other James, and then maybe swing by Deacon Jackson's house for a cigarette, coffee, and war and church stories while I picked pecans by the shirt full in the backyard.

Weesie shopped. I liked her shopping at Christmas. Of course, I'd like her regular seasons shopping better if it was for me, though most times it wasn't. Then it was the phone. Weesie would get to gossiping on the phone or would stay way too long at Essie's house, so long I started to count the beads on each strand of the divider between the kitchen and the living room. 'Cause we'd be in the kitchen, I knew it would be a long stay. With Teeta, he always sat outside on the porch drinking whatever the host offered, and when that one drink was finished, I knew it was time to go. Perfect timing.

Things started to shift between us, though, one day when Weesie woke me up to grits, sausage, and eggs warming on the stovetop. She asked me what I wanted to do with the day and, never before having been presented with such possibilities by Weesie, I shrugged. She offered her usual: Lexington Flea Market?

"I guess, since it's gonna be just us chickens, we could explore more together," she said.

It is just us chickens for spring break, so Weesie thought to surprise me with this trip, to see our new cousins and for her to connect with more family or just folks like her. I'd find something to keep me company, I always do, but I didn't bring my journal and now I wish I had—I needed something during these long days without at least Donnell as a buffer.

The first full day, Weesie and Daisy get up and go for a walk. Donnell has to take the bus before daylight to his school across town, so he is gone before I even open my eyes. It must be a grandma thing, leaving breakfast in the pan for you before you wake up. I get up and go into the kitchen to find grits, cold and stuck to the bottom of the pot, and scrambled eggs, and a sausage link. Enough for one person so it must be mine. It is good enough; could have used some more salt, but I eat it and think about what to do with myself this week. I brought the America Online CD that Daddy said to take and see if I can get Donnell online with me. It has lots of free hours loaded into the CD so if I can just set it up, we'll be good. I thought at least I might tinker with that while Donnell was at school, and I move to see the back of the CPU just like Daddy taught me. They do have a phone cord receiver so that meant they had a modem. I keep on and go to the setup window but it asks for a credit card number. Even though it says it's free. I abort the operation and doodle on the Paint program for a bit. Then I look over and see an *Encyclopedia Britannica* set and contemplate opening one—that's how bored I am, and it's just minutes after a late breakfast. Is this getting older? Growing out of the things you love, losing those you love, and trying to find something to occupy the minutes as they pass?

When I find some paper scraps I decide on writing Uncle Junior again, tell him about our plane ride, or at least plan what I'm gonna say this time so I don't have to mess up my stationery with crossing out words, and that way I'll have a copy—to know what I said the next time I write.

On the air mattress in Donnell's room with the encyclopedia as my desk, I feel a—a something down there near my stomach, and then it feels like you feel when you have to use the bathroom. I don't have to go, so maybe whatever sausage links Daisy made didn't agree with my stomach. I sit up to see if it will make me more comfortable, but that doesn't work as well as I had hoped. The feeling down there is dull, a constant call to heed the feeling, but not painful. Like someone had been pressing their palm right under my belly button and not letting up. I have never felt this before, a fullness, a pressure, but it feels like what Mama described I might feel when I'd finally get my first blood.

It had taken long enough. I had started to wonder if I even had any blood to get. Jenna told me she got hers when we were in fourth grade; she talked about carrying maxi pads like Mama and Sissy. I went home and told Mama and she looked at me and said my chest was too flat to worry about it yet, and I wondered what the chest had to do with catching blood in my panties, but that was all she said then. Jenna had said at the time she had to stuff her panties with what seemed like a wad of toilet paper, and that her mama bought her a training bra to wear under her shirt. The closest I got to that was some sports bras when Weesie saw me running up and down Redwood Court and Cedric was standing on the curb looking at me. I had associated getting your blood

with boys and more things to wear on your body but no one had
told me how it would feel as it was coming or how it would feel
when it came.

When Martina wore white gym shorts to freshman gym
class, though, during volleyball and after Labor Day, I knew something was going to happen. It had to. She fell trying to jump-serve
the ball like Coach had taught us and landed on her butt. The
girls in the class only tolerated Martina, so we only pretended to
move in to see if she was alright after she didn't spring back up
and Coach walked toward her with a look of concern. Missy gave
her an arm, and like synchronized swimmers having come close
in unison, we moved back in unison when we saw the brown on
her shorts, then the red leaking down her leg. Gloria being Gloria, though, ran to the locker room and came back with a maxi
pad.

At first I loved the idea that I didn't have to carry a stash of
cotton liners with me everywhere I went, but I just turned fifteen,
and everyone had their blood except me.

When I asked Mama, she said I should be lucky to live so long
without the pain. Whenever her blood came, she'd lock herself in
the bedroom for two days with the light off, only asking us to
bring her Goody Powders and sweet tea to wash them down.

At Cousin Daisy's house I go to the encyclopedia to see what
they say. Daddy taught me that if I didn't know something there
was always books, and now the internet, to give me the answer. I
just have to look. That's how he feels OK about not finishing college but being so good at fixing things. Books. I look up "men-
struation" because I know the technical term. Coach had said it
that day. I know not to look up "blood."

It isn't very helpful. Something about a cycle and an egg.

Nothing about stomach pressure or how long you might have between this symptom and the blood that followed. I don't know if I'll make it home to Columbia before I have to worry about Donnell seeing me with blood running down my legs.

When Donnell gets off the bus, we go for a walk around the neighborhood and I ask to meet Brian, wonder if he'll yell in real life, too. Donnell asks if I like Brian—like, do I want him to be my boyfriend and that's why I want to go to his house—and I say no, just to match a face with his AIM, but really I want to use his America Online to see what to do in case it is my blood coming now.

At Brian's, I wave and say hello and smile, because of course he looks like someone who would try to talk cool on AIM but has bottle-cap glasses and sounds like his nose is stuffed with tissue when he tries to speak his infamous line, "Waz up with you?"

I say, "Nothing, really, nice to meet you," and ask if I can check my email so I can tell my dad I made it OK. Brian says yeh sure whatever; Donnell raises his eyebrows but they go into the family room to play video games and eat whatever snacks Brian's mom set out.

On America Online I decide on another approach and use the search function and type "first blood," and the results that come back include links to a film with Rambo, who I know from some of the films Daddy watches, but nothing related to the female body, which would be relevant to me. I try again with the word Coach had used to see if there would be any information about what to do, what to expect: when I lean forward to try to take up space in front of the screen so no one can see what I'm looking up, my breasts brush the edge of the table, and they're sore—as if they only just then came into existence—and the hair on my arms tingles. I try to comfort myself by cupping my chest. It works a little. Just then I see *sore breasts* are a symptom, as well as *abdominal or pelvic cramping.*

Back home, Sissy has started to use tampons. Mama said something like only fast girls use tampons, and Sissy shrugged her shoulders. Gloria told me her mama said that, too, that's why she has maxi pads, but she wished she didn't have to use them. Sissy told Mama maxi pads made her walk like a cowboy wearing a diaper, and Kotex could fit in her pocket when she had to go to the bathroom—you could hide it better. I figure if my blood is coming while I'm in Tampa with Donnell, I need that kind. I look up "tampons" next.

The text says, *Designed to be inserted into the vagina,* and that freaks me out, but, armed with this information, I suppose I'll be somewhat ready should the time come. I clear the internet history before logging out of the online session and join the boys playing video games.

THE NEXT MORNING IT'S SILENT IN THE HOUSE AGAIN. THERE'S a note from Weesie to telling me to eat breakfast and get ready by 9:00 so I can go to the mall when they return from their walk. It is 8:30, and my legs just don't move like they did yesterday, I can't say why. It isn't because I'm sleepy, because I've stayed up later than how late me and Donnell stayed up last night. We watched the late shows and he told me about his girlfriend, and I wondered if Roger would ever see me in that way—to be liked, to be had—and I asked Donnell if he thought I had any qualities that guys like him might want in a girlfriend. Donnell looked at me in the spotlight of the TV in the otherwise dark room. He cocked his head to one side. Was he trying to see in the TV-lit room or was he trying to find the words to answer my question? In the eternity in between, I regretted having asked my new cousin to look at me that way at all, but who else did I have to ask? Donnell made a noise.

"What?" I asked.

He said, "I mean. You have a nice smile. Long hair."

I can't help but touch my hair anytime someone mentions it. A nervous response to it always being one of the nice things folks would say about me. "Your hair is so pretty and long. Jet black." Nothing else. It wasn't hair that made girlfriend material, or else why wasn't I made one? Fuck this. I changed subjects and asked what colleges he was applying to and he shrugged. "Staying close to home, so somewhere around here." He waved his hand in the shadow of the TV switching to commercial break and it disappeared.

I can't hear any compliment if there is one, because I just know that even in a pretend situation, a boy has a hard time tracking a compliment to a reason to like me like a girlfriend. I have guy friends at school. They pick me first-ish for group work because I am smart. When I was younger, I played rougher than all the girls and had a smart mouth, so they picked me first-ish for dodgeball, too. Sometimes, though, I was a smart-ass, and Mama always warned me about that. Right before spring break, even my geography teacher must have exhausted all his energy trying to bend me into submission—was that it? My refusal to do the yes sir, no sir dance—and thought that attempting to embarrass me in class, even if it was in front of Roger, wasn't going to get the response he sought.

"Mika, are you done with your journal prompt?" Ironically, we were writing a pros/cons defense of whether the Confederate flag should stay on top of the statehouse in light of the NAACP boycott. Of course, no. But my argument was you couldn't even really see it, so taking it down wouldn't stop the hate.

"Yes," I said. Maybe someone in the room had gasped. He walked around with a pointing stick, to lengthen his arms. I had snickered one day with Gloria that he had to use that stick 'cause look how short his arms were! But also, he tapped his pointing stick on desks to emphasize a point, to wake someone up, to attempt to intimidate. He walked over to me with the stick raised, and I thought about what level of contact it would make with my desk. I was already irritated in general—everything made me feel like I was going to explode if someone even looked at me the wrong way, and the night before, I'd cried uncontrollably watching the nature channel when the newborn fawn got snatched by a wolf. He tapped the desk, attention style.

"Yes, what?" Here he goes. It's the same script, different cast. I exhale loudly. Someone snickers.

"Yes, I'm finished writing why I think it's dumb for us to even write about the Confederate flag being on the statehouse or not, because white people are going to hate Black people either way and don't need a flag." I looked him straight in the eyes. You could tell he didn't expect "all that mouth," Weesie would say. He stepped back a few steps and contemplated if he was to go another round with me or not, but now my ears were burning. He took a different route.

"Seems like we have an El Presidenté in the room; someone who thinks this is their country to run." He smacked the pointer stick on the blackboard. "This is my country! Some of y'all want to overturn my rulings. I'll see you at detention, El Presidenté."

I almost said "Yes" again but didn't want to know how far he might take his smacking of the pointer stick, and I knew when I had taken my stubbornness too far.

At the mall in Tampa, Cousin Daisy and Weesie peel off to Macy's and I'm walking like I have cement in my shoes. Used to me clipping at her heels, Weesie turns around and comes back with a look of concern. Before she says anything, I say I'm alright but feeling icky, and she lifts the back of her hand to my forehead for a spell and looks up to the mall skylights to feel the temperature of my head better. She moves to my neck, and, to my embarrassment, down the neck of my shirt to feel my chest. Says I don't feel warm to her but to go to Eckerd's and get a ginger ale and they'll meet me at the food court in a bit.

Here's how you can tell you're at the Black mall: all the things teenagers like me would want (candy, soda, snacks) are at the back of the store and not just off to the right of the exit or near the checkout. On my way back to the refrigerated section I glance up at the security cameras and stick my tongue out. My hand barely touches a ginger ale before an employee pops down the aisle pretending to rearrange the sodas by turning them around and around until all of the labels are facing out. I pull out the ginger ale and feel eyes on me. I put it back in the Pepsi slot. The hands two doors down go back to spinning bottles. I pull out a Pepsi and feel eyes again. I put it back in front of Orange Crush. They don't know that, sick or not, I can play this game all day— and I would have, but then I feel something hot *down there*. I put the ginger ale back and start to walk to the front.

You know I don't have anything that's not mine or not purchased, but the bottle spinner is now done spinning the bottles and is following me. Daddy always rolled his eyes whenever we felt The Watch happening. One day in Walmart he turned around in the middle of the hardware section and said, "Can *I* help *you?*" and the employee was so startled that they jumped back and shook their head and walked away. I don't have time for games because my panties are getting hotter and I don't know what's going on but I need a bathroom to investigate. As the glass exit approaches, I walk slower through the metal detector so that no one will suspect anything because I'm leaving the store not having bought anything despite how much time I spent in the back section. Would you believe I even consider lifting my hands to show they are empty? Dead Prez calls this "the police state." Uncle Junior plays them nonstop since he made it out. One day I asked him what "police state" meant, and what he described is exactly how I feel in this Eckerds. *'Cause the world is controlled by the white male . . . and the women don't never get respected.* To signal the escape, I ask the clerk where the bathroom is, even though I know where it is, but this is the Black tax; all the extra labor, all the extra steps. The cashier mumbles something inaudible, and it doesn't matter. I am gone.

The bathroom stalls feel smaller than any normal bathroom stall, and that's prolly 'cause I am growing hotter each second that passes. All of a sudden there are too many clothes on my body and my instincts start to kick in and somehow I go from investigating what is happening *down there* to fighting not peeing on myself. The damn shirt tucked in my jeans. The damn belt. The jeans that peel down my thighs like opening a banana. I slide my hands between my legs with the same intentionality of slipping between couch cushions looking for change when the ice cream truck music makes its way through the open windows on Forestwood Drive. My hands slide out wet, smell like iron. When I finish using the bathroom the bowl is brown and all I did was pee. I slide everything up quickly and flush and hope that there is something in those metal cannisters hung on the walls with a twenty-five-cent sign. Once, when I used to have to go into the bathroom because Weesie had to go to the bathroom, I had asked her what these were, and Weesie called it sanitary pads and said if you put a quarter in you can get one. I don't have a quarter, 'cause I didn't buy any ginger ale from Eckerds—just the three twenty-dollar bills Daddy gave me for the week. So I roll toilet paper as thick as I think a maxi pad is and put it in the bottom of my panties. What I hate more about all this, more than bleeding through my pants like Martina, is that now I have to go back to Eckerd's and I have to buy something despite the fact that everyone probably thought I ran out with something I didn't pay for.

I finally get the ginger ale and choose the smallest pack of Kotex—the brand that says *compact* and *flushable* on the package, because they look small enough to stick in my pocket, and if I untuck my shirt I can make it back to Cousin Daisy's house without anyone noticing. At the food court I'm trying to decipher the folded instructions, trying to figure out how the angles work, when they walk up and I say I really need to go home and lay down. I put the back of my hand to my forehead for emphasis. They agree—only because the house is on the way to the mall on the other side of town—and I'm relieved, because I can figure this out on my own.

In Cousin Daisy's bathroom I feel a way about putting my foot on the bathtub ledge like I was doing a stretch in gym class, but there's no other way to get the right angle to see what's supposed to happen next. The applicator cardboard is waxy and slippery in my hand, and I have to balance with it in one hand and the diagram in the other. It hurt so much down there the applicator feels like rose bush thorns. I push and squeal. Thank God no one is home. When I pull the applicator out, my hands are bloody; the applicator looks like those thick peppermint sticks. It's all disgusting. I quickly throw everything in the toilet and flush. The instructions say to do this every four hours or risk *death*, so I start the countdown to the next time. Luckily there's enough to get me back to Columbia, so the rest of the days, every four hours I slip into the bathroom, do the tub-side leg lift, and lunge and quick flush. Donnell jokes and says I need to stop drinking so much water since I need to run to the toilet so much. Thank God he doesn't know I'm bleeding down there. No one does. Or else there'd probably be a bigger fuss. Sharper pains come; I breathe through each pulse. I am starting to put them into perspective: not any worse than when I fell off my bike and scraped my knees.

The last day in Tampa I wake up to my new routine. Donnell off to school, Cousin Daisy and Weesie walking. Breakfast on the stove and the note. We don't leave until late in the afternoon, so we still have time to hit a Friday Flea before we scoop Donnell from the bus stop and drive to the airport. Wiggling the applicator when it goes in makes it not feel like I'm scraping my insides all the way up now, so the whole thing doesn't feel as awkward anymore. This time when I flush, the water whirs, and the applicator starts to go down the drain but stops. Daddy taught me that if something got stuck you need to wait until you stop hearing water run before you start again, or else there won't be enough gravity to carry the bowl contents back down the drain, so I wait. The water shuts off and when I push the lever down, the water circles and circles and starts to rise. Panicking, I look around the room and under the cabinet and in the bathroom closet for a plunger. I find one and give it a go. The water has stopped rising, but the plunger just turns the water brown and the applicator is now floating in the bowl. Somehow, holding my breath makes fishing it out easier. I try to flush again, and the water thankfully drains out the bowl, but now it won't fill up. There is no winning this.

Weesie and Daisy return and I'm still in my pajamas and

haven't eaten breakfast, because I've lost track of time fooling around in the bathroom, and Weesie calls after me.

"Mika, you alright? You didn't want breakfast?"

"I'm alright, Weesie, still not feeling well," I say. Still true.

I hear them mumble something and hear someone scraping the bottom of the pot that probably had grits, hardened now— trying to make them resemble something more palatable, instead of the saucer plate they resemble when cold. What is there to do but continue with the day like nothing happened? We're about to leave; I'll be back in Columbia soon and can process this all in the comfort of my own room, in my own bed.

While getting dressed and packing up, Cousin Daisy cusses from the bathroom. She stomps into the kitchen and says she needs to call a plumber. On the phone, she raises her voice and says it's an emergency, because she has an old septic tank and she has to get her guests to the airport and it's her only toilet in the house so someone needs to come now or else the whole house might flood.

"Years ago, after the big hurricane ripped through here, we had so much water in the ground and around the systems that everyone's tanks backed up and it took me weeks to mop up all the poop out of the house. We had to change some walls because the stench soaked through the drywall," Cousin Daisy said, justifying her fussing to Weesie after she hung up the phone.

SOMEONE GOT THE MESSAGE AND CAME RIGHT AWAY. DAISY says it must be her tax dollars at work. Every *clink* the plumber makes, the pressure in my stomach increases. There'll be some mumbling, then more clinks. A grunt. Clinks. The plumber says there's a blockage and he needs better access to the pipes. Everyone is watching the clock, and each time the grandfather clock in the living room clicks, I feel it in my own gut like Uncle Junior's bass when I used to ride around town with him. How does sound move through your whole body? *Tick. Tick.*

Donnell walks in from school and stands in front of the bathroom threshold. "What's going on here?" he asks. The other night, we talked about how since his dad won't in the picture and Cousin Daisy was raising him, she keeps reminding him that he has to be the man of the house. He admitted under the TV spotlight that he didn't know what that always meant, but sometimes he thought it meant talking with a bit more bass in his voice and puffing out his chest. I giggled: "Like Tarzan?" and he laughed and said yeh, he guessed so. But it also meant acting like the authority over the residence whenever a handyman came in the house. "You'd be surprised how often guys try to take advantage of Grandmama, thinking she living by herself, but when I walk in, I see their attitudes change."

Cousin Daisy says that the toilet won't flushing so she had to call the plumber. The plumber lets out a low, guttural chuckle.

"It was a major blockage," he said. Donnell asks of what and the plumber strolls out into the living room holding the trash can, then dramatically places it in the middle of the small gathering space between the bathroom and the foyer. He looks around the room at Donnell, then Weesie, then Cousin Daisy, and locks eyes with me.

"Someone's been flushing Kotex down the toilet."

Weesie, quick-lipped as usual even though she had been silent for so much of this exchange, immediately calls out, "Mika, you got your first blood?"

All I think about is Martina's face that day in the gym, how fireball red her face turned when me and Gloria got so close we saw the river of blood down her thigh. If I was white, I'd be as red as the box of the Boston Baked Beans candy me and Sissy used to shake around the house when we were younger—Teeta's favorite candy, and so mine. But I'm Black and with my elders, and so shame manifests in no direct eye contact with anyone. Head down.

"Nothing to be shame of, baby," Weesie calls out. I look up, slightly comforted. "You just shoulda said something."

Cousin Daisy scoffs. "Yeh, we could have told you not to flush that stuff."

I try to explain to the room that the package says it's flushable. The plumber cuts me off, "But not the applicator, and especially not if you on septic, on property that's below sea level like this. Stuff ain't got no direction to go but back where it started."

How am I supposed to know the geography of this place?

Donnell looks back at me when Cousin Daisy takes the plumber outside to settle up and I know they Black, too, and my blood, but damn if it ain't feel like how I feel being watched in any store you go into as a Black teenager. I broke his grandmama's house. Our last hours together are spent trying to fix a mess I caused. I fidget with my gold hoop earrings, unsure of what else to do with my hands while I wait for Daisy to come back and throw us back into the mouth of the airport.

Weesie says again she wishes I had told her what was going on so she could help me, but it's too late now. I never want my mama, but I swear I miss her right at this moment. Then another pang—but this time, the ache of wishing I was home, my head in her lap, and her stroking her hands along the length of my hair. Then her hand rubbing my back, the heat of her touch radiating down my spine; how, even now that would make me feel like everything was going to be alright.

But, whew, to get back there, I have to get through the process of the air and the plane and the turbulence and all of that. But the way my stomach dropped when that plumber blamed all of this commotion on me and my blood was not unlike the way I felt when I thought we were about to fall out of the sky. It is a falling, though. Maybe a falling through—to a place I won't get back to no matter how small I make myself now, no matter how I plait my hair to look like those photos when I was a small girl in the days when Teeta still walked the earth. The closure I feel when Weesie says, "You're a woman now," in front of everyone like this feels not unlike the closure of understanding Teeta was *gone* gone when I walked into the funeral home for the wake.

Back at Redwood Court, Mama and Daddy come to pick me up. First words out of Mama's mouth, of course, are about my appearance. She cocks her head and just says I look different, must have been the Florida sun. I am exhausted from it all and drop my bags in the kitchen and tumble my way into the den and crumble into the corner of the couch.

Weesie announces, "Y'all, we ain't got a baby no more," and Mama stands up straight. Daddy, barely in the door behind her, grabs the corner of the countertop and I can feel the metal keys still in his hands scrape along the way. I suck my teeth.

She smiles. "Mika got her first blood while she was away and flooded the whole neighborhood by flushing all the Kotex down the commode!"

"Weesieeee," I whine. I look around the room, surprised and a little comforted by the fact that even with crossing over into supposed adulthood or whatever it is I'm supposed to be now, I can still be reduced to a whining mess back at home.

Work

You've had a friendship bracelet business since elementary school, so you know what work is. You had convinced your daddy to take you to Michael's craft store to buy the embroidery string, the safety pins, the bobbins to wrap the string around, and the clear plastic box to organize it all.

You could knot the string into intricate designs: the tornado, the V, rows of diamond-bodied fish, hearts, and rainbows. You watched your daddy build an invoice sheet for his computer business and so you built one for your business, too. Classmates/customers could custom design their friendship bracelets with the colors, and after a few days you would hand deliver the fresh wrist adornments during recess or lunch, and they would pay the seventy-five cents or two dollars, depending on what design they chose.

Eventually you had enough business to have one or two people knot the embroidery string into bracelets for you—your own employees—and so all you had to do was take the orders, give the orders, take the money, and deliver the product. Some weeks you made twelve to fifteen dollars, and after you paid your employees, you still had something like five or six dollars left over—enough to buy a Capri Sun and Cheetos for snacks, instead of the no-name-brand juice and cheese crackers. After your premium snack allotment, you decided to save the rest. You put your earnings in the seashell jewelry box you inherited after your aunt Olive died. Once, you almost had one hundred dollars tucked away in there. You didn't quite know what you wanted to do with all of that money then but were proud that you had it anyhow.

Uncle Junior stayed with y'all whenever he was out of jail for long stretches on account of Cedric, Weesie's foster boy, was sleeping in Uncle Junior's bed now, eating up Uncle Junior's sausage patties and salmon cakes and grits. Drinking Uncle Junior's ginger Chek soda. Your mama couldn't let Uncle Junior stay in the house too long either, because the Learning Funhouse Daycare was an in-house childcare operation, and the Department of Social Services loved to do unannounced visits, and if there was evidence that Uncle Junior was staying there with the six children—cousins, mostly—your mama could lose her license and they all could lose the house. Because you heard your parents argue about the cost of rent and why your mama needed to max out the six slots allotted for children instead of a more comfortable four.

The house was crowded, and on most days since he got back from jail, Uncle Junior slept on the floor of your room.

You watched Destiny for him because you loved them both. You taught her how to drink out of a straw and eat real food. You were there when she first learned to walk, unassisted by her toy vacuum cleaner for a walker.

Everyone had called you "the writer," because you always had your journals, were always asking for "the story" about something or were asking for a stamp to send someone a letter. You often thought about how lonely Uncle Junior must have been in that jail cell, all alone and no one from the outside seeing about him. Last time, you'd told him y'all would call after Christmas once enough was saved for a collect call, but it's summer and no one called since, so you wrote him again. Here's the new snippets of house gossip you had: you heard Cedric was making friends with the Newcastle Gangstahs, and had stopped working at Hardee's even though he came home with new things each week like he had a paycheck from somewhere. Y'all only found out he wasn't working at Hardee's because your daddy had stopped by Hardee's three times on three different occasions when Cedric said he was 'sposed to be working and he wasn't there. And yet he had in his room the nicest stereo with a five-CD disc changer.

Your hundred dollars went missing. You used to be able to keep your savings without problems but now that he was home, you thought it was Uncle Junior but couldn't prove it. You believed no one but you knew you had it, and so everyone's first question was: What you need to keep that kind of money for, Mika? Everyone doubted the success of your friendship bracelet business, your ability to save.

Daddy felt sorry for you in the way that he does and said he would help you replace it, so maybe don't make much of a fuss of it to everyone. It was hard to believe that Uncle Junior would go so far as to take from the only person who thought to still care about him in some way when he had been locked up, and hard for you to believe that he didn't understand that you used your nice stationery and Thurgood Marshall stamps so he could have a piece of home with him on the inside.

So, you made up your hundred-dollar deficit by babysitting on the weekends. You kept Malik and Ayanna from 10:00 A.M. until their parents came to get them at 6:00. You walked the tots through breakfast, lunch, and snack, just like you watched your mama do during the week when you were home on summer or school breaks, sad that you couldn't go to summer camp like your classmates or weeks-long sleepaway camp like on *Bug Juice*, the reality show about a sleepaway summer camp on the Disney Channel. Malik and Ayanna's moms paid you twenty-five dollars for the full day, and then Mama and Daddy both asked for five dollars per kid to replace the chicken nuggets, instant grits, and animal crackers and milk you used up. It was good, easy money.

Mr. Eliot, Sissy's program director at the Boys & Girls Club, had asked if you were looking for summer work one day when you accompanied her to the afterschool program. He noticed that you weren't restless like the other kids. Your focus on your social studies and English homework was "commendable," he said, raising his left eyebrow. You liked Mr. Eliot because he was tall like Daddy, but *he* had finished college and talked to you about Black history and Black literature and slavery in a way that Daddy never did, and of course none of your white teachers, not even the ones you liked.

He asked how old you were, and you said fifteen, and he asked if you ever worked before. You said yes. For your father's computer business, which was technically true though you never got compensated. Whenever Daddy was out of the house, customers called with their computer problems. Once, Jack Jones called to say his WordPerfect program was frozen and so you walked him through the process of finding and pressing CTRL + ALT + DEL, all three at the same time. You waited on the phone with him, listening to him breathing and calling out the commands while the computer restarted and auto recovery returned to him the flyer for the used Honda Civic he was trying to sell. Jack thanked you profusely and reported your good services to Daddy and soon enough you were his Software Troubleshooter.

Another time, Ms. White, who did Daddy's taxes, called to say her *Encyclopedia Britannica* program disc was swallowed by the computer, and you told her to get a paperclip and unfold the little piece of metal until it was one long stick. You didn't ask why she didn't have a paperclip—doesn't everyone have them?—but when she said she didn't have one, you thought quickly on your feet and asked if she had a cookie tin with sewing supplies. She laughed and asked how did you know? "Everyone has one," you said. You told her to get the longest sewing needle and use that. Go to the front of the computer tower and stick the needle in the tiny hole just beneath where the CD goes and push hard. Ms. White squealed when the computer tower relinquished the disc. You were now the Major Communications and Services Software and Hardware Troubleshooter, unofficially. Though one of Daddy's customers was so impressed that a little Black girl knew so much about computers and spoke so *articulately* about how to fix problems that you were featured on the local news segment about your knowledge—so that verified your title.

When you told Mr. Eliot this, and of course about your friendship-bracelet business and babysitting services, he first asked if you might keep his own son one Saturday or two. Then he asked for your résumé, said he might be able to help you find a *real* job—he raised his eyebrow again—to make some *real* money.

The little paperclip man in Microsoft Word had helped enough for you to draft a document that looked like the templates titled "Résumé." When you printed it and colored in the heart next to your name because you didn't have a color printer, you were proud, especially when Mr. Eliot smiled and pointed to it and said it was nice and to keep an eye out for a call from Tonya at Youth Workforce Development.

Sissy had seen you hand Mr. Eliot a piece of paper but didn't know about the arrangement. He was still smiling when he folded the hard-won résumé that you stayed up half the night to make into a small square and slipped it into his gym shorts pocket—the same pocket that had his whistles and keys and lanyard sticking out of it. Not to be defeated by his lack of care about the document he had asked you to prepare, you straightened your back when Sissy inquired and told her that Mr. Eliot had asked you for a résumé and would help you get a real job this summer.

YOU HADN'T FIGURED WHAT IT WOULD MEAN FOR EVERYONE else's life for you to have a real job, Monday through Friday, for six weeks over the summer, but here you were. When you told Daddy, he sighed. He now had to accommodate an early-morning drop-off and an afternoon pickup during the summer, when he thought he had a reprieve from normal school pickup. You told him the Department of Health and Environmental Control building was just across the parking lot from the State Archives building where you and Vanessa had gone to accept the regional and state awards for eighth-grade advanced history research papers. Vanessa's mom felt bad for you when you said you might not be able to attend to accept the award for best paper in the whole state of South Carolina because you didn't have anyone to take you and stay all day, even though it was a Saturday. There was a football game that day at the university. Those days, Daddy had to post up in his satellite hut, a small four-foot-by-four-foot room, to ensure that the broadcast went off without a hitch.

You never asked Mama to take you anywhere, and that weekend was her biweekly hair salon appointment—and it was time for her relaxer, and she could not, would not, miss it. So, it had been you and Vanessa, and Vanessa's mom. Daddy sent you with five dollars for lunch, but Vanessa's mom bought the eight-dollar sandwich and Coke and said congrats after you accepted the award.

The first few days of your real work were *real* boring. There was no other way for you to describe it when Daddy asked how it went. By Wednesday, you brought in your Discman, so at least you could listen to music while your supervisor shrugged and pretended to drum up real work for you to do. You were stationed in the water-control division where residents just outside of Columbia who had well-water sources had to bring in samples of water to make sure all of the chemicals weren't above the undrinkable amounts. You couldn't imagine there were people who didn't live with the same type of water you had—wasn't it, what, 2000 now?—but there still were, and a whole operation went along to make sure people's water was safe to drink.

You had many hours of idle moments waiting for someone to come in with a mason jar or Sprite bottle of cloudy water. You were instructed to put on latex gloves to handle the sample— a new pair each time—so as not to jeopardize the integrity of the test.

You put whatever container they brought the sample in into a gallon-sized Ziploc bag and waited for them to fill out the required intake paperwork. Everyone in the department was white, and it amazed you how many folks who may or may not have had safe drinking water reminded you of Weesie and Teeta, or any number of their friends.

When the older Black man who looked like he could have been Deacon Jackson's father shuffled to your desk, you brought out your "yes sir's" and "no sir's," and even, when you saw him struggling to negotiate the small text on the page, handed him a magnifying glass like what Teeta would have used for reading his Bible. The gentleman studied it and held it up close to his face like a monocle, so you shook your head, picked up the pen, and asked his name, address, how long had he been living at the residence with a well, etc., until the paperwork was filled out. You asked him to sign and he simply marked an X and, despite protocol, you found an empty bottle to transfer his sample from the 409 cleaning solution bottle he had brought it in, so that it would be accepted for processing.

The gentleman shook your gloved hand while he thanked you for your help. You had saved him from embarrassment, he said. You were much nicer than anyone in here had ever been to him after all these years. He said it loud enough for your supervisor to look up. The man who looked like he could have been Teeta, if Teeta had lived, smiled at you and tipped his hat on his way out.

You went home your first week of work feeling like maybe you'd made a difference, and despite the long lulls and the long lunch hours spent staring at court shows on a small television, you wondered why Daddy came home each day looking worn down.

He said because he doesn't have a "nice cushiony office job" like you.

The next week found you folded over a countertop with a mountain of labels and a barrel of empty test bottles. Your supervisor explained that because this was a work-to-learn environment for summer interns, every week would look different. You would spend this week affixing labels on ten thousand bottles for the known well-water users within a two-hour radius of Columbia. He chuckled when he said this should keep you busy, and you were so thankful you had your Mariah Carey CD and, even though you didn't care for it, Sissy's Tom Petty CD, and the Cranberries. You made do with what you had at the ready.

Because your grandfather and your grandmothers all at one point worked as cleaning people in big office buildings, and because many times you accompanied them, you smiled at the janitor who mopped the floor of the hallway outside your office every day after lunch. When Teeta retired, because he and Weesie still needed some money, he started cleaning a network of dialysis centers along Two Notch Road. You did anything Teeta did, back then in the before times when he was with y'all. Even waited in an empty dialysis room, pushing the reclining chairs back and upright, back and upright, back and upright, because what else was there for you to do? His shift started before the center closed, and you saw how the white nurses didn't look at him, nor did the patients. Once, there was a white nurse who saw Teeta walk in, and you carrying a broom behind him, and the dustpan, and out of his back pocket like a tail or wedding-dress train were the clear trash bags that he lined each receptacle with. The nurse rolled her eyes, even though Teeta said "Good evening," and she balled up whatever paper was next to her and looked at the other white nurse, who never even turned in your direction, and threw the ball of paper right at you both. It came and it came towards you like a bullet, and then it hit the floor. The nurse who didn't throw the paper said something about "missing the trash" and they both shrugged and went back to whatever it was they were not doing.

It took enough of these aggressions to teach you to acknowledge the invisible people.

When the janitor mopped his way by your bottle-label assembly line for the third time and scrubbed real hard, you looked up, nodded, and smiled like you were taught. He motioned for you to remove your headphones. You did. He asked what you were listening to, and that day you had sneaked out with Daddy's *The Best of the Spinners* and *The Best of the O'Jays* CDs. He called you "young gun" when he heard what you were listening to. He hadn't yet asked your name. One time, you heard your supervisor say he wished Tony didn't use so much water when he mopped the floors during the height of water-sample intake time, so you knew his name. You smiled when he said "young gun," and maybe you shrugged your shoulders, and you were careful to only walk on the area of the hallway he hadn't mopped yet when you walked to the bathroom, and you looked back at him so he could see your conscientiousness, and he was looking and you smiled again, and then you slinked into the bathroom.

The next day, Tony mopped by again. You didn't have to look at the clock to know it was 2:15 P.M. On time. This time your supervisor had ducked out for a cigarette break, so you were alone in the intake room when Tony stuck his head in and asked what you were up to. You told him summer work, trying to "make a dollar out of fifteen cents"—you said this knowing he would be impressed with your reference—and he went, "Tell me, sister, can you spare a dime?" And did a little jig while raising his voice. Just like the O'Jays. You laughed, thinking of Daddy. They both had goatees, though Tony's was more gray. He had a stomach that rolled over his belt and a vest that was a touch too small, and you couldn't help but think of Winnie-the-Pooh when you saw him, and wonder if he rested his arm on his belly after a good meal.

But who were you to judge? You still couldn't order clothes from Delia's or the juniors section of Belk, not since Teeta died and in the first months, everyone kept buying you chocolate and your favorite roast-beef-and-cheddar junior sandwich from Hardee's. It didn't help at all. Anyways, Tony was in the room with you, and you had a moment, and finally he asked for your name and you told him, and you heard him start to say he had something, but then he stopped. He was probably going to say "daughter." He stopped then and pulled a cloth CD case from his back pocket—almost the exact one you had hoped to buy with your first paycheck.

Tony plopped the CD case down on the table on top of the water-bottle labels and told you to peek inside. You looked at him while you opened it. If your mother saw you, she might have popped you in the mouth for the ways your eyes curved up instead of focusing on the thing you were doing. You rubbed your hands along the canvas case, admired it first. It was probably a twenty-CD holder. You asked him if he had any Michael Jackson, because that was probably what Daddy would say he liked to listen to, and Tony laughed when you opened the CD case: Miles Davis, *Sketches of Spain* and *On the Corner;* Missy Elliott, *Supa Dupa Fly,* and Nas, *It Was Written;* The Notorious B.I.G., *Ready to Die;* and Charlie Parker, *Ornithology.*

From sitting at Weesie's and Teeta's sides during spades while you were learning and not playing, you knew how to keep your face from giving up information.

Tony leaned in close on the table, and at first you wondered why he smelled familiar, then you realized it was the second-hand smoke caught in his clothes, covered by Old Spice. He said you could borrow his collection to keep you company while you were at work, and if you had a CD-W drive on your computer at home (you did, you showed off that you knew what he was referring to) you could take it home to copy the CDs and bring them back tomorrow.

You had to think about how to ask Daddy for blank CDs, and also how to copy CDs without showing him that you had these CDs from Tony to copy, because then he'd want to know how you got them, and how do you say a Black man at work gave them to you? He had shown you how to download Napster, though, and how to choose more stable MP3 files, and even though you had to clog up the phone line overnight while you waited for two songs to download, you were starting to gather some of the Mariah Carey songs you didn't have yet.

You remembered this fact and decided to just ask him for an advance on your paycheck, so that you could buy CDs to burn your Napster songs, so you could have more music at work, and of course a CD case for you to carry them in so as not to scratch them. You knew exactly which one you wanted.

Daddy told you, actually, he was planning on taking you to the credit union to open up your own savings account. You could also get a checking account because you were getting a check from a real job, but it would have his name on it, too, because you were a minor. But you could get checks, and your own stack of deposit and withdrawal slips with an account number that was especially yours. Because you now worked real hours for your real job, he met you outside the moss-covered DHEC building Thursday during your lunch hour. It shouldn't take more than an hour to set it up, he told you, and then he said that it would be ready for you to deposit and cash your check tomorrow. You didn't remember telling him that you got paid that day. He said DHEC was a state agency and he worked for a state agency, too, so the pay periods were the same. You shrugged. On the way to the credit union, Daddy tried to tell you about managing money, said that he would cut you a deal: for every dollar you put into your savings, he would put in a dollar so that your money could double by the end of the summer. You would more than replace the hundred dollars that went missing, that you tried to make up by babysitting, and you could have real money sitting in a real bank account that Uncle Junior could not touch.

You liked the idea of that and agreed to the challenge. Friday came, and Daddy picked you up again during lunch to deposit the check in the bank. He encouraged you to take out twenty dollars for next week's lunches, and you looked at him. He smiled, said, "You're making real money now, Mika." You filled out the withdrawal slip for forty dollars, and when Major asked what's that for you said to cover any yard sale or flea market shopping you would be doing with Weesie during your weekend stay at Redwood Court, and also to purchase a sweet snack from the vending machine during your work day, which was two doors down from Tony's office. You didn't mention Tony.

Daddy dropped you off back at work, and you heard the *slop, slop* of the mop coming down the hall. Because your supervisor was in the room, you sneaked off this time, saying you needed to use the bathroom. Why couldn't you talk to your colleague out in the open?

That's what you heard your supervisor call the people who go into the same office with him: "colleagues." But you tiptoed down the unmopped side of the hallway toward the bathroom. Tony stopped and watched you walk toward him, smiling.

You preempted the conversation, greeting him with an "Afternoon," saying you didn't have any leftover CDs and could you hold his CDs for the weekend and copy and bring them back on Monday? Tony said, "Sure thing, young gun, enjoy them this weekend." You motioned back to the office and scurried back to affix labels onto the water-sample bottles.

Weesie had no idea where you disappeared to when you asked her to go to Walmart to buy some "school supplies." She looked for you in all the office supply aisles and you were already at the front, checked out, and waiting with a plastic bag. You asked the clerk to double-bag the CD case and the blank CDs, so you could figure out how to bring them into the house without anyone asking. You hadn't thought this all the way through or else you would have bought some pens, or a new notebook. You would have left yourself some actual money for lunch next week, but the two purchases took up the majority of the spending money you had withdrawn, and now you had to get to next Friday (Daddy promised to take you every week to help you manage your money better) with $9.87—and the sandwiches from the cafeteria cost $7.00 after tax. You knew Weesie would take you to Walmart without questions, but the computer you needed was at home, so now you had to tell Weesie that you forgot you had to babysit Malik this weekend and actually you needed to go home tonight. You'd come back next week. Weesie looked absolutely disappointed, because she had wanted to go out into the country to the special flea market and didn't want to drive out that way by herself, but you told her you could go next week, and you told her you had a job now so you could help with gas money. Weesie drove you home.

Of course, you forgot that on Monday you were to be moved to a different department altogether because your summer internship rotated you between departments.

Monday went by and you now had two CD cases in your little purse with your Discman and you were ready to see Tony and give him his CDs back, and you smiled because it was raining that

day and you wanted to walk up to Tony and say, "Against my window / I can't stand the rain."

After buying the fifty-cent Captain's Wafers Cream Cheese &
Chives crackers from the vending machine for lunch, you returned to your computer desk. Not only were you on a new floor
but they didn't have AOL, or any internet, so you couldn't even
go online. Eventually, you gave up the lyric'd music and went for
Miles Davis's *Sketches of Spain* CD that Tony had given you. You
liked this because it was music that Daddy didn't listen to, so you
felt more educated, more . . . refined. You had jazz now. Real
jazz.

It didn't occur to you yet that Tony wouldn't be in the hallway
at 2:00 because he'd be mopping the third floor, where you were
last week, probably looking for you. You didn't think about that
when you went out to the restroom thinking you'd hear the
squeegee of the mop against the tile hallway.

The rest of the week went on like this: Daddy driving you to
work, not giving you lunch money, you typing the same three
words into small boxes, trying to learn the words to the new
music you had but no one to talk to about it, and so on. Thursday
morning, he made mention he would take you to the bank during lunch so you could get money out to go with Weesie to the
flea market for the weekend. You waited outside for him to drive
up, and of course he was late.

You told your supervisor you'd be back by 2:00, and it was
1:25, which meant if Daddy showed up at all, you would really
only have time to go to the bank and then come right back. No
convincing him to stop by Hardee's. Another cheese cracker
lunch.

On the way to the credit union, Daddy instructed you on how
to use the withdrawal slips, the whole process. While you were at

the counter filling out the paperwork, he asked you how much you thought you might need for the weekend trip. You told him you promised Weesie some gas money, so $10, plus $20 for you for the week. He reminded you: lunch money? You nodded your head, annoyed now that he'd stopped giving you money for lunch, and said, OK $50 and started to write the number five down. He stopped you by putting his hand on the withdrawal slip. You looked up at him wondering what was wrong and began to say the numbers out loud to prove you could do that simple math in your head. He told you last week you deposited $309 (he assured you that you'd get what money was taken out for taxes back next April), and only took out $40. If you took out $50 this week, you'd have $219. The credit union required a $30 minimum to maintain the account, so that left about $190. It's actually $189, you said. He nodded. He looked up at the teller and the folks piling into the credit union during their lunch hour, and then off into space in the way that he did so often when trying to say something that would annoy you to no end. You broke into the stare and said, yeh, so what? And he turned to you and said, what if he paid you back $250 next week when his paycheck came? You know, like an interest loan? What do you say?

He spilled into your silence to explain that he had to help Weesie with her insurance payments, and a neighbor had come by with a plate of greens, fried chicken, and cornbread and asked to borrow some money so her lights would stay on, and just this Monday the oil light on the car *and* the check-engine light came on, and he looked up and just like that he just needed this little bit to make it to next week.

What do you say?

He said, so then you'd withdraw $239, and it'll be like you didn't have to take out any money for yourself this weekend, because you'd get that back plus more. He looked up to the ceiling lights and started whispering numbers that suggested the math he was doing in his head.

You nod your head slowly, in agreement. And just like that, your account was empty again. Slowly, you wrote $239 and signed your name and you and Daddy almost crawled to the teller window. She smiled at you, not smiling. Daddy laugh-talked in the way he did when nervous, trying to explain you have a "big purchase" this week. He patted you on the shoulder. You ignored him and dug around in the candy dish looking for a cream soda Dum Dum. Any small joy. The bank teller didn't know who to hand the money to, and so Daddy reached out his hand, counted out $50, handed you those bills, then put the rest in his pocket. He push-tapped you toward the door and you dragged your feet back to the car like you were in elementary school again. A child. Before turning on NPR, he reminded you that next week you'd have it back, with interest, he promised. Did you want him to hold on to your $50 until you got home so you knew it would be safe? You shake your head.

It took longer than you thought it would to get back to the DHEC building. Now that you were already late, why fuss to be *only* ten minutes late vs any other amount of time?

When you got on the elevator, you pressed the third-floor button. As the elevator climbed, you smelled cleaning solution wafting through the elevator shaft. You'd have sprinted into the hallway if you didn't know that the floor would be wet. But you knew that Tony always kept one side unmopped until the other side dried, so you looked for where the WET FLOOR sign was not and sprinted toward the body bent over the mop handle. He didn't hear you call his name when you got out of the elevator because he had his headphones in. Just as he was about to lift the mop into the bucket, you ran up between his mop and the bucket and waved your hands. Tony's smile was so big. He moved to take off his headphones and said he thought you had left him, young gun. You shook your head no, no.

He said he had something for you and reached into his vest pocket. He said he kept it here, because he thought that maybe, eventually, he'd run into you. It was a little notebook, like what you'd get at Bi-Lo in the stationery section or a gas station. He said he saw you writing in a notebook once on lunch break and figured, with your new music, maybe one day you'd write songs. He said he thought you'd be famous one day—a big, big deal.

And you didn't know why, but you felt your ears go hot, and your chest tighten like you were about to cry.

Tony asked you, what's wrong, young gun? And you just shook your head. And moved in to hug him, and you felt him tense up, then relax, then pat your back and say, "It's OK, it's OK, why you crying, young gun? It's OK." He started reaching for reasons you might cry: "Is this about the CDs? Something happen to them? It's OK, young gun, they can be replaced, it's OK." You hugged him tighter and ran your fingers along the spirals of the notebooks. You told him it's all gone. So many folks only just take, take, take, take from you. He asked, take what?

You said, "Everything."

Independent Women

For the most part, I loved being a winter baby, especially a January one. I got to be far enough past Christmas to not have the stupid Christmas–birthday present mash up. And when Weesie let me start picking my birthday presents, I started to understand that usually, if what I wanted was too expensive and wouldn't come up on sale on the holiday market, it would come down to a reasonable price by my birthday so as to make way for the store's spring stock.

Daddy had started getting in on the let-Mika-choose-her-gifts train as well. I was getting older and, according to him, too fussy and too choosy. Last Christmas he gave me two crisp hundred-dollar bills and sent me off with Weesie. It was the best. Being a traditionalist, though, Weesie made me wrap anything I brought home. It didn't really make sense, 'cause the whole idea of wrapping was the element of surprise, but I learned the trick of separating them into multiple boxes so it looked like I had the most gifts when we started pulling them from under the tree. Tired of being told to hand me gift boxes, Destiny plopped her little self down in the middle of the floor and started opening one of my gifts. We all laughed, and when we cleaned up, Weesie was like, "Ain't I tell you that you would feel good opening all your gifts if you waited?" She was right. Everyone knows I monitor the Christmas tree each night and arrange and rearrange the ornaments. Whole camera rolls are taken up by my documenting the bright lights, the gold wrapping paper (Weesie insists on consistency), the angel on top. I don't go so far as to count them all total, but I do know about how many boxes everyone has under there, to know if some new presents arrived while I was at Forestwood Drive. This is my duty and I live for it, except those few years Weesie didn't put a tree up after Teeta died. Last Christmas, though, Weesie somehow slipped me a fourteen-karat gold necklace under the tree. I didn't ask how she bought it, even though one minute she'd be crying about bills and the next I'd have the exact necklace she saw me looking at, standing at the jewelry counter at J. B. White's. They say everyone speaks their love in different languages and in December and January, Weesie showers me with the world, it feels like—even when I tell her she don't have to do so much.

Having your grandma think you're mature enough for a gold necklace was a sign that there would be more shiny things to come now that I was becoming a woman, whatever that meant. Ever since we got back from Tampa, every new thing I wanted to do was "Now that you're becoming a woman" or "Since you're a grown woman," but Weesie only used that when she was trying to make a statement about my sass. Mama gave it to me when I said I didn't want to go to the skating rink with her anymore and it was "I guess since you're a grown woman now you're too good for skate nights," and maybe that was partially it, but just in general, the shine of the skating rink had started to vanish for me because we were going so often.

Mama had worked with the PTA to set up a fundraiser for the kids at the elementary school I used to go to and that most of her daycare kids went to. The more people came and rented skates and mentioned the school grade you were there to support, the more money the school got. I guess I should say, before I was becoming a woman, Mama and I used to love to go, and I got Gloria to drag her mama, little brother, and sister, and sometimes my daddy would come but not skate. He'd guard our things and drink iced tea and eat the cold pizza. Like a watchman. And every few songs, I could tell he went to the announcer's booth to make a music request, because who else but him would make the DJ play "Backstabbers" or "Rubberband Man" while school children skated? I'd be rounding the bend and see Daddy nodding his head to the music, pumping his hand to the rhythm, "Rubberbandman-Rubberbandman," and I'd be the lone school-aged person on the skate floor mouthing the words with him. *"Rubberband man get down!"*

Before I "became a woman," I loved the place, though. Growing up, Mama rounded up all of me and my January birthday friends and we all had joint parties. If I couldn't have a pool party like the summer babies, at least I could have almost a whole school grade show up in celebration, because somehow there were five of us born within a week of each other. What a way to start 1985, we always said. Me, Sherrie, the Black Ashley, Angela, Erika with a *k*. Every year. Then when Gloria joined my friend group, she rounded out the birthday crew. Six of us.

It helped that we were all friends then, and that the costs of a skating rink party were split between our parents. A deal. But last year it became clearer that convenience shouldn't be the reason for us to keep that tradition, 'cause half of the group didn't talk to each other at all. Mama still won't understand. Each time she brings it up, I huff and tell her to stop asking me about the Black Ashley (who acts white now), Angela, or Erika with a *k*. She still has to work with Erika's mom, a teacher, and Black Ashley's mom is a new vice principal at the elementary school. "Have fun. You be friends with them," I told her. But as for me, when our fifteenth birthday came and they peeled off to have a private buffet dinner at California Dreaming downtown and did not invite the rest of the crew, I knew it was the end of Destiny's Child, as we called ourselves. So me, Sherrie, and Gloria had to scramble to figure out what to do for our birthdays. It was going to look so bad. I got so mad I cried about it, then got more mad 'cause it was making me cry. At home, Mama and Daddy wrung their hands about what to do. I couldn't even bring myself to say what was wrong, because I was starting to hyperventilate just thinking about it.

"Mika, you have to breathe to speak and say what's wrong. Did someone hurt you?" she asked me.

I shook my head. I don't know what her watch could've told her about being left out of party planning and friendship back-stabbers, but she looked at her wrist. "Is it your time of the month?" I shook my head again.

"Well, what is it?"

I told them about California Dreaming and it's both because we were left out and because I knew we wouldn't be able to af-ford anything like it, even with the three of us left, and every time I thought about the yeast rolls with the honey-cinnamon butter that came to the table even if you didn't order anything, I got more mad.

That year I was inconsolable for the week, and over at Weesie's house she looked at me with such pity she said we should go out to the Lexington Flea to cheer me up. It helped, but my ears still ran warm if I thought about it. Finally, at the last minute, Daddy had gotten with Gloria's mom, and when he came to pick me up from Redwood Court, he gave me the news: "Mika, we may have a solution about the birthday situation." He said that I could invite whoever could fit into the van, and he would personally pick them up like my own New York City taxi driver and drive us around town. We could choose our own music, even. That was probably the biggest deal. On the day, after we rode around, he dropped us in front of Applebee's and said he'd come back in two hours and that we could order whatever we wanted. It wasn't California Dreaming, of course, but we had unlimited Shirley Temples and chicken fingers *with ribs,* and we pretended we were high dining—pinkies out—all night long.

But this was my sixteenth birthday, which felt important. We'd have to find a way to celebrate ourselves despite the ways of the world: George W. Bush had won the presidency even though the majority of the U.S. didn't vote for him. That's what my people say. I was chatting with Donnell online and he said things were tense in Florida. Sometimes, it's funny to think about time—how only about a year before we had thought the world was going to end with the new millennium, and now all I heard was every Black person everywhere saying we were looking at a different world ending, and truly all I wanted to do was have a normal moment where I didn't think about what it meant that the world was shifting before my eyes, but about how I was "becoming a woman" and what that might mean. I wanted to celebrate sixteen years on the earth. Sweet Sixteen. The promise of the generations to mark a moment in our lives where we turn the corner and don't look back. In ten days, I was going to *be* a woman.

During our break in after-school band practice, Sherrie, Gloria, and I brainstormed what it would look like to celebrate our birthdays this year.

"We could go back to the skating rink but make it like a throwback party," I said. I wanted to bring the shine back to one of my favorite ways to celebrate. Everyone knows that I'm the sentimental one. Sherrie picks at me and says that because I spend so much time with old-timers, I am too nostalgic and act like I'm sixteen going on sixty. Whatever.

"Nah. No one goes to Red Wing anymore," Sherrie offered.

"Movies and a dinner?" Gloria suggested.

I said that was so 2000. Sherrie was probably the flashiest of the three of us and skirted between the nerdy-mouthy crew (us) and the growing bougie crew because the leader of that crew— the California Dreamers—and Sherrie's parents grew up out in the country together. Weesie said it was a classic case of country mouse to big city mouse who forgets their roots. She had lived down the road from their grandparents, and they all came to Columbia at the same turn of the century. 'Bout the same time some Black folks made their way up north. "But some people just want to erase who they are, who they people are, where they come from," Weesie said. Won't no use reminding the Dreamers that their grandparents had dusty bare feet like mine. But Sherrie struggled with the balancing act sometimes, and it showed up in her hunger for flair and big gestures.

They went through a few more ideas that just didn't seem fit for a group of Independent Women.

"I know. I have it!" Sherrie said. "My apartment complex has a clubhouse no one ever uses, especially in winter. Let's have a no-grown-ups, invite-only Sweet Sixteen party."

She started shrugging her shoulders with her hands raised, lifting the air into the sky in a little dance. Gloria caught the moment and bounced her shoulders as well, singing, *"I wanna dance tonight / I wanna toast tonight,"* from our favorite movie, *Love & Basketball.* Sherrie pointed and smiled at Gloria like she won a prize when she started singing the song, and I wanted to do a little two-step but I didn't want them to pick at me. I don't dance, even though I have to keep time because of band; I haven't yet learned what it means to let the body move loose like a weed in the wind.

"I'm thinking we make it a boys-and-girls party."

I raised my eyebrows. I don't know about this. Daddy won't going to go for it, I knew it. Gloria was in. Before I could be in, too, I was going to have to ask Mama and Daddy.

I WAS OLD ENOUGH NOW TO KNOW THAT GETTING DADDY TO buy into something I suspected him to say no to meant getting Mama to buy in first. Age-old game. Daddy could get away from being the official "no" by saying he'd have to ask Mama, so I started going to her first with the main details, get her buy-in, then go to Daddy. This was bigger, though. Bigger than "could I stay out with Gloria after curfew 'cause the movie we wanted to see would end too late?" It was even bigger than the first time I asked to sleep over at Sherrie's house, because my family knew her family, and even though it was modern times, not like when they were growing up, all the folks we socialized with abided by the same set of Black-people codes: everyone is eligible to correct you if they see you out in the world acting a fool. Even when our friend group started to include boys, we had to assure Mama and Daddy that none of us dated or intended to date Jamal or Prince or Curtis. I still held my breath in anticipation whenever Roger caught eyes with me in the hall. Maybe one day. We three girls had to promise that nothing was going on, and Daddy practically did a background check on them before we got the OK to sit in a dark theater together or be dropped off at the mall. I still don't think he wanted to OK it, but I overheard Mama reason with him one night, reminding him that she was my age when they met and even started going steady.

"Yeah, Major, the world was different, but it also wasn't that long ago, and we are going to have to start loosening the reins."

I never imagined Mama to be the one to come to my defense, but I could tell the more my interests started resembling that of "regular" girls and not tomboys, we started to come around to each other. I figured she could be an ally with this, too, if all of the pieces were in the right place.

WEESIE CALLED THE HOUSE AND ASKED TO SPEAK TO ME. IT was Thursday and she wanted to know, when might I have time in my "busy" and "too grown" schedule for her? It was true, I had started to find ways to be out with my friends, or I had band practice and competitions or homework that piled up like all the business documents I watch Daddy gather for tax season, except homework is every weekend and I need a computer with internet I can actually use.

Weesie had convinced Daddy to build her a computer, I guess to try and entice me over there more often 'cause she said she felt like I was slipping away from her, but when he showed her how to get on America Online and she tried to call Ruby to announce her technological improvements, and realized she couldn't be on the phone and on America Online, she accepted that the internet thing won't going to happen; so the computer became an expensive gospel CD player that could also play endless games of solitaire.

"You'll at least come and spend a little time with your poor old and washed-up grandma before your birthday, won't you?" she asked.

She was trying to joke about it, but it didn't feel like a joke, 'cause there won't no Weesie chuckle. I tell her I'll try to come; I have to see how much of my homework I can get done and to see if there's anything I can do from Redwood Court to prep for "this thing" I want to do.

"What thing, Miss Missy?" she asked. It was weird talking to her over the phone and not in person, but it was just so much harder to get over there like I used to. I had to lower my voice a little, though, because I hadn't yet brought it up to Mama to bring it up to Daddy.

"Me and my friends want to have a boys 'n' girls party at Sherrie's apartment complex," I said as low as I could without whispering—or else the whisper sound would trigger Mama to pay attention; weird how it worked like that.

"Oooo wee" was all Weesie said. She was rarely speechless. "Major know?"

"Not yet. I want to have everything in place," I say, looking around. If Mama really wanted to know, she'd be by the phone asking me what was it I was talking about, or I would have heard the *click* of the receiver being picked up in another room.

"Well," Weesie said, clearing her throat. If I was with her at Redwood Court, I'd be watching her sit back on the barstool at the island and straighten up. It was one of her signature moves whenever she had an epiphany or good advice or a juicy story to tell.

"Well, Mika, who do you think planned the wedding for the young lovebirds who later became your parents, a week before your mother started her senior year of high school?" I hadn't thought of this. Or Sasha's graduation party. Or all the baby showers, Easters, and all. "Baby, let's plot this weekend. I'll help," she said. "What do you need, a new dress?"

I told her yes.

"Shoes?" Yes.

"Who's worrying about refreshments?" I told her I was volunteered.

"You know Ms. Hunter make you a red velvet every year since you were a little girl and you had told her that cake was your favorite. In fact, she called earlier today to say she was going to bring it Sunday, but I can ask her to hold it."

I say OK. Mama started making her way to the front of the house. I knew it was 'cause I had been on the phone longer than I usually am.

"We'll make it right. Come over this weekend and we'll go to the good mall across town."

WE CAME BACK FROM THE MALL LATE AND TIRED AND EMPTY-handed. I couldn't find a piece of clothing that looked anything like what *Seventeen* magazine suggested one might wear to a "festive winter party" that would (1) button or zip without cutting into my stomach or gaping open at the chest, or (2) not cost an arm and a leg.

I had found something I liked, but I'd ignored Weesie's first inquiries of how much it was all the way across the department store to the dusty fitting rooms. I was already mad we were in the Misses and not Junior section, but this dress with a velvety gold top with sequins sewn into the edges and a black flowy bottom looked cute, and maybe stretchy enough that an XL would fit me. I could pull it over my head and felt comfortable enough to walk out to show Weesie.

"Oh. Baby. It's cute, but I can see too far above your knees. It's January. You can't be running around like these little white girls who can afford to be sick."

I held the side seams and wiggled my hips trying to pull it down lower. Then I reminded her I could wear tights.

"It's still too short, though, and I don't know how much it costs yet to know if I like it enough." She smirked and opened and closed her hands like clamshells in my direction, telling me to come, come.

I know she just wants to tug the dress down and look at the tag. So I do, go to the seating area, twirl, and move in.

She sucks her teeth, then whistles. Shakes her head.

"Girl, if you don't take this 'spensive frock off!" I slink into the fitting room to discover that getting the fitted top of the dress over my boobs in the opposite direction is near impossible. I huff two times too many, then I hear my grandma call for reinforcements.

"Baby. Baby, excuse me, can you help my grandbaby in there get out of one of y'all's dresses? I figure if you help her and it tears, y'all will know what happened instead of if I go in there."

I tell her I can get it and suck in my stomach, but it's really my boobs, back, and shoulders—all things I hadn't had to really contend with before now. The clerk knocks and I open it enough to let her in without the whole world seeing us struggle. She grabs the hem of the dress and tugs firm but quick, and I shimmy.

I must have looked like a snake shedding its skin, because she stormed out, dress in hand, and pushed the door closed so hard it echoed in the dressing area.

Dressed in my street clothes again and feeling defeated, I thumbed through some black pants with elastic waistbands— what I knew would always fit me without trying them on, the kind of pants that already took up so much space in my closet— then told Weesie we could just go home.

I TOLD THE GIRLS I COULD HANDLE DESSERT AND MAYBE ASK my godmother to make her famous slow-cooker grape jelly meatballs. Gloria said her mouth was watering just thinking about it, and Sherrie dropped our dreaming and said it wasn't a family reunion. Then she asked if I was going to get a sheet cake or petit fours from Tiffany's Bakery. I said Weesie's friend was just going to make a red velvet cake like she does for me every year and Sherrie protested that we need to have enough for all our guests and I should just get about sixty petit fours, so if thirty folks come, they can have two each. I'd never bought petit fours, but Weesie always asked for "a few petty furs" each Mother's Day and Daddy only ever got enough for the *mothers*. Everyone else would watch Mama and Weesie lick their fingers. Sometimes Daddy would get some sugar cookies, but never more than four petit fours.

I didn't spend all of my Christmas money, knowing we were thinking of something to do for our birthdays, but I was not sure

I had enough to cover this fancy expense. Still without a dress or shoes, I had to figure out refreshments and how to tell Weesie to tell Ms. Hunter not this year on the cake, etc.

I told Weesie the girls wanted petit fours and she sucked her teeth. "Y'all not old enough for that delicacy," she said. When I told her I had to figure out how to buy them and also convince my parents to let it happen at all, she shook her head.

"Y'all at least got flowers? What's the décor gone look like?" I shrugged my shoulders, 'cause I figured, what's the use going so deep on an unapproved party?

After church and after after-church supper, Weesie gathered me from the den and told me to take a walk with her around the Court. We skipped Reggie's house, and Mrs. Jackson's car wasn't there, so we skipped it, too. Weesie said she thought she'd seen Calvin help her son clear out the garage so they could put the car in there so folks wouldn't know if she was in or out. "I ain't never seen someone live in a community so 'sistent on secrecy," Weesie said, walking by. "Either way, we ain't going there."

We went to Dot and Buddy's house first. Weesie unfolded the manila folder she had slipped under her arm on our way outside.

"Dot, you know our baby going to be sixteen in a couple of days and I want to make sure she has the best birthday yet." Weesie started at the porch. "I'm not coming inside, 'cause we determined to get as many folks in as possible. Our baby having it at a clubhouse, and you know how they be having expenses we can't even dream of. But I think we can send her in style with a nice corsage and maybe some flowers," she said. "For the ambiance."

Dot looked at me. "Sixteen, huh? I remember when you were riding up and down the Court on your Big Wheels."

I smiled. "Yes, ma'am."

Weesie started again. "Anyways, Dot, whatever you can give. I know it's not our usual kitty use but I just thought—"

Dot stopped Weesie from explaining and disappeared and returned with ten dollars. Weesie handed me the pen and told me to record it. Like usual. We went up and down and around the Court. Folks saying happy birthday. Singing the "Sixteen Candles" song. When we got back, Weesie took the folder and said she'd take care of the rest. She called Mama and Daddy then, too.

"Yes, Rhina. I think it's a good idea for our little woman," Weesie said, twirling the phone cord around her fingers. "Imagine if I was like this when Major just appeared like out of thin air across the street." She looked at me. Only Weesie could cut through to them, truly. Who was I to think I could take this on alone?

"I imagine there will be adults somewhere, because sixteen-year-olds can't just rent a building." I shook my head. Weesie's mouth dropped open in disbelief. Oh. "I mean, the girls want to be independent. Do you remember what that's like? We didn't chaperone all of y'all's dates." Weesie winked at me, then rolled her eyes at whatever Mama must have been saying on the phone.

"Major. Hi, yes. I think y'all should let her have this."

She did some more convincing in the flavor of Weesie, then hung up, letting out a big sigh.

"That's how I feel every night," I said.

"Whew. Baby, how do you do it?"

We laughed.

SO I HAD TO TELL SHERRIE AND GLORIA THE COMPROMISES that got Daddy to say yes, including these very specific concessions:

1. We had to give him a copy of the names of everyone who RSVPed.
2. Unless they were our cousins, they had to go to our school.

We'd gone over this at lunch, so I saw their eyes roll. I continued.

3. He was uncomfortable with the no adults bit, but he would do ID check and folks had to show their school IDs or driver's licenses—no one over twenty-one.

Sherrie's hand slapped the table. "It keeps going," I said.

4. Daddy *may or may not* choose to stand outside, in the cold, the whole night.

When he demanded this, I protested. Everyone knows who my dad is, and even if they didn't, we literally had the same face! He said he'd stand off to the side, covert style. I reminded him about the winter thing and he said they teach you inclement weather operations in basic training, he'd be fine.

Exasperated—understandably—Sherrie and Gloria asked if there was anything else.

"He wants to speak to y'all's parents to make sure all of the parents are OK with the plan. I guess to make sure we're not hiding anything," I said.

Sherrie looked down at her lunch tray. I asked what was wrong. She admitted that her big sister had pretended to be her mom to reserve the clubhouse.

Gloria spoke for the both of us. "You mean your parents don't know about this? What do they think we're going to be doing?"

"Dinner and a movie," Sherrie said. We threw our hands up in disbelief.

ON OCCASION, EVER SINCE SISSY GRADUATED HIGH SCHOOL and moved out of the house, she would remember she had a little sister, me, and would call me up and we'd go to a restaurant, and out for a spell. Because she knew I loved to read and wanted to be a writer, Sissy took me to the big library downtown, where I could get as many books as I wanted on any topic. When she called to see what I wanted to do around my birthday I asked her if we could go look for a dress (again)—and shoes. Maybe if we went to Bakers I could find some cute ones that could match whatever dress I found, and also Bakers because I knew they carried WIDES in most styles.

Sissy asked a few questions about the party then told me we could go after school one day this week, but she'd call me once her work schedule was confirmed. She was still so young and so new at Applebee's, everyone else got calendar priority before her.

Sissy decided we were going to go looking for shoes and things on Thursday evening, and it was super close to the day of the party—to not raise alarms, Sherrie's big sister had reserved Sunday night: still a weekend but technically a school night—so whatever I found during that trip was going to have to be it. When she honked the car horn, I thought it was weird that she wasn't going to come inside. No one ever talked about it, but Teeta almost died in the room with her, and so no one really blamed her when she had started to find reasons to stay out of the house more and more. And then when she graduated from high school a few months later, almost no sooner did she have her diploma than she announced she was moving out. Daddy tried to pull the "You're only eighteen" line, but she had already signed the apartment lease and paid the deposit.

I went outside with my purse and jacket, ready to go, and Sissy was reaching in the trunk rustling a big bag.

"You can help me get your dress out of the car instead of watching me struggle," she said.

"My *what?*" I asked, moving to the back of the car with her. Sissy had something covered in a Michael's dry cleaning bag draped over her arms and another bag marked Claire's Fashion Jewelry. There was a glimmer of lilac flashing through the only piece of the plastic that wasn't opaque, and I got excited, hopeful, and cautiously optimistic at once. It was the right color, at least. I tried to peek into the Claire's bag on the way inside, but whatever it was clinking around in the bag was covered by tissue paper.

Inside, Mama turned off the television when I walked in, like I was the only one not clued in to what was going on. She had a huge smile on her face. Sasha hung the dress on the back of a dining chair and pointed at it like a game show girl revealing my prize.

"I was asking around at work about where I could help you find a cute dress that would fit you when Weesie told me about the mall trip. My homegirl Michelle, she's almost about your size but a little taller. She said she was in a wedding and the bride made her wear purple and it's a shame because the dress was cute but it was purple. So she can't imagine wearing the dress again and asked if I wanted to see if it would fit you."

This was probably the most I had heard my sister talking about something that didn't really have to do with her. Talk about Freaky Friday.

Mama jumped in. "Weesie and I found a dress in your closet we knew fit you just so, and we took it to your aunt Jesse to help her hem this one. So it should fit first try."

I started to unwrap the dress, and it was almost exactly the same style of dress as the one that would not come off in the dressing room—except instead of sewn-on sequins, it had a shiny, lacy short cover jacket. I tried it on and it slipped down my body like a waterfall—so easy, without obstruction. I walked back to the living room and Mama and Sissy were smiling.

"Look at my baby," Mama said. I twirled and laughed—of course Weesie would see to it that Aunt Jesse hemmed it below the knees. I still liked it, though.

"Your sweet-sixteen baby," Sissy corrected. She pulled out three tiaras from the Claire's bag and told me to pick one and I could give the other two to Sherrie and Gloria. She helped me put it on and whisper-sang, *Cinderelly, Cinderelly, lovely dressy Cinderelly.*

I TOLD SHERRIE I COULD SHARE MY RED VELVET CAKE WITH the party but I couldn't do Tiffany's Bakery. I didn't have to buy a dress, thank God, but the shoes I wanted and that could fit me made up most of the difference that I saved, and I needed a dress coat. I couldn't wear my hand-me-down Member's Only jacket with this dress. Weesie charged what she could, and I used my Christmas balance. I was tapped out. There would still be flowers and some bites, and I saw on Weesie's back porch the ingredients for lime sherbet 7 Up punch. That was all we could do, and more than enough. Sherrie said forget it, she'd take care of the cake situation, and Gloria got her brother—over twenty-one, but an exception—to agree to DJ the party so folks could do requests and stuff.

We hand-delivered forty-five invitations and got thirty-eight RSVPs. Out of courtesy we gave invites to the former crew but didn't expect them to RSVP, and they didn't. It'd be a nice group. Roger was on the list, and high up, so that meant he replied early.

"You going to ask him to dance?" Gloria asked when she saw me looking long at the list and knew I was thinking about him.

"I don't know. I guess," I said. I was just glad he'd be there, and glad I knew that at least I'd look nice.

WEESIE TOLD ME SHE HAD ONE MORE THING FOR ME, SO I should stop by Redwood Court before I headed out to the party. Because Sissy knew how paranoid Daddy would be about the whole thing, she'd requested time off so I could get there without having to hitch a ride with the party bouncer. She drove me out to Redwood Court, and there were cars in the driveway and along the curb, kind of like how folks had lined up for cookouts back in the day. I half expected Teeta to pop his head from the back gate; that's the feeling I got pulling up. There was Aunt Viola's car, Ms. Hunter's, Betty's car. Reggie's doors were open, so they were home and probably inside with Weesie.

When I walked up to the door, I could see the surprise. There were balloons bouncing along the ceiling: IT's YOUR DAY! HAPPY BIRTHDAY! SWEET 16, and so on. I walked in and all the mouths started singing the Stevie Wonder birthday song. You know the one. Weesie had her hands in the air like she was the choir con-ductor. She cued them for the last round, and Ms. Hunter came out of the living room with my favorite red velvet cake and a few lit candles. I hadn't expected any of this, and I channeled my ner-vousness by trying to straighten the tiara and make sure my dress was still looking right.

"Baby, make a good wish, now," Weesie said. I looked around the room and said, "Thank y'all so much. I love y'all."

Ruby moved to put the corsage on my wrist and told me it was from everyone. Two deep-purple calla lilies and baby's breath. I held my wrist out to look at it, and almost with the same unified voice as with the birthday song, everyone who'd crowded into 154 Redwood Court crooned at the sight, so I twirled my whole completed outfit and Sissy Vanna Whited me again.

Weesie cut through the "sookie-sookie nows" and called out: "Y'all let this baby make her sweet sixteen birthday wish so she can get some of this real cake and food before she rides off to her ball."

Ms. Hunter, still holding the cake in one hand, moved the other hand that was shielding the candles. My first thought was a wish about Roger and maybe a dance, but whatever is going to happen to us will be what it's supposed to be. No use wasting my good wish on that. What I thought about next felt something like what a grown adult would say out of the novels I've been reading, or the Great Book Grandma Annie speaks about all the time. I was moving into a new space. Grandma Annie loved the Corinthians verse "When I was a child, I thought like a child. When I became a *woman*," she would edit it, "I put away childish things."

I figured either Roger was going to notice me at my party or I was going to find the right person for me. But moments like right now seemed worlds away from the event about to start on the other side of town. I looked around the room, the folks gathered, and took mental pictures, swearing never to forget any of it. What would Teeta say to me? I took a deep breath and whispered, "May I always feel *this* big love," and blew out all of the candles.

Acknowledgments

Redwood Court was made possible through the unwavering support of my loving husband, Curtis Caesar John—who over the last few years spent hours with me talking through or listening to early drafts of the stories that comprise the book. It's no coincidence that the final gathering scene in *Redwood Court* is his favorite, because it takes as its model the John and Caesar family clans, of which I have become a part through him, and their undying commitment to celebrate big and with big love.

Through this project, I know what literary partnership and having the right team behind you should look like. Victoria Sanders read the short story "Work," called me out of the blue, and said we could do great things together. I am here to say it is true. I am honored to have a fierce advocate in Victoria for literary representation; she restored my faith in the industry—and more, she matched me with the dreamy team at The Dial Press: Maya

Millett and Whitney Frick and all of the collaborators behind *Redwood Court*'s production.

Just at the moment in my life that I needed her, I know now, Renée Watson and I became sisters. I remember the day I read *Piecing Me Together* and I texted her how much I wished a younger me would have had her books—to be able to so fully see myself in a novel. But also in friendship and writing (and the industry), I have never felt so seen by someone as by Renée. She was one of my first readers for and helped edit "Work," and she encouraged and reminded me to submit the story to *Kweli Journal*'s spring 2020 issue on Black girlhood. If she had not texted me at the last hour to send it—despite my paralyzing fear of rejection—who knows where I'd be? Where Mika and her Columbia community would be? Like my own experience, *Redwood Court*'s interior world is held up by Black women who love each other.

This book was brought to the world by the love and work and support of Black women in my life: Laura Pegram of *Kweli*, your vision for a publication platform and community for voices like mine quite simply changed my life; Abba Belgrave, your friendship and clear-eyed reading and critique of my work, from the NYU poetry workshop table to the final leg of the work for *Redwood Court*, sustained me; Jessica Lynne, chile—your friendship and sisterhood, all of the conversations and writings, our musings, brought my home of Columbia, South Carolina, to such light . . . the place that made me, of which I had never imagined its extraordinary ordinariness until our friendship was deepened by being two Southern Black women living in New York City, leaning South.

Of course the list of Black women holding me up is long, long, but I'll name here my Red Olive team members, each of them over the ten years, especially Damaris Dias and Sharbreon

Plummer. Finally, Maya Millett at The Dial Press, who said "yes" to this project, and continued to encourage me, push me, reassure me throughout the process that *Redwood Court* was worthy of being in the world. I am very aware of how lucky I am to have a Black woman as an editor for this project, and I hope many more to come.

Growing up in a Southern suburban town as a dark-skinned Black girl was made bearable and sweet by the community of friends, elders, and of course my family who supported my dreams in ways I'm still uncovering. My maternal grandparents, Louise B. Melvin and James E. Melvin, showed me how to create safe, nurturing, restorative spaces, and how to fill them with those who see and love you. My mama, Lavoris Rena' Dameron, and daddy, Thomas W. Dameron, Jr., helped me understand that it's not what you have that fulfills a life, but what you make what's around you beautiful, and that you must share it. I wanted for not much in their care though I understand now the sacrifices it must have taken for me to grow up believing I could make of myself whoever I dreamed to be—even if there wasn't a model in my family for it. I could make the model.

As I was completing the final stages of *Redwood Court,* having returned some few years earlier to my hometown, Renée Watson came to Columbia to do an author visit at the Richland County Main library branch. It was such a full circle moment, and I got to share with my literary sister how my blood sister Tressa T. L. Dameron brought me here weekly and waited patiently for me to select *whatever* books I wanted to take home with me, and then took me out to dinner. It was during those trips, as a middle schooler, that I was able to expand my world by reading bell hooks's *Wounds of Passion* and *Killing Rage, The Autobiography of Malcolm X,* Richard Wright's *Black Boy* and *Native Son,* Toni Morrison's *Song of Solomon,* and Zora Neale Hurston's *Their Eyes Were Watching God.* I would not be the writer I am today without those trips to my library, without those words expanding my understanding of story, Blackness, witness, troubling the status quo, all of it—without my sister taking me out weekly for such a small gesture that has rippled for the rest of my life.

Finally, as I was preparing *Redwood Court* to be sent out into the world, my first, and only, fiction writing teacher, Randall Kenan, left us. When I was a young college student still finding my voice, Randall encouraged me to experiment with style, to bring my background in music onto the pages, and give my characters the voices and lexicon and phrases of the places they were from. Because I wasn't formally studying creative writing, I could only take his intro class, but in a later semester he and I designed an independent fiction writing course—complete with his specially curated texts that reflected my international historical study—and each week I'd journey to his office and sit at his feet; still today I feel so honored to have been able to share conversations about craft and stories about writing the Black South. Ideas and storylines for *Redwood Court* were brought to life sitting across the desk from Randall—I will be forever grateful for his quiet mentorship.

May we all have a community of folks—blood and chosen blood; cheerleaders and coaches—surrounding us all of our days.

ABOUT THE AUTHOR

DéLana R. A. Dameron is an artist whose primary medium is sto-
rytelling. She is a graduate of New York University's MFA program in poetry and holds a BA degree in history from the
University of North Carolina at Chapel Hill. Her debut poetry
collection, *How God Ends Us,* was selected by Elizabeth Alexander
for the 2008 South Carolina Poetry Book Prize, and her second
collection, *Weary Kingdom,* was chosen by Nikky Finney for the
Palmetto Poetry Series. Dameron is also the founder of Saloma
Acres, an equestrian and cultural space in her home state of South
Carolina, where she resides.

delanaradameron.com
Twitter: @delana_writes
Instagram: @delana.r.a.dameron

The Dial Press, an imprint of Random House, publishes books driven by the heart.

Follow us on Instagram:
@THEDIALPRESS

Discover other Dial Press books and sign up for our e-newsletter:

thedialpress.com

The Dial Press, an imprint of Random House,
publishes books driven by the heart.

Follow us on Instagram:
@THEDIALPRESS

Discover other Dial Press books and
sign up for our e-newsletter:

thedialpress.com